SHADOWED

LEGEND OF THE IR'INDICTI SERIES, BOOK 2

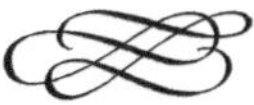

CONNIE SUTTLE

To Walter, Joe, Larry, Lee, Dianne, Sarah and Mark.
Thank you.

ACKNOWLEDGMENTS

As always, this book is the result of collaboration. If it weren't for the support of my editor, my cover artist and my beta readers, it would be less than it is. All mistakes, as usual, are mine and no other's.

About the Author:
Connie Suttle lives in Oklahoma with her husband and a conglomerate of cats. They have finally banded together to make their demands, which has proven disconcerting to all humans involved.

You may find Connie in the following ways:
Facebook: Connie Suttle Author
Twitter: @subtledemon
Website and Blog: subtledemon.com

Blood Destiny Series:

Blood Wager

Blood Passage

Blood Sense

Blood Domination

Blood Royal

Blood Queen

Blood Rebellion

Blood War

Blood Redemption

Blood Reunion

Blood Destiny Series Boxed Set (Books 1-10)

Blood Recall

Blood Alliance*

Legend of the Ir'Indicti Series:

Bumble

Shadowed

Target

Vendetta

Destroyer

Legend of the Ir'Inditi Boxed Set

~

R-D Series:
Cloud Dust
Cloud Invasion
Cloud Rebel

~

Latter Day Demons Series:
Hot Demon in the City
A Demon's Work is Never Done
A Demon's Due

~

Seattle Elementals Series:
Your Money's Worth
Worth Your While*

~

BlackWing Pirates Series
MindSighted
MindMage
MindRogue
MindMaster*

~

Black Rose Sorceress Series
The Rose Mark

Rose and Thorn

Black Rose Queen

Queen of Thorns and Roses

Future Wars Series

Buffer Zone

Black Zone*

Other Titles from SubtleDemon Publishing:

Malefactor

Transgressor

Underhanded*

by Joe Scholes

*Forthcoming

FOREWORD

CHAPTER 1

"Dude, you can't let it bother you." Sali glanced sideways at Ashe as they walked away from school.

Three weeks.

Three more miserable weeks of school before summer break. Ashe had been taunted (again) by Chad and Jeremy as they drove away from Cloud Chief Combined in Jeremy Booth's new car. Jeremy's parents had given him an early graduation gift and both boys boasted about the shiny, red automobile whenever possible. Granted it wasn't the sports car Jeremy had bragged he'd get, but it was a new car, nonetheless.

The Grand Master had recently approved Mr. and Mrs. Booth's application to adopt Chad Daniels into their family, although it was unheard of for shapeshifters to adopt a werewolf child. Ashe knew it would mean trouble the moment the Grand Master's signature came back on the required paperwork. That meant that somehow, Chad would likely end up with a new car, too.

Ashe and Sali were finishing eighth grade and Ashe would turn fourteen in a few weeks, with Sali's birthday a month after that. Jeremy and Chad had gone back to calling Ashe *empty*, though everyone knew about the bat. The tiny, insignificant, mostly embarrassing *bumblebee bat* that was Ashe's alter ego.

"If they knew what else you could do, man," Sali kicked at a stray clump of dirt, sending the offending clod and a trail of brown dust sailing into the field beside the road.

Only a narrow, graveled lane ran through Cloud Chief, enabling the residents to drive to and from scattered rural homes or away from Cloud Chief and onto a nearby county road.

No humans knew that Cloud Chief was anything other than a ghost town, hidden away on a western Oklahoma prairie. Ashe's vampire father and Nathan Anderson, Cloud Chief's other vampire resident, helped keep it that way. They were aided in their efforts by concealment spells a traveling witch placed around the community every year.

"Dad says we can't tell anyone about the misting," Ashe grumbled. Ashe could turn to mist in a blink, becoming invisible to everyone. Not only was he undetectable to the werewolves who had keen scenting ability, he could sail right through the smallest of cracks and could somehow travel through solid surfaces if he wanted. It was a bit disorienting if he did that, so he kept it to a minimum.

"Yeah. My dad says the same," Sali kicked at another clump of dirt, but this one disintegrated when he made contact instead of rolling into the field as the last one did. "What do you think you'll get for your birthday?"

"Mom still says no on the cell phone," Ashe had resigned himself to living without any sort of communication technology for another year. He and Sali desperately wanted cell phones. Their parents said fifteen was the magic age for that bit of technology. "I think I might get a new tablet, though."

"Not the same," Sali grumped. "Marco might come home after school's out in Austin," he added. Sali's older brother attended the University of Texas, studying engineering.

"For how long? Is he gonna work for Mr. Winkler again?"

"I think so. Mr. Winkler pays for Marco's classes and gives him extra money for working over the summer with his security company. Wish I could do that."

Ashe watched Sali closely. Sali was back to being envious of his older brother, it seemed. William Winkler was a security magnate with a nationwide company that provided armored car services, guards and electronic security for banks and other businesses. Ashe had been quite impressed with the Dallas Packmaster when he'd met him more than a year earlier.

"Come on, Mom pays us for working at Cordell Feed and Seed."

"Yeah. But it's not the same as working security for Mr. Winkler."

Ashe didn't point out that neither he nor Sali had turned fourteen yet—they were much too young to work for Mr. Winkler's company. Sali's werewolf had grown, though. He was quite impressive when he turned, now. Ashe had also grown—he was barely under six feet tall but still quite thin. Aedan, his father, smiled whenever Ashe's mother suggested that he would be as tall as his dad.

"The good news is that we'll be ninth graders next year and Chump and Wormy will be in college," Ashe said, squinting in the bright afternoon sunlight. He had sunglasses, but Principal Billings didn't allow anyone to bring personal items to school. The Principal had also suggested uniforms for the students, but there hadn't been enough support from parents for that to be pushed through at a school board meeting.

Ashe had used nicknames for Chad and Jeremy—he was careful to say them only when he was away from the young werewolf and his shapeshifter best friend-turned-brother.

Weldon Harper, Grand Master for all werewolves, had approved Chad's adoption after lengthy consideration. Ashe would never forget the circumstances surrounding Chad's mother's death; she'd attempted to kill him, Sali and their mothers after compulsion was laid by Dark Elemaiya.

Ashe often wondered about the Elemaiyan race—he was of the Bright Elemaiya, but still knew next to nothing about that part of his ancestry. When he'd asked his father if there was anything written about them, Aedan immediately directed the conversation to other topics.

"Yeah. They'll have to find someone else to insult at college. I hope it's somebody bigger and badder," Sali muttered, referring to Chad and Jeremy.

"And Mrs. Booth is so nice," Ashe said.

"She makes good cookies," Sali agreed.

"Dude, are you hungry again?"

"Well, duh."

"I think there's microwave popcorn in the pantry," Ashe offered.

"That might get me through till dinner," Sali grinned. Both boys took off running toward Ashe's house.

"Mom, we're home now," Ashe said over the phone as the microwave dinged across the kitchen. Sali waited impatiently in front of the kitchen appliance while Ashe phoned his mother at Cordell Feed and Seed. "How are sales?"

"I wish we could enlarge the store, that's how busy we are, and I'm running out of everything," Adele Evans sighed. "And I wish you and Sali were old enough to drive. I could use your help right now."

"Mom, I could get Sali and me there in a few minutes," Ashe offered. He could. All he had to do was turn to mist and fly to Cordell.

"Ashe, you know your father wouldn't like that."

"Yeah." Ashe sounded so hopeful for a moment, causing Sali to look up from the freshly popped bag of popcorn he was devouring. The young werewolf watched as Ashe's face fell when his mother rejected the idea. Misting was the safest way to get anywhere and Ashe's parents wouldn't allow him to use it.

"Hon, you could be placed in danger because of that," Adele cautioned.

"I know." Ashe's day had definitely gotten worse. First the taunting and now this.

"Ashe, don't be depressed about that. Look, I have to go. I'll bring chicken and dumplings home from Betsy's." Ashe hung up when his mother did.

"Dude, that sucks," Sali said sympathetically, holding the popcorn bag out to Ashe. Sali had vacuumed up more than half the bag in the space of a few seconds.

Waving the nearly empty bag away, Ashe slumped onto a barstool at the kitchen island. The house wasn't even a year old—the last one had been blown up by Paul Harris, the former English teacher for Cloud Chief Combined—with a little help from the Dark Elemaiya. The Anderson home had also been destroyed; Paul Harris was prejudiced against anyone that wasn't werewolf and Nathan Anderson, being vampire, was a prime target.

Aedan Evans and Nathan Anderson, the community's two remaining vampires, rebuilt afterward. Aedan had built a larger home this time, giving Adele the spacious kitchen she wanted and a deck outside the solarium.

Ashe liked the kitchen, too; windows lined the walls facing east and north, but the north window was wide and curved at the top, overlooking the sink. Just as before, the garage was through the kitchen door on the west side of the house.

Ashe and his parents had spent the past year replacing personal items destroyed in the blast. The loss of his library grieved Ashe the most; he was still struggling to find copies of favorite books that had gone out of print.

"Come on, dude, let's watch TV," Sali pulled Ashe toward the door leading to the lower, underground level of the house. They clumped downstairs and settled on the sofa in the media room. His mind wandering instead of focusing on the program Sali had chosen, Ashe wished he were anywhere except where he was.

"This is all that's left?" Bill Jennings, Director of the Joint National Security Agency and Homeland Security Office, glanced up at his assistant. Six names on a piece of official letterhead had been passed to the aging Director. Bill was two months away from retirement and the President and other high-ranking officials were already vetting candidates to fill his position.

Bill shook his head at the list of children still living. Another piece of paper resting under his hand listed the names of the dead. There were nearly seven hundred of those and he still wasn't sure they'd gotten information on all the children involved. He worried about many other children listed as missing—had they been abducted? How could he explain these things to the President, let alone someone coming in to take over his job? Bill sighed heavily. "Where are they now?" he asked.

"These six," Vince Jordan, Bill's assistant, tapped the paper containing the names of the half-Elemaiyan children still living, "are relocated, but we've seen how unsuccessful that has been in the past. You know where the seventh one is, through Mr. Winkler."

"Yes. I do know where the seventh one is," Bill agreed. His once dark hair was now completely white and had thinned over the years. His brown eyes now required glasses to clear fading vision. His face, too, he barely recognized in the mirror most mornings. When he had time to examine it, that is. Wrinkles and lines—that's mostly what Bill saw when he looked.

Winkler, the werewolf security mogul who provided the government with facial recognition software and other security measures, being what he was, still appeared quite young. Most people would think him thirty or so, although Bill knew the Dallas Packmaster was more than one hundred years old.

"Do you think, sir," Vince mused aloud, "that we might put these six," he tapped the paper again, "where the seventh one is?"

"Director, what do you need?" William Winkler saw Bill Jennings' phone number displayed on his cell before answering right away.

"I have an unusual request," Director Jennings said. "I need your help. And the help of a few folks in Oklahoma."

CHAPTER 2

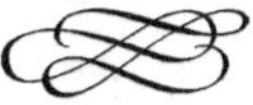

"I think it would only be for a short while, and there's always compulsion afterward," Winkler spoke with Weldon Harper on his cell. He had to get the Grand Master's permission first and then obtain permission from the Head of the Vampire Council before calling Director Jennings back with an answer.

"We need the support of the community, too, don't forget that," Weldon pointed out.

"I think most of the community would agree. There might be a couple of holdouts."

"True. I can override those. I realize those kids are in danger—how many are there?"

"Only six families, Grand Master. One family has an older child that's eighteen from the mother's first marriage. The child the Elemaiya are after is sixteen. The other families have children ranging from fifteen to seventeen. That seems to be the age the Bright Ones are taking them."

"I'll allow this and have a word with a couple of people in Cloud Chief," Weldon said. "Do you want to contact Wlodek, or shall I?"

"I'll let you handle that," Winkler said. "And I'll arrange for temporary housing inside the community. If we're lucky and can place those families in Cloud Chief, maybe the summer is all we'll need to throw the hunters off their trail."

"I hope the same thing; I'm not sure how those kids might fit into a paranormal school, although I'll instruct the Principal to allow it if necessary."

"Understood, Grand Master. Perhaps Bill will have something else worked out by that time. What I still don't know is whether those families understand exactly what we're dealing with." Winkler blew out a frustrated sigh.

"Will they understand werewolves and vampires? Not to mention shapeshifters," the Grand Master said dryly.

"There's that," Winkler agreed. "I'll talk to Bill again. Let me know what Wlodek says."

"I'll leave a message—he's asleep at the moment. Do you think Ashe Evans might be able to help with those children? He's the same, except for his parents."

"Yeah. Those other kids don't have a vampire father." Weldon snorted a laugh at Winkler's comment. "Or a mother that flies whenever there's a full Moon," Winkler went on, grinning. "I have to go. I'll call Bill and get back with you."

"Good enough." The Grand Master terminated the call.

"Charles!"

Charles nearly dropped the stack of files he carried two floors below Wlodek's private study. Wlodek, Head of the Vampire Council, and his staff occupied a rather large manor house in England, hidden in the countryside of Kent. Wlodek seldom shouted—Charles could hear a near-whisper from the ancient vampire while standing on the ground floor of the spacious home. Dropping the files on his desk, Charles sped through the house, up two flights of stairs and stood in Wlodek's study in less than three seconds without a hair out of place.

Wlodek studied his personal assistant before saying anything.

Charles was eternally curious and loved information of any kind. His hazel eyes held a question as he, in turn, studied Wlodek. Wlodek's official title, *Sanguis Rex*, was seldom used. Instead, he was addressed as *Head of the Council* or *Honored One*. It gave the illusion at times that Wlodek's vote was only one of nine. The Council (and Charles) knew that he often made decisions on things that never reached the Council for a vote.

"Charles, make arrangements to send this amount to William Winkler in Dallas," Wlodek handed over a slip of paper.

"Might I inquire what this money is for?" Charles displayed no emotion, although three quarters of a million dollars was quite a large sum to be sending the Dallas Packmaster, who held sufficient wealth of his own.

"Temporary housing," Wlodek replied. "And if we're lucky, information on half-Elemaiyan children that might make fine turns one day. When they're of sufficient age, of course."

Charles knew not to blink or to show shock, surprise or any other emotion to the Head of the Council. "Of course, Honored One," Charles replied. "I'll have it done immediately." Turning quickly, Charles almost disappeared, he moved so swiftly.

"Good," Wlodek muttered and went back to sifting through a pile of requests.

"I've received a transfer of funds for temporary housing. What do you think that means?" Winkler asked the Grand Master over the phone. "Seven hundred fifty thousand. That's a lot of temporary housing."

"Wlodek never does anything in half-measures, or generally anything at all unless there's something that will benefit the vampire race in it somewhere," Weldon Harper grumbled. "We just don't know what that is at the moment. Doesn't matter. Tell Director Bill he can bring the families to Cloud Chief for the summer. How quickly can you get those prefab homes in place?"

"I've already made arrangements; all we have to do now is inform the community that they'll be hosting humans during the summer." Winkler didn't really want to be the one to make that announcement.

"I'll leave that to you," Weldon said, causing Winkler to grimace. Grateful that the Grand Master couldn't see the face he'd just made, Winkler said, "I'll get on that immediately," and hung up.

~

"What's going on?" Sali slid onto a cafeteria bench beside Ashe. Principal Billings' announcement on the intercom had interrupted their last class of the day.

Billings seldom used the intercom for announcements, and the device had crackled and grumbled as the principal instructed all students and faculty to gather in the cafeteria.

In Ashe's opinion, the intercom's difficulties were likely due to lack of use. Benjamin Billings preferred to bellow at wrongdoers and anyone he suspected of wrongdoing.

This time, the electronic intercom was used instead and all students were instructed to attend an unscheduled general assembly. Tables had been hastily folded up and shoved against a wall, leaving benches and chairs for seating inside the recently constructed school. The old school building had been destroyed a year earlier by a tornado.

"Dude, there's a bunch of people walking down the hall," Ashe hissed, his acute hearing detecting many footsteps and the banging of doors on the north end of the schoolhouse.

"Look," Sali whispered, nodding toward the wide doorway leading into the cafeteria. His mother, Denise DeLuca, led a crowd of Cloud Chief residents inside the lunchroom.

Principal Billings, surrounded by the faculty of Cloud Chief Combined, watched as representatives from the community took seats in the swiftly prepared assembly. When all was quiet except for a few coughs and throat-clearings, Principal Billings stepped to the podium.

"I have a special guest here today, with an announcement from the

Grand Master and the Head of the Vampire Council," Principal Billings began. "Most of you know him already—he was here for the investigations a year ago. Mr. Winkler, if you'd like to come in, now." Principal Billings held out his hand and William Winkler strode through the door, coming to stand next to the Principal.

Taller than Billings by a good six inches, while his presence overshadowed that of Cloud Chief's Principal, William Winkler smiled and nodded at the assembled crowd before taking Billings' place behind the podium.

"I realize this meeting is a surprise to most of you, but I have a prepared joint statement from the Grand Master and from the Head of the Vampire Council," Winkler began, his nearly black eyes scanning the crowd. "I ask you to remember that they helped put these communities together, and it is our duty to follow their instructions. Here is the statement." Winkler pulled a folded paper from his shirt pocket and opened it.

Dude, this is weird, Ashe sent to Sali, who nodded in silent agreement. "It is agreed between the werewolf and vampire races," Winkler began, "that we should provide shelter and protection for the families of the half-Elemaiyan children who have been preyed upon by the Elemaiya. These children face kidnapping or death if we do not act. It has been requested by the authorities within the U.S. Government that we provide homes for these families until a more permanent solution may be found."

"*What?*" Sali mouthed at Ashe. Whispers and murmurs interrupted the silence in the cafeteria—students and adults were expressing their surprise and alarm at this strange turn of events. Everything from curiosity to animosity was uttered between neighbors and classmates. Winkler held up a hand and silence resumed.

"What that means," Winkler went on, "is that there are only six children left. Six who haven't been kidnapped or killed, out of hundreds. The government has attempted to relocate the families, but even that hasn't worked. They've lost at least fifteen others since they started the relocation program. They're asking us now to take the remaining six families in until a better solution can be arranged at the end of summer. The Grand Master has decreed it," Winkler offered a hard stare to the werewolves around the room.

Ashe watched one particular person, knowing he would be the barometer for the racism and bigotry that would likely ensue—Principal Benjamin Billings, PhD., *werewolf*. If there were a more sour expression attainable on the Principal's face, Ashe was never destined to see it. Billings was angry, with a capital A. His gaze turning from Billings, Ashe searched out the other two—Chump and Wormy.

Chad and Jeremy were already huddled together, whispering. Ashe might have heard what they were saying if the cafeteria wasn't already buzzing with micro-conversations.

"Where will they live?" Mr. Dodd, the History teacher raised a hand.

"Temporary housing will be trucked in," Winkler answered. "All paid for by the Vampire Council. I believe the Council has arranged to have vampire assistance tomorrow evening to put everything in place. You won't be expected to do anything except treat our guests with respect while they're here."

"But they're all humans," someone else spoke up. "Except for their *half-human* kids." Ashe recognized the derision in Chad's voice. Jeremy's mother, Diane, frowned at her son from a seat near the door.

"Don't tell me this isn't Ashe Evans' fault," Jeremy chimed in.

"What did you just say?" Winkler was now examining Jeremy Booth with guarded interest. Jeremy, a shapeshifter, wouldn't fall under as much scrutiny as Chad, his adopted werewolf brother and best friend.

"Nothing." Jeremy knew when to keep his mouth shut around older, stronger adults. His animal was a wildcat, but a younger werewolf could take him down easily.

"Are the humans aware that they'll be among those who aren't human? Do they even know we exist?" Greta Rocklin, the Transformational Arts teacher, asked. Also a werewolf, she was married to Micah Rocklin, Second to Marcus DeLuca, Cloud Chief's werewolf Packmaster.

"I am joining Bill Jennings, Director for the Joint NSA and

Homeland Security Department in Dallas tomorrow morning. The families will be informed at that time," Winkler replied. "Many of you know already that werewolves and vampires work in a special division of Mr. Jennings' department. He, the Grand Master and the Head of the Vampire Council all wish for us to protect these children inside Cloud Chief's hidden boundary. These families have not been informed as to what their children truly are and why they are hunted. The Director and I will attempt to explain things tomorrow, and I'll be taking one of you with me to meet these families so they can see a werewolf and shapeshifter for themselves."

"No self-respecting werewolf will agree to that," Principal Billings almost exploded, causing Winkler's head to turn swiftly in the Principal's direction.

"I was going to do it," Winkler said, "so they can see a wolf. I'm taking Ashe Evans with me because he has something in common with those children. Shall I report your reaction to the Grand Master?"

"No." Principal Billings hung his head immediately. Ashe knew the Principal wasn't sorry for what he'd said, just as Chad and Jeremy weren't. He raised his hand.

"What is it, Ashe?" Winkler lifted an eyebrow in Ashe's direction.

"Where will you put the temporary housing? Will they really be protected by the witch's boundary?"

"That's our hope. The Elemaiya haven't found their way back here after your father placed compulsion on the two that came last year. The housing will be in the field behind your home, I think. Water and electrical lines were laid there in case Cloud Chief ever increased in size. The location will also make it easier for your father and Nathan Anderson to guard them at night."

"Have you talked to my parents? About me going to Dallas?"

"Ashe," Winkler smiled, "I spoke with your father last night. I have your parents' permission."

"Okay, just wanted to check," Ashe huddled into his seat, feeling slightly embarrassed.

"How many will be coming?" Mr. Dawkins, the Math teacher, asked.

"Seventeen will be coming to Cloud Chief," Winkler answered. "Ten parents, six half-Elemaiyan children and one human child. Trace and Jason will be back to help guard the community and run errands —the families won't be leaving Cloud Chief once they arrive. They have to stay hidden. I warn you to treat them as any other member of the community, at the Grand Master's command. Their names and whereabouts are to be kept confidential. You understand why, I hope."

"Those lives depend on it," Miss Campbell nodded. She was the only shapeshifting teacher in Cloud Chief, becoming an exotic leopard at the full Moon. Larry Garnett, the newly hired werewolf English teacher, was content to stand beside Principal Billings without saying a word.

"Gonna teach human kids to be empties?" Chad sneered at Ashe on the way out the door. Most of the adults had either left the school or gone into Principal Billings' office with Mr. Winkler to voice private concerns, leaving Ashe at the mercy of Chad and Jeremy.

"Want to say that to my dad?" Sali shoved his way through a knot of students, causing Wynn and Dori to smack him on the shoulder for being rude.

"Your dad wouldn't care if the empty disappeared," Jeremy snickered.

"That's not true," Sali growled, his eyes going feral. The threat of Sali's werewolf forced Jeremy to back up.

"That's enough, boys. Chad, Jeremy, air your concerns with the Principal or with the Packmaster," Greta Rocklin appeared and pointed the older boys toward the door.

Ashe hunched his shoulders. If his parents would only allow him to mist, he could avoid those two bullies easily. Instead, Chump and Wormy always accosted him in public but generally away from adult eyes, and Ashe was prevented from doing anything to protect himself.

Not wishing for the Second's wife to report any infractions, Chad and Jeremy raced toward Jeremy's new car. Sali and Ashe watched them leave, feeling a bit of envy as the two boys drove away.

"I'm gonna have a car when I turn sixteen," Sali muttered, his eyes returning to normal. Stuffing hands in his pockets, Sali walked toward the gravel road that led to Ashe's house.

~

"Here," Ashe set a plate of nachos in front of Sali before picking up the phone and calling his mother. "Mom, we're home. I'm feeding the tapeworm now," Ashe announced when his mother said hello.

"Honey, did Mr. Winkler talk to you today?" Adele sounded worried.

"Mom, he talked to all of us."

"No, I mean about the trip to Dallas."

"He announced it to the entire assembly," Sali said, stuffing another cheese-laden tortilla chip in his mouth.

"He didn't," Adele heard Sali's comment and became concerned immediately.

"After stupid Jeremy said it was my fault that the humans were coming," Ashe grumbled.

"I'm calling Marcus when I get home," Adele fumed.

"Mom, it'll just make it worse—they don't bother me unless there's nobody around to stop them," Ashe pointed out. "Besides, they'll go off to college in the fall. End of problem."

"Ashe, the Dallas trip is supposed to be fun for you—to meet others who might be like you in some way. You'll stay the night with Mr. Winkler and talk with those children when they're brought in. Mr. Winkler wants you to show them the bat."

"But not the mist, huh?"

"That's dangerous and you know it. If word of that got out," Adele didn't finish.

"Yeah, I know," Ashe said glumly. If anyone, particularly the Vampire Council, learned of that specific talent, Ashe might become a desirable target for more than just the Elemaiya. "Mom, I gotta go before Sali eats the last two nachos."

"All right. We'll talk more when your dad wakes."

Ashe hung up the cordless with a sigh. Sali handed over the plate with the designated two nachos on it. "Dude, you really are a tapeworm," Ashe said.

~

"I heard him, Marcus. He said this was Ashe Evans' fault. Everybody inside the school cafeteria heard it," Denise DeLuca said. Marcus had just walked through the door of their Cloud Chief home after a busy day at DeLuca's Locksmith Services in Cordell.

"Denise, we've known for a while that those two bully some of the younger ones. If it were only Chad, I could have a talk with him, but Jeremy is a shapeshifter. We don't have that much control over them."

"You don't think Chad put him up to it?"

"The boy lost both his parents. I expect Chad to be rebellious."

"That's no excuse to be cruel," Denise went to pull dinner from the oven. "Sali's on his way home. Mr. Winkler will come by before he leaves with Ashe tonight."

"I'm glad it's the weekend," Marcus said. "Have we heard from Marco?"

"Mr. Winkler says he'll come home for a week before going back to Dallas and working for him the rest of the summer."

"I'm worried that our oldest will become a member of the Dallas Pack."

"There are worse things to be," Denise said softly. "Being a member of the Dallas Pack holds a certain amount of prestige."

"Oh, and being a member of the Cloud Chief Pack isn't important?"

"You know that's not what I meant."

"Sorry, it's just too near the full Moon."

The full Moon was in two days, on Sunday, May third. Everybody in Cloud Chief felt it. Marcus wondered how Winkler was going to handle getting humans to their hidden community around that event.

Shrugging off the thought, Marcus went to wash his hands. The back door clicked shut as Sali walked into the kitchen; Denise told him to wash up, too, while she put dinner on the table.

~

"We have to get this out of the way fast; full Moon is Sunday," Winkler said, driving down I-35 toward Dallas three hours later. Ashe, buckled into the passenger seat of a Winkler Security van, listened while the Dallas Packmaster spoke.

"Mr. Winkler, do you know anything about those kids?" Ashe asked quietly, his blue eyes focused on the Dallas Packmaster's face in curiosity.

"I don't think those kids know much about themselves. How can we know anything? I'm not sure Bill gave them any kind of explanation when they relocated their families; just that someone was hunting them." Winkler turned dark eyes briefly on Ashe before directing his attention to the highway again.

"I assume they know about the deaths and disappearances of the others? How many of the disappearances do you think are actual deaths and how many are kidnappings by the Bright Elemaiya?"

"Kid, you worry me at times, knowing more than you should," Winkler tapped the steering wheel absently as he drove through the Arbuckle mountains in south central Oklahoma.

"I know the Bright Elemaiya went to that clinic for a reason. What reason, other than getting children, could there be? And if they wanted children, then they *wanted* them, instead of letting humans keep them. Doesn't that make sense? It's like the cuckoo, laying its eggs in another bird's nest."

"Yes—they sound like brood parasites, don't they?" Winkler agreed.

"But the cuckoo chick pushes the eggs or the nestlings of the parent birds out so it can get more food," Ashe pointed out. "You haven't heard of that happening, have you?"

"No. But we don't know much at all about these families. If Bill will consent to answer questions, I suggest you ask him."

"Bill Jennings, the Director of the Joint NSA and Homeland Security Department? That Bill?"

"Yeah. That Bill." Winkler grinned at Ashe. In the dim interior of the van, Ashe barely saw it.

"Sounds like you know him pretty well."

"I do. We've been working together for twenty years."

"You really are connected to National Security, aren't you, Mr. Winkler?"

"Yep. But don't let that out. It's a secret."

"Got it." Ashe turned to look at the cut-rock sides of mountains through which they traveled. They shone in the nearly full Moon overhead. "News said it might rain tomorrow," Ashe added.

"I hope it doesn't rain on Sunday," Winkler chuckled. "Wet fur and mud isn't fun."

"I just stay inside and flap around the house," Ashe said. Winkler laughed.

∼

"This is your house?" Ashe stared openmouthed at the three-story mansion.

"No, my house is next door," Winkler said, leading Ashe up the wide, multicolored brick walk to a mansion. "Mine is a little bigger. I bought this one for someone before she died," he added. "Never had the heart to sell it afterward. The families will be brought here initially, for the announcement. Trace and Jason are inside—they'll stay here with you."

"When are the families coming?"

"Tomorrow morning," Winkler replied. Ashe watched as Winkler unlocked the substantial front door and punched a code into the security alarm keypad just inside the house. A massive, gleaming wood staircase split and went up both sides of a gallery; the tiled, oval floor of the entryway was of polished marble and shone in the dim light. Winkler hit a switch, bathing the entire foyer with brightness.

"How's the bustling metropolis of Cloud Chief?" Trace walked in with a soda in his hand. He'd heard Winkler and Ashe enter the house and walked in from the kitchen to greet the new arrivals.

"There's nothing bustling about Cloud Chief or anything else within a hundred-mile radius," Ashe grinned at the nearly seven-foot werewolf. Jason followed Trace and hugged Ashe.

"How are you, son?" Jason smiled.

"I'm good, Mr. Landers," Ashe assured the older werewolf. Trace had told him the year before that Jason was more than a hundred fifty years old.

"We'll be coming to Oklahoma with you, to help out with those kids," Jason said. "And we'll be giving regular reports to Mr. Winkler and the Director."

"So I'd better behave, huh?"

"Yup. Hate to have to ground you," Trace ruffled Ashe's slightly curly, light-brown hair.

"Being grounded sucks," Ashe nodded.

"Come on, kid, you're on the second floor between Jason and me," Trace said. "Is your bag in the van?"

"Yeah. I can get it." Ashe turned toward the door.

"Nah, Trace will handle it. Come on, want something to drink?" Jason motioned for Ashe to follow him. Ashe trailed Jason and found the largest kitchen he'd ever seen at the back of the house.

"Mom should see this," Ashe breathed. The kitchen island was ten feet long and held a separate sink and dishwasher.

"Do we have transportation to Cloud Chief arranged?" Winkler spoke with Jason over Ashe's head.

"All done. Six vans plus drivers and security for each. Trace and I will take the kid, here, in a separate vehicle. Bill is providing an agent for each van."

"Real agents?" Ashe blinked at Jason, a surprised expression on his face.

"Real agents," Winkler chuckled and patted Ashe's shoulder. "You saw Radomir last year—kid, that vampire is better than any agent I've ever seen. And he's not the best I've ever known."

"Who was the best, Mr. Winkler?"

"That would be Lissa," Trace set Ashe's small bag on the kitchen floor. "She saved my brother's life once. I saw the recorded footage. You wouldn't have believed it."

"Lissa?"

"We'll talk about that some other time," Winkler growled. "Jason, show Ashe to his bedroom." Winkler stalked out of the kitchen.

"Boss gets a little touchy about her," Jason murmured. "This was her house. Come on, kid, there's a big TV in your room."

"So she's the one who's dead?"

"Yeah."

CHAPTER 3

Jason cooked bacon and eggs for breakfast the following morning before Bill Jennings arrived, followed closely by six families with seven children. One was completely human—a child of a previous marriage. Ashe studied all of them—the adults seemed tired and worried, their children (all teens and older than Ashe), curious and cautious at the same time.

"This is Ashe Evans. His mother went to the same clinic," Bill Jennings introduced Ashe to the newcomers. Ashe stared in mute surprise—two of the teens had pointed ears.

"Why do we have to move again?" one of the boys whined. He had blond hair and green eyes, but no pointed ears.

"Hush, Philip," his mother warned.

"It's time we were more open with the information available," Bill Jennings sighed into the silence that came after. "Ashe, here, will help explain things to you. Mr. Winkler, if you would?"

Winkler led everyone into a large media room with theater seating and a huge television screen mounted on the wall. "Take a seat and get comfortable," he instructed. Ashe sat between Trace and Jason at the back of the room. Winkler stood in front of the large screen to make his announcements.

"Now," Winkler began, "More than thirty years ago, all this began. I know some of you may have difficulty believing any of this at first, but I assure you, everything you hear will be the truth. I hope it doesn't change anything with you or your family; it just is. This is why they're after these children here, and why so many have died or been abducted." Winkler clicked a tiny remote and the television screen came to life behind him.

Ashe stared—he hadn't known they'd taken photographs of the two Dark Elemaiya from last year's attack. One looked human—except for the pointed ears. The other, a hybrid, had a very tall, mostly human body with the head of a doglike creature. It looked similar to pictures he'd seen of Anubis, the Egyptian god of mummification and the afterlife. The head certainly resembled a jackal's with tall, pointed ears. The feet, too, were long for a human and bore claws instead of toenails. Ashe had detected the hybrid a year before, using echolocation. He just hadn't known exactly what it was as it ran away from him.

"What is that thing?" Philip spoke loudly, his words blunt and irritating as he pointed at the Dark hybrid's image on the screen.

"That is a hybrid—his race manipulated his birth, I believe," Winkler replied dryly. "Now, you'll be happy to know that you're not related in any way to these two. You may be related, however, to some of these." Winkler clicked the remote again and another set of images appeared.

Ashe drew in a breath. It was video this time—someone was walking through a field at twilight, but there were people—people with pointed ears—all around. The camera was attached to clothing somewhere—Ashe couldn't see anything of the wearer.

The camera stopped before a woman who obviously thought herself beautiful. She had long brown hair and wore many jewels and a richly embroidered dress. A carved gold band circled her head and her green eyes flashed angrily. *"I'm not sure how you knew to contact us,"* she informed the camera-wearer coldly. Ashe recognized the voice of the camera bearer, though, when he spoke.

"That doesn't matter," Winkler said to the Queen of the Bright

Elemaiya. *"What does matter is that your dark cousins have discovered your attempt to increase your numbers and they're picking them off, one at a time."*

Ashe gaped at the images as he listened to the conversation between the Bright Queen and Winkler a year earlier. Winkler handed over a folder of information to the Queen's attendant.

The Queen, obviously skeptical, hadn't believed Winkler at first. After Winkler's evidence had been presented, the Queen offered two guards to help eliminate the Dark Elemaiya terrorizing Cloud Chief with help from Paul Harris, the former English teacher. When the screen went blank again after the recorded confrontation, the room erupted.

"Calm down," Bill Jennings, who was aging and unused to dealing with teens, now stood before the crowd, all of whom wanted to talk or ask questions at once. Ashe sat quietly in his seat at the back, knowing that he'd react the same way if he were only now learning of his ancestry. The Bright Queen and her people, though—that had been a shock. He, like the others, was seeing them for the first time and it was frightening.

"Who were those people?" one of the fathers demanded.

"Bright Elemaiya," Bill replied. "The first images you saw—the dead ones? Those were Dark Elemaiya. The Dark Ones are at war with the Bright half of their race. The Bright Ones donated eggs to the clinic in St. Louis. They have also donated to fifty other clinics over a thirty-year period, with the clinic in St. Louis being the most recent. We had no idea what was going on with the child disappearances over the years until someone made the connection to the St. Louis facility." Bill sighed and shook his head.

"These six children were born as a result." Bill went on, sweeping out a hand to encompass the six teens. "And no, it is not romantic to be a child of an alien race. That's what they are—they are not native to this world."

Ashe blinked at Director Jennings' words—there'd been other clinics and other kidnappings or killings. That had come as an unwelcome surprise. Director Jennings' statement brought another spate of overlapping conversations—Ashe even heard a bit of profanity—before the Director restored calm.

"You're saying that my dad isn't my dad?" a girl asked tearfully.

No, your father is your father. You are a half-human, half-Elemaiyan child. Ashe, will you come up here, please?"

Ashe rose reluctantly and walked unsteadily toward Director Jennings, turning to face the crowd when he arrived. "Ashe is what you are," the Director stated. "With a few differences, I think. Ashe, tell them about your parents."

"My mother is a shapeshifter," Ashe began nervously, his blue eyes betraying a bit of concern over spilling his parents' secrets to humans. His first admission caused a ripple of murmurs throughout the room. "My father—my dad—is a vampire." The room exploded.

"That has to be a lie," a mother stood and pointed a finger at Ashe.

"No, ma'am, not a lie," Ashe shook his head, nearly quaking before the disbelieving crowd.

"Ashe is also a shapeshifter," Winkler, who'd leaned against the wall beside the television screen, straightened and came to stand beside Ashe. "Show them, Ashe, what you are."

Ashe gulped anxiously before allowing his clothing to drop. Fluttering and hovering as the bat, his audience sat in stunned silence for seconds before riotous discussion began. People pointed at him and spoke in incredulous whispers to others. It made him uncomfortable. Once conversation died down a little, Ashe flapped toward Trace and Jason at the back of the room.

Now what? Ashe sent to Trace as he dipped and bobbed before the tall werewolf's face. Without a blink, Trace snatched Ashe's tiny bat from the air and tucked him onto the top of his shirt pocket. *Thanks,* Ashe said mentally, folding his wings and getting comfortable on Trace's shirt.

"No problem, kid," Trace said softly, grinning.

"We are moving you to a special, paranormal community in Oklahoma," Winkler informed the crowd while attempting to hide a smile. He'd witnessed Trace's quick grasp of Ashe's tiny bat. "It is inhabited by shapeshifters, vampires and werewolves."

"Just when I think my life can't get more messed up than it is," Philip grumbled as he climbed into a van with his mother.

"Director Jennings assures me it is safe," his mother hissed, climbing onto the back seat with her son.

"Why can't we ride with Luanne?" Philip muttered.

"For safety," the agent in the passenger seat turned and said. "It'll take four hours or more to get there. We'd prefer not to make any unscheduled stops on the way." He turned back in his seat, accepting no argument from Philip.

"Mom, this can't be happening," Luanne Jansen shook her head in confusion as she huddled in the back seat of a van between her parents.

"Honey, don't worry about it," Linda Jansen soothed. "This is to throw those people off our trail. Director Jennings says we'll leave at the end of summer and go somewhere else—somewhere *normal*." The driver cleared his throat, causing Linda Jansen to fall silent.

"I think our driver is one of *them*," Luanne whispered.

"He is and can hear better than you ever will," the driver retorted, backing up to allow the lead van through. Luanne gripped her father's arm, suddenly terrified.

"That bat was so cool," sixteen-year-old Edward Pendley loaded into a van behind his father. "Dad, do you think I might be able to do that? I'm half, too."

"Son, I don't know," Steven Pendley replied distractedly. "Talk to that boy—he may know."

"I will," Edward declared and clicked the lap belt around him. "Do we still have to finish our lessons?"

"If you want to graduate, you do."

"Darn." Edward had always been homeschooled—his mother died shortly after he'd turned three and with pointed ears, his father had little hope that his son wouldn't be ridiculed at a public school.

Using the insurance money from his wife's death, Steven Pendley had worked evening jobs and schooled his son at home. Now they both knew the source of what Edward's doctors had thought a slight deformity; Edward had inherited his pointed ears from another race.

∼

"Mom, I want to go shopping," Elizabeth Frasier pouted, her arms crossed angrily over her chest. "I haven't gotten new clothes in forever." She'd watched enviously as they'd passed shopping center after shopping center on their way through Dallas the day before. Now they were leaving all of it behind.

"Lizzie, hush, this is hard enough for your mother as it is," Francis Frasier helped his daughter into a van. Mary Ellen Frasier attempted to control the shaking in her hands, but wasn't having much success.

"Come on, hon, get in. We'll be all right," Francis did his best to calm his frightened wife. Elizabeth wasn't helping, whining about shopping when she should be worried for her safety. Francis sighed over the whole thing and climbed into the van after his wife and fifteen-year-old daughter.

∼

Sixteen-year-old Keith Caldwell stared out the window as the van drove away from the huge mansion. A Denton, Texas, city limit sign blurred past as the vehicle drove northward toward Oklahoma.

Keith thought of himself as practical and still had trouble believing what he'd been shown and told earlier. Another race? That had to be a trick of some sort. Leaning back in his seat, he convinced himself that he was part of an experiment—the government was testing the effects of stress on teens or something. That had to be it.

His half-brother, Bryce, sat in the third row of seats in the van. Older by two years, Bryce had cast puzzled glances at Keith after they'd received the information earlier.

Keith took one look at his parents' faces—Jeanine and Michael Caldwell appeared pale and worried. Leaning against the locked door of the van, Keith closed his eyes to sleep during the trip.

∼

Macy Hill gripped both her parents' hands as they sat in the back of a van speeding toward Oklahoma. Of all six children, she'd been closest to capture—if the car full of drunken college students hadn't hit one of the men trying to take her, she'd be gone already.

Her job at a pizza parlor in Athens, Georgia, kept her out late on weekends. One Saturday evening six months earlier, she'd been walking toward her car when the two had attempted to abduct her.

Thinking at first that she was tired and failed to notice their approach, she now knew they might have used other means to come at her unawares. Four male college students in an ancient Buick had driven through the small parking lot and run one of the men down. Except they probably weren't men. Macy had rushed inside the pizzeria to phone the police and her parents.

Although the police arrived quickly, there was no sign of either abductor at the scene. Only four college students and a dented car remained in the parking lot. Macy and her parents had been relocated immediately.

Now, she sat in the back of a van between her mother Ramona and her father Rocky, both parents holding her hands and doing their best to comfort her. Macy felt alienated—from everything. Her world had just turned inside out and she was lost.

∼

"Well, we've stocked the basics plus a few extras," Greta Rocklin stared at the last of six pantries. She, Denise DeLuca and Sharon O'Neill had gone shopping for the human families, buying what every family would need—flour, sugar, coffee—the things they always stocked in their homes.

Pads of paper lay on kitchen counters for lists of other necessities. No computers were allowed in any of the temporary homes—Director Jennings had forbidden that type of communication, along with landlines and cell phones. There would be no contact with the outside world for nearly three months.

"They should be here anytime," Denise checked her watch. "Mr. Winkler called Marcus and said they left four hours ago."

"Are we supposed to invite them to dinner or what? There's spaghetti and that sort of thing, but we'll have to get someone to run to the store after they tell us what they need," Sharon sounded worried.

"Billings isn't happy," Denise admitted reluctantly. "I thought he and Marcus were going to go after each other's throats. This isn't the best time for this to be happening—the day before a full Moon."

"Aedan and Nathan will have to watch them tomorrow night just to make sure they stay indoors," Greta agreed. "I know they'll place compulsion when they leave, too, but what about while they're here? This could turn out so badly," she stared at her hands. "If those kids become curious and get anywhere near a couple of people, we could have trouble."

"Let's hope that doesn't happen. Somebody will have to warn them to stay away from certain individuals," Sharon nodded.

"This is it? Man, this is the middle of *nowhere*, Philip snapped angrily as the van pulled through the barrier separating Cloud Chief from the human world.

"Philip," the agent turned in his seat for the second time after listening to Philip's complaints for four hours, "this is to save your life. Do you want to live or not?"

"They're all double-wides," Steven Pendley, Edward's father, sighed at the six prefab houses spaced ten yards apart in an Oklahoma field.

"They're tied down as well as they can be and there's a new storm shelter between the third and fourth houses," Jason came to stand beside Steven. "The women did a little grocery shopping for you, but there's paper on the counter to make a list for other needs. We'll bring dinner for everyone tonight, but get those lists back to Trace soon if you want to eat after that. We'll have a meeting over dinner to give you the dos and don'ts. Tomorrow is the full Moon, so it goes without saying that you need to stay indoors. The vampires will be standing guard, just in case."

"Are we in danger on full Moons?" Edward now stood beside his father, staring up at Jason curiously.

"Not unless you jump between a werewolf and what he's hunting," Jason grinned.

"Cool," Edward breathed. "Dad, this is so cool!" Edward went racing toward the house they'd been assigned.

"It's cool," Steven smiled tentatively at Jason.

"Lizzie, the furniture and everything is new. What is there to complain about?" Francis Frasier leveled a look at his daughter.

"Daddy, this is nowhere. Do you see that field out there? It leads nowhere!" Elizabeth flung out an arm helplessly.

"I need to take a pill," Mary Ellen spilled her purse onto the kitchen counter, searching for a Valium.

"Dude, you can see all the houses from here," Sali whispered as he and Ashe stood on the deck behind the Evans home.

"Yeah. Good thing they put in a big storm shelter—those double-wide mobile homes won't last five seconds in a tornado," Ashe grumped.

"They look okay—like regular houses," Sali tilted his head to examine the mobile homes. "If you like rectangles," he added.

"Wow, geometry did sink in," Ashe bumped Sali's shoulder with his own.

"Werewolves don't need geometry," Sali side-kicked Ashe.

"Planning on living in the woods?" Ashe teased. "Where will you hook up your computer? I don't think pines have electrical outlets."

"They've evolved. They're the new, improved pines," Sali declared.

"Yeah, Wi-Fi pines. You think there's an app for that?" Ashe grinned as they watched the new arrivals unload suitcases from vans.

"With special docks for MP-3 players," Sali agreed.

"Well, I've heard of singing pines," Ashe said.

"But these could be blasting disco," Sali observed.

"Sounds like a good way to scare off your dinner," Ashe said. "I hear rabbits and deer hate disco." Both boys watched as one of the new arrivals began walking in their direction.

"What's his name?" Sali asked quietly before the boy arrived.

"I think that's Edward," Ashe said. "He's okay."

"Hello," Edward said shyly, once he stood in front of Ashe and Sali. "I'm Edward. Edward Pendley." His dark-brown hair was slightly curly and fine, lifting in the Oklahoma breeze as he gazed curiously at Ashe and Sali with hazel eyes. Freckles littered his face and moved just a bit as he grinned shyly.

"I'm Ashe and this is Sali—Salidar DeLuca," Ashe introduced Sali.

"Hi," Sali said.

"Are you like Ashe?" Edward shaded the afternoon sun from his eyes as he looked Sali over.

"Nah. I don't think anybody is like Ashe," Sali grinned. "I'm a werewolf. My dad's the Packmaster for Cloud Chief."

"Really? You turn into a wolf? That is seriously cool," Edward sighed. "I now live in the best comic book ever."

"Talking with the local fauna, Eddie?" Philip walked up and stared impolitely at Sali and Ashe.

"Better than talking with the flora," Sali said, bristling at Philip's rudeness.

"Yeah, you don't want to talk to the plants—the pines play disco," Ashe said, sending Sali into a snorting fit of laughter.

"Really?" Edward was ready to believe anything.

"Nah, we're just teasing," Ashe said. "Want to come inside the house for a soda?"

"Uh," Edward glanced behind to see if his father was looking.

"I'll tell him," Ashe said, sending mindspeech.

Steven Pendley nearly dropped the suitcase he carried when Ashe's voice sounded inside his head. *Edward is coming to my house for a soda. He'll be back in a little while. By the way, the mindspeech is a secret. I think you can keep secrets.*

"What is it?" Trace set another bag down inside the Pendley's temporary home.

"Nothing. Just had a thought, that's all," Steven set about unpacking.

Ashe and Sali hadn't intended for Philip to come along, but he did. All four boys sat at the kitchen island and drank sodas, finishing off the tortilla chips that Sali opened two days before to make nachos.

"So, is this all there is—a kitchen, garage and a sun room?" Philip looked around him.

"That's all there is," Sali nodded sagely. "*Above* ground."

"My dad's a vampire, remember?" Ashe said, crunching on a chip.

"Can I see the rest?" Edward was nearly vibrating with excitement.

"I have to get permission from my dad, first," Ashe said. "He wants to know everyone that I invite over."

"What does it matter? He's dead right now anyway," Philip said.

"Were you born rude or have you cultivated that attitude?" Ashe slid off his barstool, angry in a blink.

"Philip!" Jackie Raymond walked into Ashe's home, searching for her son.

"It's the truth, Mom."

"You don't have any idea what the truth is. Come with me, I need your help unpacking." Philip grumbled as he followed his mother out of Ashe's home.

"Ignore him, all the others do," Edward said softly. "He's gloom and doom all the time."

"He's rude with 'tude," Sali agreed.

"Hey, no more rhyming in this house," Ashe tossed a tortilla chip at Sali, who ducked it easily. "Dude, we should get back to your new house before your dad wonders what happened to you," he said, turning to Edward.

"All right." Edward took his soda bottle with him and he, Ashe and Sali walked along to Edward's temporary home.

"Dad, this is Sali. You've met Ashe already," Edward introduced his new friends.

"Need help, Mr. Pendley?" Ashe offered.

"That bag over there has a few photographs and things in it. Want to unpack those?" Steven Pendley asked, searching through the fridge for something to drink. "Good, they got a few sodas." Pulling a cola from a box, he popped the tab and drank while Sali, Ashe and Edward unloaded framed photographs of Edward when he was small, posing with a pretty, red-haired woman.

"That's my mom—I don't remember her," Edward said, tapping the photograph Ashe held. "She died when I was three. In a car crash."

"Sorry, dude," Ashe said. He didn't say that his own mother had almost been killed the same way a year before.

"It's okay," Edward shrugged. "She was on the wrong side of the car when the ambulance came," he whispered to Ashe. "Buckled in. Nobody in the driver's seat." He cut his eyes toward his father. "Dad gets upset if I talk about it." Ashe glanced quickly at Steven Pendley, who was drinking his soda and staring through the living-room window at the prairie beyond.

"Dude, we need to talk soon," Ashe whispered back.

Cordell Mayor Jim Taylor was terrified. The man threatening him had taken him by surprise, knocking him out as he'd walked from the barn toward his house earlier in the evening. Now that Jim was conscious inside his kitchen, his assailant was asking strange questions.

"Tell me!" The black-haired man demanded, gripping Jim's shirt tightly in a fist. "What did you see?" Jim Taylor saw the scar on the man's upper lip, his face was so close.

"S-six big mobile homes," Jim stuttered, flattening himself against the wall in his kitchen. "I-I didn't see them myself. Heard about it fr-from s-somebody who lives on highway f-fifty-four."

"Where are those mobile homes now?"

"D-don't know. Didn't say where they w-went."

"And the name of the person who did see them?" The name barely left Mayor Taylor's mouth before he died.

CHAPTER 4

$\mathcal{A}$she wanted to talk to his mother about Edward and the way Edward's mother had died, but he'd never admitted to either parent that he'd been involved in saving Adele Evans from a dangerously weaving truck while she lay unconscious on the passenger seat.

Ashe had driven the old Ford home from west of Cordell, terrified the entire time. If he told his parents about that now, he'd be grounded forever. Judiciously deciding to keep it secret, Ashe set plates on the kitchen island. His mother had brought home takeout from Betsy's again—Cordell Feed and Seed was so busy, Adele was too exhausted to cook.

"Chicken and dumplings, with two pieces of cornbread, as usual," Adele smiled at her son and sat down on a barstool to eat her own meal.

"I'd like you to meet one of the new kids," Ashe said. "He's sixteen but shorter than Sali. He has pointed ears. And freckles."

"Pointed ears? Really?" Adele dipped mashed potatoes onto her plate—she'd ordered pork chops with potatoes and gravy.

"Yeah. One of the others has pointed ears, too—I think her name is Macy. She covers them up with long hair, though."

"Do you think it makes them feel different?" Adele's brown eyes watched Ashe, prepared to weigh his answer.

"Don't know," Ashe ate chicken and dumplings for a while. "Edward—I think he's homeschooled. His dad said something about homework when Sali and I left. Edward wanted to explore a little."

"Where did he live before?" Adele asked, curious.

"Edward says they lived in Missouri until his mom died, and then they moved to Memphis. That's where they were until Director Jennings relocated the families."

"Director Jennings is getting old," Adele said. "He's done a lot for the country, though."

"Mr. Winkler says Mr. Jennings is about to retire."

"I hope they find somebody good to take his place."

"Yeah. He took over after Anthony Hancock got killed." Ashe admired Anthony Hancock; the previous Director was a national hero and died in the line of duty. Ashe had written a history paper about him.

"How are the newcomers fitting in?" Aedan Evans walked through the middle door and came to sit next to Adele.

"Some better than others," Ashe said, taking his plate to the dishwasher. "There's one kid who's really rude. His name is Philip."

"Honey, you may have to overlook that—these kids have been uprooted from their lives, homes and friends. I can't say I'd be happy about it, either," Adele admitted.

"Aedan?" Ashe and his father both heard Nathan Anderson's voice outside their home. Nathan hadn't bothered with the doorbell located beside the garage door—he'd known that Aedan would hear.

"I'll get it," Aedan held a hand out, stopping Ashe from going to the kitchen door that led into the garage. Soon Nathan Anderson stood inside their kitchen. Nathan was tall but not as tall as Aedan, with dark blond hair and green eyes. He smiled at Ashe.

"How's Cori, Mr. Anderson?" Ashe asked. He hadn't seen her at school the day before.

"Enrolled at the University of Oklahoma for the fall semester," Nathan's smile widened. "As of yesterday."

"Cool," Ashe breathed.

"Aedan, I just heard something on the news," Nathan said, his expression becoming serious. "The Mayor of Cordell was found murdered in his home."

$\sim$

"Do you think the murder has anything to do with these families?" Aedan asked as both vampires walked through the field behind the Evans' home. Aedan and Nathan could see the six new houses clearly in the deepening twilight.

"Surely not—why would anyone kill someone with such a high profile? That's foolish."

"True. But we've seen plenty of that during our lifetimes."

"Also true. But what would the Mayor know? Those houses weren't trucked through Cordell—they came through from the opposite direction. Mr. Winkler is smarter than that." Nathan shook his head.

"It's probably an unrelated incident," Aedan decided. "Did the news say anything else?"

"They'd just found the body so there wasn't anything. You know humans; proceed with caution and keep information away from the public as long as possible."

"We'll be on our guard to see if anyone else is harmed or killed," Aedan nodded. "We'll investigate if that happens."

$\sim$

"Director, Cordell's Mayor was just murdered," Winkler spoke over the phone to Bill Jennings. Bill had flown back to D.C. earlier in the day.

"I'll send two agents," Bill said. "Will you notify the Grand Master, just in case this is connected? How did the man die?"

"Broken neck," Winkler replied. "My contact in Oklahoma City confirmed it."

"So, someone strong, then. Any clear motive?"

"Not that I know. So far, they haven't found anything missing, but there was some sort of flap last year between the Mayor and his opponent during the election."

"I'll have my agents look into that as well. Is there anyone inside the community who might be able to help them? Someone awake during the day?"

"Yeah."

"Who is that?"

"Marcus DeLuca. He's ex-Special Ops."

"You mean I'm just now learning that the Cloud Chief Packmaster was Special Ops?"

"Under a different name—he's eighty-seven, Director. Of course he'd have to use a different name. Most of us do."

"Of course," Bill muttered softly. Winkler still heard.

~

"Haven't seen you before." Philip stared at Aedan and Nathan. He wasn't supposed to be outside this late at night, but his mother was cleaning up the kitchen after dinner. Philip had sneaked out.

"Young one, why are you out at this hour?" Nathan asked the blond teen.

"Why are *you* out at this hour? And who are you anyway?" Philip returned in his usual, rude manner.

"We guard the community at night," Aedan replied. "You will go inside and not come out again this night," compulsion was thick in Aedan's voice. Philip turned immediately and walked toward his new home. Aedan and Nathan watched as he walked through the door, closing it behind him.

"That must be the one Ashe doesn't like," Aedan muttered as he and Nathan resumed their rounds.

~

"Dude—Dad just got a call from Mr. Winkler," Sali whispered into the phone.

"What about?" Ashe asked on the other end. Ashe was in his bedroom; his mother was tending her plants upstairs in the solarium so Ashe didn't have to whisper.

"The Mayor of Cordell was killed earlier, so two agents are coming. They want Dad to help them investigate since he's awake during the day. Mr. Winkler said to get your dad or Mr. Anderson to help at night."

"They think the murder has something to do with these families?" Ashe asked.

"I think so—why would they send agents if they didn't suspect something?"

"True," Ashe agreed, setting aside the book he'd been reading. His bedroom was bigger, now, with even more bookshelves. Because of the explosion the year before, however, only half the shelves were filled. "Or maybe they just want to prove that it didn't have anything to do with the families. Better to know, don't you think."

"Yeah. I guess," Sali reluctantly agreed.

"When are they coming?" Ashe asked.

"Tomorrow. They're supposed to stay in Clinton tonight and see dad at the locksmith's shop tomorrow afternoon in Cordell. Dad has to remind them that tomorrow night is the full Moon."

"Surprised they didn't think of that," Ashe chuckled. "Those guys are supposed to be smart."

"They're not used to werewolves, I bet."

"Or vampires." Ashe and Sali snickered for a moment.

"Dude, want to play football or Frisbee tomorrow?" Sali asked.

"Sure. Call before you come over." Ashe and Sali hung up.

"Keith, why haven't you unpacked your bag?" Bryce Caldwell sat on the end of Keith's bed.

"Why? We'll be moving again soon—Mom said so."

"Two and a half months. Are you prepared to wear wrinkled clothes the whole time? Come on, we have a washer and dryer. You need to wash some of that stuff. Those jeans are so dirty they may fall apart in the laundry."

Keith and Bryce couldn't be more different. Keith had blond hair while Bryce's was nearly black. Keith's green eyes gazed steadily at his older, half-brother. Bryce looked like Jeanine Caldwell, their mother. Keith favored Michael Caldwell, Keith's father.

Bryce, Jeanine's son from her first marriage, hadn't seen his father for three years after Bruce Stinnett's parental rights had been terminated. Michael Caldwell adopted Bryce afterward. Bruce Stinnett had fallen on hard times after leaving Jeanine and Bryce behind when Bryce was barely a year old, turning to petty crime. He'd been jailed after stealing a few cars and selling them to chop shops in Florida.

"If my jeans fall apart, will I get new ones?" Keith picked at a scab on his right thumb for a moment, but now he raised his eyes to his brother again.

"I think we're allowed a few new things—we just have to go through that Marcus DeLuca guy to get stuff online."

"What do you think he looks like—when he's a werewolf? I gotta tell you, that Winkler dude scared the heck out of me." Winkler had become a huge, solid black wolf with gleaming, golden eyes.

"He wouldn't have growled if Philip hadn't tried to touch him," Bryce pointed out.

"Philip's an ass."

"A general consensus," Bryce sighed. "I don't know that there's any hope for him. Can you see him working at Easy-Stop someday?"

It started as a snicker, but soon Keith was lying on his side and laughing uncontrollably. He could easily see Philip snapping rudely at the customers of a self-serve gas station and convenience store.

"Come on, bro, let's hang up your clothes," Bryce said, hefting Keith's suitcase onto the bed.

～

"Mom, do we have the ingredients to make cookies?" Macy asked. They'd cleared away the dinner dishes after having pizza for their first meal at the new home.

"I think we can make oatmeal or sugar cookies—I saw a bottle of vanilla and a box of oats in the pantry." Ramona Hill smiled at her daughter.

Macy had long blonde hair that covered the delicately pointed tips of her ears, and blue eyes that now pleaded with her mother for cookies. Macy had been beautiful and thin all her life. Ramona struggled with her weight constantly and her brown hair frazzled and curled furiously in any sort of humidity. Macy's hung like a river of gold down her back.

"Did I hear cookies?" Rocky Hill walked into the kitchen. He had darker hair and brown eyes; Ramona's eyes were green. Ramona always believed it to be the donated egg that had given her daughter blue eyes and blonde hair—although the clinic had tried to match features as well as they could. At least they thought they had.

Ramona was still trying to understand the information handed out earlier—still struggling to make things go back to normal. Or at least as normal as they could be. They were surrounded by werewolves, shapeshifters and—she shivered for a moment—*vampires*. Cookies sounded like an excellent idea.

"Let's make oatmeal cookies," Macy decided. Ramona pulled out the sugar and the box of oats.

~

"Liz?" Luanne tapped on Elizabeth Frasier's bedroom window.

"Luanne, what are you doing out there?" Elizabeth hissed, struggling with the locked window and heaving it upward. "Shouldn't you be inside? What if those people are out there?"

"What people would you be meanin', lass?" Aedan allowed the Welsh lilt to come out in his voice. Luanne shrieked at the sudden appearance of the vampire.

~

"Your voice is different now," Elizabeth cast an accusing glance at Aedan. She and Luanne sat on the sofa inside the Frasier home, huddled fearfully together. They'd been caught first thing by one of those—*vampires*.

He'd admitted it freely when he'd escorted Luanne into the Frasier's home moments earlier, introducing himself as Aedan Evans to Mary Ellen and Francis Frasier.

Linda and Peter Jansen, Luanne's parents, were on their way—all the families had walkie-talkies provided by Bill Jennings' department and Francis had notified Peter that Luanne had sneaked out and gotten caught by the Cloud Chief night guards.

"I have several accents," Aedan replied frostily. A very good judge of character, Aedan disliked Elizabeth, finding her a bit on the shallow side. Elizabeth's black hair was styled carefully, while her brown eyes flashed with anger and defiance toward Aedan.

Dressed in a silk blouse and designer jeans, Elizabeth also wore red heels, diamond earrings and multiple bangle bracelets. Luanne sat quietly beside her friend, dressed more appropriately in jeans and a T with athletic shoes on her feet.

More subdued than Elizabeth's fiery character, Luanne had light-brown hair and hazel eyes. Prettier, too, if you looked past the makeup that Elizabeth wore nearly to excess.

"Lu, I can't believe you left the house without telling us," Linda Jansen rushed in, a Georgia accent plain in her voice.

"Mom, I only wanted to check on the others," Luanne muttered, staring at her hands.

"I'm so sorry, I'll make sure it doesn't happen again," Linda turned to Aedan.

"It's not a problem tonight, but it will be tomorrow," Aedan nodded to Linda and her husband, Peter. Peter frowned at his daughter as he walked into the Frasier home but chose not to say anything at first, allowing his wife to handle the situation.

"Why will it be a problem tomorrow?" Francis Frasier demanded.

"Full Moon," Aedan replied. "Unless you want to meet up with just about every resident in Cloud Chief. As animals."

"They really do that? On the full Moon? That's not a myth?" Peter Jansen finally spoke, a bit of worry in his voice.

"Yes. That's not a myth. Nor is this," Aedan reached out and casually snapped off a piece of granite from the breakfast bar, which separated the kitchen from the living area. "Stay inside at night unless you notify us ahead of time. Young miss," he gave Luanne a stern look, "use your walkie-talkie next time. You can visit with your friends during the day." Aedan handed the chunk of granite to Francis Frasier and left the house in a blink. Shocked, Francis dropped the heavy piece of granite and cursed.

"We were threatened," Francis Frasier snapped at Marcus DeLuca early the following morning. If Francis knew anything about werewolves, he wouldn't be accosting the Packmaster on the day of a full Moon. Nevertheless, Marcus listened as patiently as he could while Francis ranted about Aedan's visit the night before.

"How?" Marcus, sitting at the breakfast table, crossed arms over his chest. "How were you threatened?"

"He told us to stay inside at night unless we cleared it with him or one of you-you, well, *your* kind," Francis floundered uncomfortably.

"Didn't Director Jennings say the same thing? Didn't his agents tell you exactly that before they left?" Marcus was beginning to think Francis Frasier a fool.

"But this," Francis tapped the piece of granite he'd brought with him. "That *vampire*—snapped it right off our counter. If that's not a threat," Francis' voice held agitation.

"Do you want protection or not? Is your daughter in danger or not?" Marcus scooted his chair back and stood, nearly growling at Francis Frasier. "You," Marcus pointed a finger at Francis, "are more of a danger to us than we are to you. We've learned how to live among humans.

You, on the other hand, with just a careless word, could expose us to the outside world and certain death. Yes, we're strong, but your kind outnumber us. We'd be just as dead, one way or the other, if you let this secret out." Marcus had to stop for a moment to calm his anger.

"We agreed to allow you to live here," Marcus continued, "because we offer some sort of protection against what hunts you. And yes, they hunt you. Have you seen the numbers of the dead—all those children across the country that have died or been abducted? Is that what you want for your child? Is it? Aedan is trying to protect you as well as your child. Have you seen the information? At least sixteen sets of parents were killed with their children." Marcus was wound up and ready to turn.

"Marcus," Denise walked into the kitchen, giving the soft warning to her husband.

"I'm all right, Denise," Marcus blew out a calming sigh. "Mr. Frasier, you weren't threatened by Aedan Evans. If you had been, you'd still be hiding inside your home, too frightened to come out. Go home. I'll have someone fix your counter."

"Fine." Francis lifted the heavy granite with difficulty. "I see we have no voice in this community." He stalked out of the DeLuca home with as much dignity as he could muster.

"You weren't meant to have a voice," Marcus growled as Francis slammed the front door behind him.

"I heard the whole thing, dude; that Frasier guy said your dad threatened him. Dad told him if your dad did threaten somebody, they'd pee their pants." Sali crunched into the snack crackers Adele had given them before they'd retreated to Ashe's bedroom on Sunday afternoon.

"Your dad did not say pee their pants," Ashe grinned at Sali.

"Nah, but that's what he meant." Sali shoved his hand inside the box of snacks, pulling out another handful of crackers.

"The first time that man's daughter walks into a field in her high heels, she's gonna sink right into the ground," Ashe snickered.

"I hope I'm there to see it," Sali said, stuffing crackers in his mouth.

"Come on, dude, stop eating and let's go play Frisbee."

A few moments later, Ashe, carrying his ancient, lime-green Frisbee (which was liberally pierced with Sali's teeth marks), trundled up the steps, closely followed by a nearly grown wolf. Of the few things to survive the explosion the year before, Ashe's Frisbee had sailed through the blast almost untouched.

"Is that Sali?" Ashe grinned at Edward's question. The curious teen had shown up as if called when Ashe and Sali began playing. Ashe tossed the Frisbee; Sali chased after it and caught it in his teeth, at times leaping high off the ground to snag the flying disk.

"Yeah. If you want, go down there," Ashe pointed toward Sali, who now sat patiently on the new spring grass in Ashe's front yard, the Frisbee dangling from his mouth. "You can toss the Frisbee back after Sali catches it."

"Cool." Edward returned Ashe's grin and trotted toward Sali, who willingly gave up the Frisbee. Edward's toss wobbled on its way to Ashe, but it did make it.

"What's this? The *empties* playing with the dog?" Chad and Jeremy had driven up on the gravel road in front of Ashe's home. Ashe gave them a hard stare—he figured they'd come to check out the temporary housing and the new arrivals to Cloud Chief.

Trace, Jason—Chad and Jeremy are in front of my house and I'm worried about Edward, Ashe sent to both werewolves. Trace, dressed in jeans, no shirt and sunglasses, ran up while Chad continued to taunt Ashe, Sali and Edward, calling them empty and worthless. Jeremy chimed in that humans didn't belong anywhere in the community. Edward's freckles stood out as his face paled at Jeremy's insults.

"How would you boys like to sit down with the Packmaster?" Trace walked up to the car from the driver's side while both boys faced the other direction to do their taunting. Chad and Jeremy jerked around at Trace's words.

"Who are you?" Jeremy demanded.

"One of William Winkler's wolves," Trace grinned. "Try saying that three times fast. Now, you can either move along and not bother any of these people again, or I'll report you to Marcus. Your choice, of course."

Without answering, Jeremy shoved the car into gear and drove off, flinging gravel and raising dust in the afternoon sun.

"Everything all right here?" Trace pulled off his sunglasses as he walked up to Ashe.

"It was fine until Chump and Wormy showed up," Ashe replied softly.

"You can't let them upset you," Trace said as his cell phone rang. Pulling it from his jeans pocket, Trace checked caller ID before answering. "What is it, boss?" Trace asked. Ashe, with his enhanced hearing, knew from the voice that it was Winkler calling.

"There's been another murder—a farmer about two miles away," Winkler said.

CHAPTER 5

"Ashe, will you and Sali walk Edward home?" Trace said after he hung up. Winkler had asked Trace to call Marcus and coordinate with the two agents Director Jennings had sent to investigate the Mayor's murder. Ashe could tell Winkler was concerned about this second death from his cell-phone conversation.

"Sure," Ashe agreed. "Edward, we have to take you home. Come on, Sali, let's go."

"What happened?" Edward asked as they walked toward the temporary housing while Sali's wolf trotted alongside.

"They're investigating something. Might not mean anything," Ashe hedged. He didn't want to frighten Edward, who was already worried. No names had been given over the phone and Ashe wasn't sure who lived two miles away—in any direction.

Itching to follow Trace instead of seeing Edward home, Ashe calmed himself and focused on the task Trace had given him.

"Hi, Mr. Pendley," Ashe said as he, Edward and Sali walked inside the Pendley's home. Steven Pendley was reading a book in an easy chair in their living room.

"Hello, Ashe. Who is this?" Mr. Pendley eyed Sali's wolf.

"That's Sali," Edward's enthusiasm was back. "Isn't that cool?"

"It is," Steven Pendley marked his place and set the book down. "Can I get anything for you boys? Water or a soda?"

"Water would be nice; soda isn't good for Sal when he's a wolf," Ashe grinned. Sali sat on his haunches and grinned, his tongue lolling from his mouth. Ashe and Edward got glasses while a bowl was set before Sali, who lapped up water happily.

"Does it hurt when you change?" Edward thought to ask when he'd nearly emptied his glass.

"Nah. It's sort of like a brief flash and suddenly you're something else," Ashe explained. "No pain involved."

"But those werewolf movies," Edward began.

"Are mostly wrong," Ashe finished. "Most of those say you have to be bitten to become a werewolf. That's not true." Ashe watched while Sali, expressing his opinion of werewolf films, yawned hugely and flopped onto the Pendley's kitchen floor.

"So, what about the vampires, then?" Steven Pendley asked.

"Can't talk about that," Ashe replied. "And I wouldn't ask my dad or Mr. Anderson, either. That's a closely guarded secret. I don't even know and dad won't tell me."

"Mr. Frasier came by this morning," Edward muttered.

"I heard about that," Ashe nodded while watching Sali, who was about to fall asleep on the floor. "Dad didn't threaten Mr. Frasier. He was doing his best to warn him. He can't protect everybody if they won't cooperate."

"Not a surprise that Frasier would exaggerate; he was an investment banker before all this happened," Mr. Pendley sighed.

"We should go," Ashe said, nudging Sali with a toe of his sneaker. Sali had begun to snore softly.

"It was nice seeing you again; come back anytime," Mr. Pendley said as Ashe and Sali walked out of the house. Ashe waved at Edward before he and Sali trotted toward his home.

"Mom, is there anything on the news about a farmer getting killed two miles from here?" Ashe asked as he and Sali walked into the kitchen. Adele was putting a chicken into the oven to roast.

"I don't know, hon. Turn on the television and check."

Ashe turned on the small television on the kitchen counter while Sali trotted downstairs to turn and retrieve his clothing from Ashe's bathroom. Clumping up the steps again a few minutes later, Sali sat down with Ashe at the island and watched for any information.

"Look—there it is," Ashe pointed to the crawler across the bottom of the screen. "Mom, it says a Cordell rancher was found murdered inside his barn," Ashe read the information on the screen. "No suspects in the case," he finished. "Now they're saying that this may be related to Mayor Taylor's death two days ago."

Adele now stared at the screen in alarm. "I wish your father were awake," she said.

"Trace got a call from Mr. Winkler, that's where I heard it," Ashe said. "Mr. Winkler told Trace to contact Sali's dad and get with the two agents Director Jennings is sending."

"Honey, I'm sure it's just to rule out any connection with our new residents," Adele soothed. "These victims are local humans. How could they possibly have any ties to the ones out back?"

"I don't know," Ashe shrugged.

Sitting inside his bedroom later and with Sali looking on, Ashe surfed the Internet, searching for additional information on the recent murder.

"Sal, look," Ashe pointed at his computer screen. "An unofficial source reports that Mr. Sparks was strangled with a chain found inside his barn."

"So, Mayor Taylor's neck was broken and Mr. Sparks was strangled with a chain," Sali looked over Ashe's shoulder to read the information for himself.

"Oh, no," Ashe said, staring at further information. "He had a family. A wife and two kids, who were at church when the murder happened."

"Definitely not cool," Sali breathed.

～

"Who the hell are you?" Washita County Sheriff Cliff Watson stared at the four men who walked up to the crime scene.

"Special Agent Nick Lawford," Nick held out his identification for the sheriff to see. "This is Special Agent Derik North," he introduced the second agent. "These two," Nick jerked his head toward Marcus and Trace, "are helping us with an investigation."

"And what investigation would that be?" Cliff Watson demanded.

"This one—and the Mayor's death, of course. Our department isn't completely satisfied that the proper suspect was accused of the murders last year. We want to make sure these aren't connected in some way."

"But that woman had the gun in the back of her van," Sheriff Watson blustered.

"And no evidence whatsoever that she was anywhere near either crime scene," Nick snapped. "You know that as well as I do. The OSBI still lists the case as inconclusive." Nick referred to two human deaths the year before—Megan Lindley, a high school senior and Terry Smith, Randy Smith's father.

"So I get no call and you just show up?" Cliff was still grumbling. He hated it when his authority was questioned.

"This crime hadn't happened when we were dispatched," Nick said. "We were notified about an hour ago. Are you going to let us in or do I have to make a call?" Nick held up his cell phone.

Nick, a tall black man, had worked for the agency for eleven years. Derik, brown-haired, blue-eyed and with only three years of experience, was happy to allow Nick to do the talking. Trace and Marcus stood a few steps behind, content to watch as the agents handled the local sheriff.

"Fine," Cliff wiped a hand over a nearly balding head before pulling away crime scene tape and allowing the four men inside.

"Smells human, but those Elemaiya smell similar to humans; there are only a few differences in the scent," Marcus growled as he and Trace sniffed unobtrusively around Granger Sparks' barn. The body lay on the floor nearby, covered with a sheet. "Unless they were part animal, like that one Winkler dealt with." Marcus referred to the hybrid that Winkler and two Bright Elemaiya had tracked and killed the year before. "That one smelled half animal, just like he looked."

"Let's take a look at the body," Nick suggested, leading the two werewolves in that direction.

"Definitely strangled with a chain," Marcus said when Nick carefully pulled the sheet back. The marks stood out in sharp contrast against the farmer's paler skin. "This would take a strong human—that's a large chain." Marcus nodded toward the chain that lay on the dirt floor close by.

"No fingerprints on the chain, so the perp wore gloves," Derik offered.

"Same with Mayor Taylor," Nick agreed. "No fingerprints found at that scene either, according to local authorities. They may have lifted one fingerprint here, but we're all waiting for the results."

"I might be able to tell if the same scent was in both places," Marcus suggested.

"We can try, but there's been a lot of traffic in and out of that place," Nick said. "Don't worry; I've worked with a couple of werewolf agents in the past. I know the drill." Nick dropped the sheet, allowing it to cover the victim's head and neck. "I'll have to ask permission to get into the Mayor's house." He grimaced at the thought of going to the Sheriff to gain that permission.

"There's a way to get in without it," Trace offered.

"We just need to borrow Ashe for a little while; we don't have much time," Marcus explained to Adele. "We'll drive into Cordell, park in a secluded spot and Ashe can take us from there."

Ashe watched in fascination while Marcus, Trace and two agents spoke with his mother. He was going to get to examine the murder scene with them. He was going to get to mist them inside the Mayor's home.

Ashe was excited about the prospect. After all, he'd never told anyone, not even Sali, that he'd followed his father and Radomir, the

Council's Enforcer, a year earlier when several crime scenes and James Johnson's body had been examined.

"All right, but keep him safe," Adele warned. "Ashe," she turned to him, "Do everything they say."

"I will, Mom." Ashe would agree to almost anything if it meant he could go.

"Come on, kiddo, let's go," Trace ruffled Ashe's hair. Ashe followed them out of the house, loaded into the agents' rented van and sat in the third row of seats as Agent Nick Lawford drove toward Cordell.

"I saw Ashe get in a van with Trace and three others," Philip reported to Luanne. Philip always felt calmer around Lu. Calm enough to act and feel close to normal. Keith and Bryce, who'd already sought out Luanne earlier, listened while Philip described what he'd seen.

"Which way did they go?" Bryce asked.

"Toward the entrance to this lost continent," Philip grumped.

"Why would he leave with them? Doesn't make any sense," Keith, the practical one, pointed out. "What did the others look like?"

"Two were dressed like the agents that rode up here with us," Philip said. "So I'm guessing they're the same. The third one I didn't recognize wore jeans and a pullover."

"So, two agents, one werewolf and one we don't know, took that Ashe kid with them off the reservation," Keith summed up what they knew. "Who can ask the kid later what's going on?"

"I don't think anybody here knows him well enough to ask," Luanne said. "But Edward does."

"Let's go find Eddie, then," Philip suggested.

Agent Lawford parked half a mile from the Mayor's farm, on the southern edge of Cordell. A church parking lot was chosen and Ashe wondered if it were the same church attended by the second victim's family as he climbed from the van. "You'll be safe enough in my mist; I've carried others this way," Ashe reassured the adults. He had carried others, just not these four.

"Randy Smith," Marcus coughed into his hand.

"Are you gonna get onto me about that now, Mr. DeLuca?" Ashe turned questioning blue eyes on the Cloud Chief Packmaster.

"No, kid. You did what you thought was right. If you hadn't been right, though, we might have had a conversation."

"Glad I was right, then," Ashe muttered. "I'll get you there as quick as I can."

Lifting the others inside his mist, Ashe zipped toward the first crime scene.

"Kid, if you were older, the Department would definitely come knocking," Nick Lawford stared at Ashe after he'd set all four adults down inside the Mayor's home. Two police cruisers were parked outside, with two officers guarding the scene, completely unaware that Ashe and the others were now inside the house.

"Body found here," Derik North pointed to the spot designated by a numbered marker on the floor.

"Don't disturb anything, Ashe," Marcus cautioned as he and Trace began sniffing through the home.

Ashe stood near the front door, watching the others examine everything while stepping carefully around markers set out previously by the local authorities. "You're right," Marcus admitted after a while. "Too many people have been in here. The scents are confused."

Ashe studied his shoes for a moment before allowing his eyes to wander to the doorframe. "Look," he said, pointing toward two small threads stuck to a tiny, splintered gouge shoulder-high on the frame.

"How did they miss that?" Nick came to investigate. "This gouge looks fresh, like the assailant ran into it while bringing the Mayor inside the house." Taking a small plastic bag from his jacket pocket, Agent Lawford removed the threads with a pair of tweezers and stuffed them into the bag.

"Wait, let me sniff that," Trace said. Ashe and Nick moved away, allowing the tall werewolf to scent the doorframe. "Kid, you're a genius," Trace grinned at Ashe. "Marcus, check this out—the scent is the same as the one in the barn."

"It was small, Director, and the locals may have been focused on the area around the body. The door was ten feet away from where the Mayor died," Nick spoke into his cell later. Ashe had been returned to his home and the werewolves were beginning to feel the pull of the Moon. They'd taken off in a rush as soon as they exited Nick and Derik's rented van.

"And you say the kid found it?"

"Yeah. We assumed the locals had collected all the evidence. They missed one piece. One important piece. The wolves say the scent is the same. We may have a serial killer on our hands."

"Are the two victims connected?"

"Sheriff says they knew each other pretty well."

"So, you think the Mayor gave up the second victim's name, somehow?"

"Could be. We'll have to look into that."

"Find out everything you can," Director Jennings said. "I need to know whether this is related to those families or not. Keep me informed."

"Ashe, keep an eye on your mother," Aedan put an arm around Ashe's shoulders just before he went out to guard the community.

"I will, dad. I'll use echolocation."

"Son, I wish I knew how you did that," Aedan tightened his hold on Ashe before letting him go. "Contact me if there's any trouble."

"I will." Aedan Evans usually went out to watch Adele fly on full moons. Tonight, he was watching the newcomers instead. Ashe would have to take responsibility for his mother's safety. "Dad, does everybody know to stay away from those houses?"

"They do, but if a few of the younger ones want to make things difficult," Aedan replied. Ashe nodded, thinking of Jeremy. Chad was expected to run with the Pack. Would Marcus know if the young werewolf slipped away? If Chad and Jeremy met up while in animal form, they could definitely cause problems for the relocated families.

"Son, Nathan and I will watch for trouble," Aedan reassured Ashe. "Just send mindspeech if you notice anything amiss." Aedan was still astonished that he could hear Ashe's mindspeech—most vampires with mindspeaking ability could only send to someone else with the talent. Grateful for what Ashe had been given, Aedan smiled at his son before walking out the kitchen door to join Nathan.

"Ashe, are you ready?" Adele asked an hour later.

"Yeah, Mom."

"You go first." Adele would wait until Ashe was away before dropping her robe and shifting to peregrine falcon. "I'll make sure the doors are locked and the alarms set," she added.

"Okay." Ashe didn't need to lock the doors behind him—he could sail right through locked doors as mist. "I'll drop my clothes outside, Mom," he added, walking out the door. Adele watched as her son shifted to the bumblebee bat and flapped away before allowing her robe to drop. Soon a peregrine falcon flew through the bright moonlight illuminating Cloud Chief.

Chad, in werewolf form, ran behind the rest of the Cloud Chief Pack, just as he and Jeremy had planned. Jeremy, as a wildcat, had arranged to meet Chad near the six temporary homes located behind Ashe Evans's house.

The vampires had to guard the entire community, giving the boys an opportunity to approach the new addition while Aedan and Nathan were checking the hidden entrance half a mile away.

Chad and Jeremy intended to have a bit of fun and perhaps frighten the humans—*the empties*—enough to make them leave. And if somebody got hurt in the process, well, that wouldn't upset either of them. All they had to do was coordinate a little, making sure the vampires were elsewhere before they struck.

Veering away as the Pack ran through a copse of trees, Chad knew he'd get away without being missed. The Pack had scented a deer and that was a fine meal to chase on a moonlit night. Feeling a small amount of regret for leaving the hunt, Chad slowed and reversed direction, trotting toward the eastern edge of the property and the six mobile homes waiting there.

Luanne loved scented candles; had a collection of them that she lit at times, just for the comfort of the dim light inside her bedroom. Two now burned brightly on her bedside table, giving her enough light to read. Limited on the number of books she could carry into exile with her, Luanne was rereading a well-worn and much-loved novel from a favorite series.

"Lu?" The walkie-talkie lying on the comforter beside her crackled with Macy's voice.

"What is it, Mace?" Lu pressed and released the talk button.

"Just wondering if you'd seen anything. Do you think any of them will come close enough for us to see?"

"I doubt it," Luanne replied, setting her book aside. "I can barely see outside, even with the full Moon."

"How dangerous do you think they are?" Macy went on.

"No idea. This is something new, and I doubt they're willing to talk about it. I'm curious, too, Mace. Maybe we'll see something before we leave. That would be nice. Maybe they'll trust us enough to show us something besides the little bat."

"That's a bumblebee bat—they're endangered," Macy said. "I did a paper on bats for a science class before all this happened."

"Are you still going to read vampire books after this?" Luanne teased.

"Well, I always thought they were fiction. Now the real thing shows up. I don't know what to think anymore. Lu?"

"What, Mace?"

"What are we going to do? Do you honestly believe we're half—whatever it is? Do you?"

Luanne breathed a troubled sigh before punching the talk button again. It was something she'd gone over in her mind, leaving the night sleepless and the day nearly listless. Her parents were putting on an act around her, but Luanne knew they were just as confused and upset over the information as she was.

"I don't know, Mace. But why did the others die? That's what I can't figure out. I can't see that any of us are special—not like that bat kid. None of us can do that."

"But what if we can? What if we just haven't concentrated or something? Admit it, we didn't know we weren't completely human. If what they say is true, anyway. And those two guys who came after me outside the pizzeria? What if they'd got me instead? I could be dead or somewhere else right now."

"I guess it comes down to whether we want to stay with our parents or go to those others," Luanne shuddered. "I want to stay with Mom and Dad. I want to go to college and do something. Here. Not somewhere else. Think about it, Macy. If they were desperate to increase their numbers and they're at war with the other side, then we'd be fighting the others with them. Wouldn't we?"

"I don't even want to think about that."

"Mace, the battery is about dead on my walkie. I'll talk to you later."

"All right."

Luanne got up to find the charger for her walkie-talkie when her bedroom window crashed inward, knocking candles onto the floor and setting her curtains afire.

~

Dad! Ashe sent desperate mindspeech to his father. *Dad, I got a signal from something and now one of the mobile homes is on fire!* Ashe had followed his mother as instructed, keeping her within distance using echolocation.

It was only when Ashe had banked in flight, sending signals out in the opposite direction that he'd caught two—likely Chad and Jeremy —nearly upon the six temporary homes lined up neatly behind his own. And then the unthinkable happened; fire bloomed on one side of a mobile home, engulfing the structure quickly. Thinking swiftly, Ashe knew he had to help. Turning to mist, he rocketed toward the burning home.

CHAPTER 6

*A*edan and Nathan were already at the home, but it was burning so brightly the vampires couldn't go in without risking death—fire could easily kill a vampire. It was far too late to haul out the community pumper truck. The other new residents were all outside their homes, screaming and crying.

"Do something!" Macy begged Aedan and Nathan to help—Luanne and her parents were still inside the burning structure. Macy screamed as the house exploded in a fireball behind her.

"They're safe," Ashe appeared, dropping all three members of the Jansen family in front of his father. If they'd wanted to keep his misting secret, he'd just blown that by saving Luanne and her parents.

Luanne was on her knees, coughing. She'd gotten the worst of the smoke and flames while her parents had rushed toward that end of the home to rescue her. If Ashe hadn't come, they'd all be burning inside the house.

Aedan pulled his shirt off swiftly and wrapped it around Ashe, who stood naked in the light from the fire. There wasn't enough water pressure to the temporary homes to save the house, and with the other Cloud Chief residents either shifted to animal form or too young to help, there was nothing to do except watch the home burn.

"You all right?" Ashe clutched his father's shirt tightly around him and knelt before Luanne, who was being comforted by her parents. They'd just lost everything they owned in the fire. "Dad, will the witch's shield keep the humans from noticing this?" Ashe jerked his head toward the burning home.

"I sure hope so, son. Nathan, let's get water on the grass around the home so the fire doesn't spread," Aedan muttered grimly. Ashe watched as his father and Nathan Anderson went to find hoses to do what they could.

The heat from the burning home was almost unbearable, so Ashe helped Luanne stand and walk farther away. Other parents assisted Peter and Linda Jansen. They followed Ashe and Luanne, eventually turning to watch as the two vampires sprayed the field surrounding the burning home.

"How did you get us out?" Peter Jansen thought to ask Ashe.

"It's just something I can do," Ashe shrugged. "Not important. Ask my dad about it." Ashe knew his father would place compulsion, but it couldn't be helped. He'd rather expose himself than allow three people to die. "Look, if you don't need anything else, I have to go find my mom." Allowing his father's shirt to drop, Ashe turned to bumblebee bat and flapped silently away.

Sending out echolocation signals again, Ashe found whom he believed responsible—two forms huddled beneath a tree roughly a quarter mile away. Ignoring them for the moment, Ashe went in search of his mother's falcon.

Chad and Jeremy sat inside Principal Billings' office while Marcus paced. Benjamin Billings waited outside, listening in on the conversation. "So you thought you'd get away with this," Marcus DeLuca growled.

Chad was the one whose condition had given them away—he had burns on his hands and across his chest. His cheek, too, bore a cut from broken glass. Chad had already offered an insincere apology to the Cloud Chief Packmaster; the feigned contrition hadn't escaped Marcus' harsh scrutiny, however.

"We just wanted to scare them," Jeremy whined.

"Shut up!" Chad hissed.

"You burned the whole damn house down," Marcus exploded. "What do you expect me to do about that? What kind of punishment do you think you deserve? They were frightened enough to begin with. Now they're terrified. We offered them hospitality, and you do this? Chad, if Ashe hadn't acted, those three would be dead now and the Director of the NSA and Homeland Security Department would be here asking questions. As it is, he still may come and I may turn you over to him. Is that what you want?"

"I didn't mean it, Packmaster," Chad lied, groveling before Marcus.

"I'm taking this to the Grand Master and allowing him to make a decision as to punishment, Chad. Jeremy, I know you were in on planning this, but the school administrators will hand out your punishment." Marcus was one of the three administrators, along with Nathan Anderson and Jonas O'Neill, Wynn's father. All three of Cloud Chief's races were represented.

"Go back to the cafeteria; you'll know soon enough what your punishment is," Marcus said. Both boys left Principal Billings' office quickly; Ashe misted away right behind them.

"It's the empty's fault we got caught," Jeremy hissed as he and Chad walked down the hall toward the History classroom. They'd decided to skip the noon meal; everybody would be staring and whispering if they walked into the lunchroom now. Jeremy was obviously upset; not that he and Chad had done wrong; just that they'd gotten caught.

"Yeah. Packmaster DeLuca pats him on the back for saving the Jansens, and he blabs that he found us afterward by echolocation. You can't convince me he did that. He was making a stab in the dark, man. He accused us with no evidence."

"Too bad you got burned and cut up a little. Most of it was healed up already, but you still have a cut on your cheek and your hands are blistered. No way to convince the Packmaster we were innocent, once the stupid bat pointed him in our direction," Jeremy cursed softly under his breath. This was Ashe Evans' fault; start to finish. The empty was becoming more of a problem every day.

"We'll get back at him," Chad snarled. "It may take a while, but we'll get him."

~

"Dude, the Grand Master is gonna hand out punishment for Chad, but the school administrators have to decide what happens to Wormy," Ashe settled into his cafeteria seat next to Sali. He'd misted straight to the lunchroom after leaving Principal Billings' office.

"What do you think they're going to do?" Cori had helped hide Ashe's absence from Mrs. Rocklin, who was supervising the crowded cafeteria. She and Sali had huddled together to conceal his disappearance from the other students, too—all of whom were eating, laughing and engaging in boisterously noisy activity.

"No idea. Cori, those people could have died," Ashe muttered, staring at his now-cold cheeseburger. Making the best of congealed meat and cheese, Ashe bit into it and chewed.

"Dad said the girl was burning candles in her bedroom. Chad wouldn't have set the house on fire if she hadn't done that."

"Cori, don't take their part in this," Ashe lifted his milk carton. "None of this would have happened if Chump and Wormy hadn't decided to terrorize those people. Now the Jansens are living in Old Harold's house because theirs burned down, with everything they owned inside it."

"I know. Mom is going through our stuff to see if we can donate anything." Cori crumpled her paper napkin and dropped it onto her tray.

"I think those two agents are working to get furniture for them; Old Harold didn't have a lot and most of it was ancient," Ashe said. "They'll need clothes, too."

"I think Mom is taking dishes over; Aunt Marcie had a bunch of stuff she didn't need." Sali's Aunt Marcella now lived in Pat Roberts' old house. She'd moved to Cloud Chief after leaving her husband and two sons behind in Phoenix.

"Mom said she'd go by the grocery store on her way home tonight," Ashe said.

"But this separates that family from the others," Cori pointed out. "They're more than a quarter of a mile away."

"I get the feeling that the other kids lean on Luanne a lot," Ashe observed. "I overheard that Philip kid saying he wanted to ride with her on the way up and Macy, one of the other girls, had just talked to her on her walkie-talkie before Chump set the house on fire."

"Even I can't believe he did that," Cori shook her head. "Talk about dumb."

"Well, they've never been particularly intellectual," Sali grinned.

"Sal, you just used two five-syllable words back to back," Ashe pounded his friend on the shoulder.

"Just checking to see if you were listening, dude," Sali said.

"No, I don't have any idea why someone would target the Mayor or my husband," Wanda Hicks wiped tears away as Agents Nick Lawford and Derik North questioned her. She was only now learning that the same person was responsible for both deaths. "They knew each other, but," she tossed out a hand in helpless frustration. "There wasn't any reason for this. None."

"Ma'am, we don't have a lot of information, other than the same person likely committed both crimes," Derik said as gently as he could. "We're just trying to figure this out."

"When you do, please let me know," Mrs. Hicks wept. "So I'll know why my children no longer have a father."

"Boss, look at this," Trajan, Trace's older brother and Winkler's Second in the Dallas pack, set a paper copy of a map in front of Winkler the afternoon following the full Moon.

"What's this?" Winkler lifted the map and studied it.

"The route they took to deliver those mobile homes," Trajan pointed out. Like Trace, Trajan was nearly seven feet tall with dark hair and dark eyes. With martial arts experience and a sports background, Trajan was a capable Second for the Dallas Pack.

"So, the Mayor was off the path, but the second victim wasn't? You think there's some connection?" Winkler studied Trajan's face.

"Well, the two men knew one another. Who knows? I might be reading more into this than there is, but what if there's a leak somewhere? Besides Director Jennings, who else knows where those families were relocated? Even knowledge of a general location for those families could be dangerous. What might happen if the murderer had vague news of their whereabouts and then went looking for information on people moving into the area or anything unusual going on?" Trace settled into the chair beside Winkler's desk.

"And six mobile homes moving along a two-lane road is definitely unusual."

"Yep. Not easy to hide that, boss."

"You think I should contact Bill and ask him to investigate his own department?"

"Well, it isn't like that sort of thing hasn't happened in the past."

"It's worth a try," Winkler agreed. "I'll give him a call." Winkler's phone rang before he had a chance to dial Director Jennings' number.

"Weldon?" Winkler recognized the Grand Master's number on his cell.

"Winkler, two of those kids from Cloud Chief managed to burn one of the mobile homes to the ground last night." Winkler was on his feet and cursing immediately.

"Ashe, I think we should talk to those people. Maybe show them we're not all prejudiced and nasty," Wynn and Dori stood beside Ashe's locker, surprising Ashe and Sali. Hayes, Larry and Jeff, three other classmates, stood behind the two girls.

Hayes and Jeff were werewolves; Larry was a bobcat and Mrs. Campbell's son. Wynn, already very pretty and showing signs of growing into a beautiful woman one day, brushed back long, white hair unconsciously as she pleaded with Ashe to take her and the others to the remaining mobile homes.

"How do you plan to do that? Chump and Wormy did their best to destroy any trust they might have," Ashe grumbled. "And most of them are decent. I was hoping Edward could be included in activities and stuff, and then the others might come along. Now," Ashe shrugged in near-resignation.

"Let's give it a try at least," Hayes offered. "Make a peace offering of some kind. I'm willing to take my new games over."

"I'm willing to turn for them." Ashe stared in shock at Wynn—she never volunteered for that. When she changed for the full Moon, she stayed close to her mother, Sharon, a shapeshifting mare, and her father, Jonas, a rare bald eagle.

Wynn was a unicorn that shone brightly in the moonlight—Ashe had flapped over her many times as the bat just to get a glimpse of perhaps the rarest shapeshifter in existence.

"Wynnie, are you sure you want to do that?" Ashe used the nickname that most people were afraid to use—Sharon called her daughter by that name but Wynn usually got upset if anyone else did.

"I will," Wynn seemed determined. "They have to understand that we're not all like Chad and Jeremy. Stupid twits," she muttered.

"Look, why don't we meet at Ashe's house in an hour?" Hayes suggested. Jeff and Larry nodded in agreement.

"All right," Wynn said. "Let's go, Dori." Dori followed Wynn toward the front doors of the school. Ashe watched both girls walk down the polished tile hallway that separated classrooms at Cloud Chief Combined.

"You're sure about this?" Ashe turned back to Hayes, Larry and Jeff.

"We have to do something," Jeff said. He, Larry and Hayes were best friends, much like Ashe and Sali, but occasionally the three boys came to Sali's house—they seldom visited Ashe. All of them enjoyed playing video games, but generally hated playing Ashe. If he concentrated on the game, Ashe was very hard to beat. The others liked to win once in a while, so they played mostly with Sali.

"I'll offer some of my books to Luanne; Trace said this morning that all her books got burned," Ashe sighed, nodding to the three boys. "Meet at my house in an hour and we'll go." Hayes, Larry and Jeff, their athletic shoes squeaking on the polished tile, walked quickly toward the school entrance.

"Sali, I know I'll get in trouble if Mom and Dad find out, but we can't go empty-handed. Want to mist into Cordell and buy snacks?" Ashe gazed hopefully at his friend.

"Yeah. Let's go," Sali breathed, excited to be sneaking away from the community. Ashe, making sure nobody else was inside the deserted school, became mist. Pulling Sali into his mist, he blazed toward his home to raid his allowance stash before racing invisibly to the nearby town of Cordell.

Waiting patiently while a man wearing a studded leather jacket purchased a few items ahead of them, Ashe totaled snack items in his head. Sali had been more than generous, dumping multiple bags of chips and cookies into their basket.

"Having a party, boys?" The woman at the register rang up the sale. The pile of cookies, snacks and soft drinks traveled along the conveyor belt while Ashe and Sali watched the cashier scan all of it. Ashe pulled a handful of bills from his pocket to pay—he barely had enough to cover everything.

"Yeah, we're inviting friends over," Ashe agreed, handing money to the cashier. Sali was already gathering up bags of purchased snacks.

"Haven't I seen you at Cordell Feed and Seed?" The woman asked, her brown eyes kind as she handed change back.

"My mom owns it," Ashe said. Cordell was small enough that everyone knew everybody else.

"You're Adele's son. Now I recognize you," the woman placed hands on ample hips as she smiled at Ashe and Sali. "Well, have fun."

"We will. Thanks," Ashe lifted what Sali couldn't carry and they walked through the door of Jerry's Super Saver Market and Bakery.

"Come on," Ashe nodded toward the opposite side of the grocery store—cars were parked where Sali was walking. They had to find a good place for Ashe to turn to mist.

"Here," Ashe hissed, walking between the brick wall of the store and the two large dumpsters behind it. Turning himself, Sali and everything they carried to mist, Ashe flew toward Cloud Chief.

"Luanne, I'm really sorry about your house," Ashe apologized later. Luanne and her parents were visiting with Macy, Ramona and Rocky Hill, having walked from Old Harold's house to the mobile homes parked in the field behind Ashe's home. "We're inviting everyone over to Edward's house—his father gave permission. We've got video games and I've got a list of books from my library that you're welcome to borrow if you want."

"Plus we have snacks and sodas," Sali nodded enthusiastically behind Ashe.

"Mom?" Luanne blinked at Linda Jansen, asking permission. They'd spent the previous night huddled inside Old Harold's underground home, wondering what would become of them. Now, several members of the Cloud Chief community had brought clothing and household items, and these children were asking them over to play games and have fun.

"I think it's all right," Linda nodded. "We might be over after a while; I'd like to talk with Macy's parents a little longer."

"Go with Luanne, Macy," Ramona agreed. "Have some fun. We haven't seen a lot of that lately."

Macy and Luanne followed Ashe and Sali out of the house. "We just wanted you to know that we're not like Chump and Wormy. Trust me, they'll be punished," Ashe said to Luanne as they walked through the field toward Edward's mobile home.

"Having a get-together?" Jason and Trace were assigned to guard during the day, so they were well aware that something was going on at Edward's home.

"Hey, Trace. Hello, Mr. Landers," Ashe nodded to both werewolves. "We wanted to get to know everybody, and Hayes always looks for an excuse to play video games," Ashe grinned. *And we wanted them to know we're not all arsonists*, he added mentally, causing Trace to snicker.

"Have a good time. If you need anything, just call," Trace waved them on.

"Will do," Sali said.

"This is Wynn and this is Dori," Ashe introduced both girls to Macy and Luanne. "And this is Hayes, Larry and Jeff," he added.

Hayes and Jeff were already deep into a video game with Bryce and Keith. Larry watched the action while Philip sat nearby, engrossed in the game and unusually quiet.

Edward, crunching away on cheese puffs, grinned at Ashe. The only one refusing to have a good time was Elizabeth, who sat on a corner of the Pendley's sofa, sipping a soda and gazing sourly at Hayes and Jeff.

"Luanne, I think Wynn wants to show you her animal," Ashe said as Wynn gave Ashe a suggestive jerk of her head. "And you have to realize that Wynn won't do this for just anybody."

"What is it?" Luanne asked, giving Wynn a puzzled look.

"It'll be a surprise," Wynn said shyly.

"Edward, can we borrow your bathroom?" Ashe asked.

"Sure. Need anything?" Edward slid off his barstool and came to stand next to Sali, offering the bag of cheese puffs to the young werewolf. Sali grabbed a handful and began crunching.

"No. But we'll have a surprise for everyone in just a couple of minutes."

Dori followed Wynn toward the bathroom—she'd have to take Wynn's clothing, after all.

"How sturdy is the floor?" Sali stopped eating long enough to ask.

"Why do you need to know?" Edward asked curiously.

"You'll see. Just wait out here," Ashe directed. He, Sali, Luanne, Macy and Edward waited at the edge of the hallway that led to the mobile home's main bathroom. Wynn and Dori walked inside the small room and shut the door.

"I think you might like this," Ashe turned to tell Luanne when she and Macy, staring down the hall as the bathroom door opened again, gasped in amazement, their eyes widening in surprise. Macy, coming back to herself, squealed and clapped her hands.

"Oh, my gosh," Luanne whispered.

"There are unicorns?" Elizabeth rose from her seat to stare at Wynn, whose horn shone nearly golden in the afternoon light, her white coat glowing. Delicate hooves stepped carefully across Edward's living-room carpet. Blue eyes gazed at the assembled teens, who stared helplessly spellbound at her.

"Don't touch—it's just like somebody trying to touch you—without your clothes on," Dori warned as Bryce held out a hand.

"How many are there?" Elizabeth's voice was filled with awe. Ashe was surprised—of all of them, Elizabeth and Philip were the most jaded.

"Wynn is the only known unicorn in the United States. We're not sure about Europe—she may be the only one living on the planet."

"That is awesome," Luanne breathed. Edward's father, Steven, had already sent a message on his walkie-talkie to other parents, who were now crowding into the Pendley's living room. They stared, too.

"This is Wynn—Wynn O'Neill," Ashe introduced Wynn's unicorn to the gathered parents. "Her mother is a palomino mare; her father is a bald eagle."

"I become an ocelot," Dori said. "I'm Dori Anderson. My Mother is a lioness and my sister Cori is a panther. You've seen Ashe's bat; Larry is a bobcat and the rest here are werewolves."

"We've lived among humans all our lives," Hayes had abandoned his video game as soon as Wynn walked in as the unicorn. "Ashe's mom owns a store in Cordell. Not all of us are like those two last night, just as all humans aren't alike. Packmaster DeLuca will make sure those two are punished. In the meantime, we'd like to be friends. If that's all right with you."

"This is the coolest thing ever," Bryce said, still staring at Wynn. His half-brother Keith nodded in silent agreement.

"I think Wynn wants to change back," Ashe said softly. Dori followed Wynn into the bathroom again while the Pendley home burst into conversation.

"It's a secret we guard with our lives," Hayes said. "Can you imagine what might happen if word got out about what we are? Some people will want to kill us. That's why we stay hidden."

"But there are some officials that are aware?" Rocky Hill asked. "The Director, for example?"

"Yeah. Some people know, and they're sworn to secrecy," Ashe agreed. "I heard that a few of our kind work for National Security, keeping all of us safe."

"Has your community ever been discovered?" Steven Pendley asked.

"When one of us showed them the way in, and that problem was eliminated last year," Marcus DeLuca walked into the house. "We're guarding against that happening again," he added. "The Grand Master has handed out punishment to the werewolf boy, and the school administrators have decided what will happen with the shapeshifter. Since both boys live in the same home, the punishments will be served together." Marcus now had the attention of everyone inside the home as Wynn and Dori walked out of the bathroom to join the crowd.

"Chad must pay restitution. That money will come from an emergency fund set up by the werewolf government, and Chad must work to pay that money back within a reasonable amount of time. Should he not do so, he will be judged again—as an adult. He also will serve a sentence through the rest of the summer—he is under house arrest and will be caged during the full moons."

Sali, Jeff and Hayes stifled gasps—being caged during the full Moon was the equivalent of solitary confinement. Wolves were compelled to run during the full Moon and it was bad enough that those under the age of fifteen were confined to their homes. A cage was very small—barely large enough to hold a werewolf.

"What about the other one?" Peter Jansen asked.

"He will be caged during full moons as well, and is under house arrest just as the other one is. And since he received a new car as a graduation gift; that will be taken away and parked elsewhere. I don't want them sneaking out somehow and driving off, so I have the keys." Marcus held up the keys in question and jangled them.

"But they'll have to finish school and graduate with the rest?" Ashe asked.

"Yes, but all the teachers and the Principal are expected to keep a close watch on them. If they act up or cause trouble, they may be doing their final assignments from home. One or both parents are expected to pick them up from school every day."

"Poor Mr. and Mrs. Booth," Ashe sighed.

"It's only for two weeks, Ashe, and they won't get to deliver a speech at graduation. Part of the punishment."

"In their case, that might be a reward. Have you seen their writing skills?" Dori huffed. Sali snickered.

CHAPTER 7

"What did you write your end-of-year essay about?" Sali asked as he caught up with Ashe on their way to school the following day. The essays were due that morning in English class. Sali hated that English was their first subject of the day; Ashe didn't mind at all.

Mr. Garnett, their new English teacher, was utilitarian at best, but he was a werewolf and that suited the community. He followed at Principal Billings' heels whenever possible.

Ashe couldn't figure out if Mr. Garnett wanted to take the Principal's position someday or if he was merely trying to fit in as best he could. He'd taken Paul Harris' post—and his home—after Cloud Chief's previous English teacher had been captured the year before.

"I wrote it on the economic feasibility of a community such as ours," Ashe replied to Sali's question. "I mean, there are certain expenses that are shared by the community, and we grow our own vegetables during the warmer months. The O'Neills supply beef and mutton to the community because they raise sheep and cattle, plus they bale hay for the others that keep horses. The Thompsons raise chickens and turkeys, so we can get eggs and poultry that way—Mom seldom buys much of that stuff from the store. The trick, I think, is in keeping the communities small so we can raise enough vegetables and meat on the hoof to keep everybody. And we have to worry about keeping it small enough that we can stay hidden."

"Dude, that's something a senior ought to write," Sali said. "That makes my essay on the relationships between shifters and werewolves look like grade school crap."

"Sali, that's important and a really good idea. I wish I'd thought of it," Ashe sighed. "Sal, you're smarter than everybody thinks. I don't know why you try to hide it."

"Too much work, man," Sali grinned. "Come on, race you to school." Both boys took off at a run.

~

"My Queen, it is time." Hilbah hated to interrupt Friesianna at anything—she held a short and volatile temper and was inclined to use the crown she wore as extra power to hurl unsuspecting subjects against convenient trees or walls. Her methods of displaying her displeasure with those who tried her patience were legendary. Hilbah, dark-haired, blue-eyed and inwardly quaking, had dressed in his finest gold silk to come to the Queen.

He should have come months earlier, but he was afraid. It was he who'd suggested the seeding of the Elemaiyan eggs in the fertility clinics, and he'd congratulated himself secretly on the cunning plan he'd devised. They'd only managed to collect a mere three hundred seventeen half-Elemaiyan children. More than two hundred of those children had already fallen in the war with their Dark cousins. Friesianna might not accept compliments and respectful groveling much longer.

"Ah, my Miriasu," Friesianna greeted her Seer. Breathing a mental sigh upon finding her in a good mood, Hilbah bowed low and repeated his statement. "My Queen, it is time. Time to gather the last of the children. Only a few remain and it would be wise to take all of them now."

"You have the tokens from each mother?" Friesianna asked, lifting a shapely eyebrow at Hilbah.

"Yes. Here," Hilbah handed an intricately carved wood box to the Queen. "I have had them since the beginning. These six are all that remain."

"Do you have any suggestions to bring them to us quickly?"

"Send out the *Call*. Have them come to us," Hilbah bowed. He knew what the *Call* would require. It was not a simple thing to do and the Queen's Jewels—her elite guards that held the ancient talismans—might object; they were powerful in their own right and the talismans made them stronger. Diamond and his brothers would not take kindly to being weakened while the Queen borrowed their talismans to perform the *Call*.

"I will consider this," The Queen rested her chin on the tip of a delicate finger, the heavy gemstone rings she wore winking in the fading afternoon light. "And I will consult with the spies that my Jewels have found for me. That will tell me much. I will give you my answer in three days."

Dismissed, Hilbah bowed again and walked away, dignified and slow. He wished to slump and hurry, but that was unbecoming of the Queen's Miriasu. Gone were the days when the Queen would heed her Seer's advice and take immediate action. No—Hilbah held not the talent to command that respect and Friesianna, upstart Queen that she was, held not the wisdom.

"My King." Rend, the Dark King's Chief Destroyer stood before Baltis, King of the Dark Elemaiya and Prince Beldris, Baltis' only brother.

"Rend?" Baltis rested his chin on a fist, gazing across the wilds of Canada while his brother spoke of days long past when their numbers had been fifty times what they now were. Before Friesianna had taken the Bright throne and war between the two races had begun. Rend now stood before Baltis, interrupting the King's thoughts and his brother's speech.

"My King, our spy reports that Friesianna may send a *Call* for the remaining children. Only a few, as I understand."

"Will our informant know when the *Call* is sent?" Baltis was now sitting straight on his throne, his interest focused solely on Rend's words. How a werewolf spy could know these things puzzled Baltis, but he was grateful for the information. Obediah Tanner, a rogue werewolf, had been feeding the Dark Elemaiya information for years. For a price, of course.

"He will know—and he has not led us astray so far," Rend said respectfully.

"Then pay him and keep me informed. We will track and destroy," Baltis commanded. "Those Bright fools still don't realize there's a seventh one out there. I'd like to eliminate him before Friesianna learns of his existence." Baltis mused for a moment. "Very well, kill the others when you find them, and keep watching for the opportunity to destroy the hidden one." Baltis escaped his reverie and waved a careless hand, commanding his Destroyers. "See to it."

"As you will it, my King." Rend bowed and walked away.

"We will bring the Bright Queen down," Prince Beldris smiled at his brother.

"Of course we will," Baltis nodded regally.

"I heard Chad and Jeremy's essays won't be considered," Cori said as she walked out of Cloud Chief Combined with Ashe and Sali.

Sali had gotten into an argument with Wynn and Dori during Math class, destroying the temporary peace that existed between them and reinstating the old feud.

Ashe shrugged over the whole thing and resolved to wait it out. Again. At least Cori was still speaking to him, even if she was giving Sali dark looks now and then.

"That's what Marcus told us yesterday. It's no surprise, but I don't think they had a chance anyway," Ashe said. "I figure somebody in your class will get it, though."

"I could use the money when I go to college," Cori said. "But dad promised to give me a little money to fix up my dorm room."

Sali and Ashe had given their best to the essay because both wanted a cell phone. Ashe figured they would be forced to wait the extra year to get one. The five hundred in first-place prize money was the amount specified by their parents or a cell phone wouldn't be allowed before the boys' fifteenth birthdays.

"Dude, we're just not destined to communicate outside mindspeech until we turn fifteen," Sali muttered dejectedly after Cori broke away from them to walk toward her home. "And that's a little one-sided at the moment."

"Hey, Ashe. Sali," Edward was waiting outside Ashe's garage when he and Sali arrived.

"Edward, what's up?" Sali grinned.

"Not much. I had to promise Mr. Landers that I wouldn't be any trouble before he'd let me out of his sight," Edward said.

"Come on in, I think Mom replenished the supply of microwave popcorn," Ashe said, inviting Edward inside.

"Luanne and Macy can't stop talking about Wynn and Dori," Edward said as they waited the prescribed time and listened to popcorn thump against the inside of the bag as it popped. "But Lizzie is back to her grumpy old self. Philip caught it from her, so now we can't stand either one of them. Again."

"I think Wynn and Dori wouldn't mind if Luanne and Macy came to visit," Ashe said, portioning out the hot popcorn into three bowls. Sali would take the lion's share if he didn't.

"Let me call Macy. Luanne is with her right now," Edward pulled his small walkie-talkie from a jacket pocket and pressed the button.

"Edward, what is it?" Macy asked.

"Ashe says that Wynn and Dori might not mind if you went to visit," Edward said.

"That would be cool, where do they live?"

"Hang on while I get Wynn on the phone; they're at the O'Neill's this afternoon," Ashe said and lifted the cordless to dial Wynn's number. Soon Wynn had her mother's permission for the girls to visit.

"We'll be there in a minute to take you," Edward said. He, Ashe and Sali raced out of the house; Edward and Sali waited impatiently while Ashe set the alarm and then they all ran toward Macy Hill's mobile home.

"Be back by six, I'll have dinner ready around then," Ramona Hill called after Macy and Luanne. Luanne's parents were visiting again—they didn't like being cut off from the others.

"You guys walk everywhere, don't you?" Macy asked as they walked across a grassy field toward the O'Neill's farm.

"Just about. People don't drive much inside the community," Ashe agreed. "Sali runs to my house as wolf, sometimes. I have a couple changes of clothes for him when he gets there."

"What does it feel like—to change?" Luanne asked Sali, who nearly blushed at the attention.

"It doesn't hurt—it just is," Sali replied. "The first time I changed, I was ten. Marco—that's my older brother—was teasing me, telling me I wouldn't ever be a wolf. It was self-defense," he shrugged.

"The first time for me, I didn't even realize it," Ashe said. "I was sleeping and woke buried under the covers. At first, I thought I was dreaming. It took forever just to wriggle out of bed."

"You changed while you were asleep?" Macy stared at Ashe.

"The first time, yeah. Scared the dickens out of me."

"You had dickens in you? Must be awful coming out," Sali teased.

"Yeah, it's slimy and green," Ashe said, poking Sali in the ribs and running away.

"You can run but you can't hide," Sali shouted. "Get back here. We have guests."

"Yes, Mom," Ashe contritely trotted back. Edward snickered.

"This is cool," Macy and Luanne, hair blowing in the wind, stood on the lower rung of the white board fence and watched the sheep in one of the O'Neill's pastures, while Wynn and Dori talked about the farm the O'Neill's ran.

"You can't really have livestock if you turn into a predator," Dori sneered at Sali, who patently ignored her. "That's why the Pack always avoids this place and the Thompson's—they raise chickens and turkeys and shapeshift into a buffalo and a swan."

"So, not many pets, either?" Luanne asked.

"No. Dogs and cats would be curious when all the shapeshifters and wolves went out on the full Moon. Not a good combination," Wynn sighed. "And I always wanted a dog."

"We can send Sali over next month," Ashe offered.

"Ashe Evans, don't make me chase you," Wynn flipped white hair back and glared at Ashe. Ashe grinned at Wynn, who couldn't help but smile back.

"This is how it's supposed to be—friends having fun," Luanne breathed in the Oklahoma air and tilted her head back to revel in the afternoon sun.

"It hasn't been fun for a long time, has it?" Dori asked.

"No. Not for a while," Macy agreed.

~

"They've found a single fingerprint from the second murder site," Director Jennings informed Winkler over the phone. "I've also had someone investigating the department. Right now, there's no conclusive evidence—no ID on the fingerprint and the investigation has failed to turn up anything."

"Trajan thinks information was handed over to the Mayor by the second victim regarding the mobile homes—we trucked them in at the same time," Winkler said.

"You mentioned that before, but mobile homes move around in Oklahoma all the time. Why would it raise a lot of curiosity?"

"Because they all disappeared. Nobody can say one way or the other just where they ended up, and that's usually not the case, Director."

"So, if they were all dumped in a field somewhere so everybody could see, then the mystery would be solved?"

"Maybe. But we can't move another six in, just to cover for the first six; we're down to five now, thanks to those two delinquents from Cloud Chief."

"I'm glad there was a vacant house for them to take," Bill observed. "Else we would have moved another one in."

"And potentially alerted the murderer. The jury's still out on that theory," Winkler said.

"I agree. We have next to no evidence, so we'll have to keep digging. Lawford and North have hit a dead end."

"If it's a serial killer, he'll strike again," Winkler said.

"That's what worries me," the Director sighed.

"Where is Philip's dad?" Sali asked as he, Ashe and Edward walked Macy and Luanne back to Macy's house.

"He's dead," Luanne replied. "I think Philip was ten when that happened. His father was killed in an accident at work."

"According to Philip, anyway," Macy said. "He doesn't talk much about that."

"So, no explanation about how he died?" Ashe was curious. He still hadn't talked to Edward about Edward's mother's accident, which likely wasn't an accident at all.

"None. We don't know and we didn't want to pry. You've seen how prickly Philip can be."

"Yeah."

"Poor Philip, I don't think he knows where he is, most of the time," Luanne said. "He doesn't bother me, but I understand I'm in a minority."

"Of one," Macy agreed.

"Ashe," Edward began.

"What?"

"Some of us saw you get into a car with two agents, Trace and somebody else a couple of days ago," Edward said uncomfortably. He'd been selected to ask questions about the incident.

"Oh. Well, I can't talk about that," Ashe scuffed his athletic shoe on a prickly pear that had sprung up during the warmer weather.

"Really? You can't?" Edward was pleading for information.

"Edward, don't ask. I can't talk about it," Ashe repeated.

"Macy, how was your visit?" Ramona Hill smiled at all the teens as they walked inside the Hill's home.

"Mom, it was really cool. We watched sheep and cows grazing. You should see the new lambs—they are so cute."

"It was great," Luanne agreed. "And they invited us back. Mrs. O'Neill said we could feed the calves next time."

"Excuse me," Trace stood at the door, tapping on the doorframe softly.

"What is it?" Rocky Hill went to let Trace in.

"I have to see Ashe," Trace said.

Ashe, who'd been listening while Macy and Luanne described their visit to the O'Neill's farm, turned to follow Trace out the door.

"Ashe, they found a third victim in Cordell," Trace said. "A woman who works for the grocery store. When she didn't show up for her shift this morning, somebody went to check on her. They found her body inside the house. We need to get inside that house, Ashe. We'll be by after dinner tonight and drive you to Cordell."

Ashe stared at Trace for a moment. "Trace, do you know her name —what she looked like?"

"I don't have the particulars—those agents called Jason a few minutes ago, asking for you to come along and get us past the police that are guarding the crime scene. We'll get more information when they show up, I figure."

"All right. I'll tell Mom when she gets home," Ashe said.

"Go on back," Trace nodded toward Macy's house. "Don't let this bother you, kid."

"I'll try," Ashe said, but he already felt ill over the whole thing.

～

"Mom, Trace didn't know anything," Ashe said, pushing lasagna around on his plate. Normally he loved lasagna, but the queasiness he'd felt after talking with Trace had only increased.

Ashe left the Hill's home shortly after his conversation with the tall werewolf, Sali following closely behind and asking questions. Ashe had to promise to tell Sali later. Disappointed, Sali trotted toward his home.

"Ready, kiddo?" Jason came in to collect Ashe half an hour later.

"Yeah." Ashe slid off the barstool he'd occupied after helping his mother with the dishes.

"He didn't eat much dinner, Jason," Adele pointed out as Ashe followed the werewolf out the door.

"Understood," Jason nodded. "This doesn't bother you, taking us inside like you do?" Jason asked as he slid the side door back so Ashe could climb into the van. Marcus was already inside the vehicle, sitting in the second row behind Agents Lawford and North.

"No. I'm upset because I know most of the people who work at the grocery store," Ashe said. "So I might know this person."

"I understand," Jason said, sliding in beside Marcus and slamming the door, once Ashe was inside and buckled in. "Let's go."

"Here is where the house is and what it looks like," Nick Lawford pointed out the home near the center of a narrow street. Ashe stared at the photograph—they'd downloaded the satellite image, he could tell. Like before, they'd parked in the church parking lot to allow Ashe to take them as mist to the location.

"It'll be the one with all the yellow crime scene tape around it," Derik North patted Ashe's shoulder. "Just get us inside, like last time. Any problems, let us know."

"Okay." Ashe took one last look at the photograph before turning to mist and then turning everyone else.

Agent North was correct—Ashe could see the crime scene tape from a distance. Worried that local authorities might still be inside, he misted through the entire house before dropping his passengers in the living room.

"Here's where she died," Nick Lawford knelt to examine the worn carpet. Ashe was no longer listening; he stared instead at the photographs on a shelf just inside the door. Smiling back at him was the image of Amy Long, cashier from Jerry's Super Saver Market and Bakery.

"Mr. DeLuca," Ashe's voice was barely a whisper.

"What is it, Ashe?" Marcus and Jason both came to stand next to Ashe.

"I know this person," Ashe pointed to the photograph. "When did she die?"

"Monday night, shortly after she got off work," Agent Lawford replied.

Ashe gulped. "Uh, Mr. DeLuca, I have a confession to make."

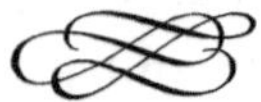

CHAPTER 8

"You sneaked into Cordell to buy snacks." Aedan growled as Ashe hunched miserably on the sofa inside their belowground living room.

"The cashier said she recognized me—from Cordell Feed and Seed," Ashe muttered unhappily. "She knew Mom's name, too. I didn't give her mine—I don't do that," Ashe hurried to say.

"And this happens just before she's killed," Marcus said, pacing behind Aedan. Ashe was forced to admit that he and Sali had gone to Cordell at Ashe's suggestion—he made sure they knew that—to get snacks.

"A man was in the line ahead of us, buying a few things," Ashe said. "He wore a leather jacket, with those sharp studs on the shoulders," Ashe tapped his arm. "One of those could have caused a gouge in the doorframe at the Mayor's house."

"Son, why didn't you tell me this before?" Aedan frowned at Ashe. Ashe knew he was in enough trouble as it was.

"Because Sali and I were talking and I wasn't paying attention. I only thought of it now, while you were asking questions."

"Did he pay with a credit card?" Agent Lawford asked.

"No—he paid cash, just like we did."

"See if the grocery store has a security camera," Nick Lawford told Agent North. "Kid, do you still have your receipt or remember the time you were there?"

"I think I have the receipt. Let me check my pants pockets," Ashe said.

Adele, who'd stood quietly in a corner while her son was questioned, followed him silently down the hall toward his bedroom. Searching through his hamper, Ashe pulled out the jeans he'd worn Monday afternoon and stuffed his hand inside both front pockets.

"Here it is," Ashe handed the crumpled receipt to Agent Lawford a few minutes later.

"The time is stamped on it; ask them to pull up the images around that time," Nick Lawford handed the paper to Derik North, who walked toward the stairs and the upper portion of the house.

"Dad, how would anyone connect me to anything?" Ashe thought to ask. "I think that man might have realized that Amy knew just about everybody in town. He may have tried to get information from her."

"That's true," Agent Lawford agreed. "Do you think she knew that you don't attend any of the schools in Cordell?"

"I don't know," Ashe shrugged. "Would that man be asking about me or about the others?"

"Good question," Agent Lawford nodded. "If he asked about the mobile homes from the other two victims, it stands to reason that he'd do the same, or ask about those children," he added. "And this is all speculation on our part. It could be completely unrelated."

"Do we know for certain that all three victims knew one another?" Marcus asked.

"Pretty sure—like Ashe pointed out, Amy knew just about everybody in the area, because of her job."

"Yeah. She said she recognized me from Cordell Feed and Seed," Ashe repeated. "So maybe they were hoping she'd recognize and remember somebody else, or would have heard something. They must really like killing, because she would have told them anything they wanted to know in the checkout line."

"Kid, you scare me sometimes," Marcus muttered.

~

Director Bill Jennings watched the entire scene play out before him. He'd asked Agent Lawford to attach a button camera to his shirt and he'd seen everything Nick witnessed and experienced, even while Ashe had everyone turned to mist. Going right through the front door of the latest victim's house had been disorienting but more than impressive. Vince, Bill's assistant, had watched with the Director during the course of the evening, shocked that a thirteen-year-old could accomplish such amazing feats.

"You know to keep your mouth shut," Bill reminded Vince before Vince went back to his duties.

"Of course I do, Director," Vince replied and walked out of Bill's office, closing the door softly behind him.

~

"I don't recognize him, but the image is so blurry," Jerry Southard, owner and manager of Jerry's Super Saver, muttered as Agent Derik North pointed out the image of the man in the checkout line.

"You should upgrade your system and clean the lenses on your cameras," Derik grumbled. He could see—barely—the images of two teens behind the man in question, but it would have been difficult to use those images to identify Ashe and Salidar.

"And you say the two boys saw the man's leather jacket, decorated with studs?" Jerry asked. Jerry, a bit overweight with thinning brown hair, had owned his business for twenty years, taking the supermarket over when the previous owner had retired and put it up for sale.

"That's what they say. I can sort of see the black jacket, but I can't make out any details," Derik squinted at the screen.

"I'm sorry. If I'd known that this could have led to the arrest of Amy's killer," Jerry sighed regretfully, pointing to the images on the small monitor. Amy was a popular cashier at his store. Everybody knew and liked her and now she was dead.

"We don't know that; he's just a suspect at this point. But if he comes in again," Derik said.

"I'll call right away. I'll have the staff on the lookout as well."

"Tell them not to give themselves away—this is a murder suspect," Derik pointed out.

"Then I'll only tell my assistant manager; he's here if I'm not," Jerry said.

"Grounded," Aedan said as soon as Marcus and the others left. "You will come straight home every day and study, read or do homework. For two weeks." Ashe hung his head as his father pronounced doom. "Salidar and the others may not visit and you may not call them. And they may not call you." Aedan was so angry his eyes were blood red. Ashe was glad his father was tight-lipped when he spoke—the fangs were likely showing.

"Sorry, dad," Ashe muttered regretfully, lowering his eyes.

"Son, we can't protect you if you leave the confines of Cloud Chief without an adult. You know that," Aedan snapped and left the room so swiftly Ashe almost didn't see it.

"The older ones get to go all the time," Ashe mumbled.

"Ashe, don't force me to add another week to your grounding," Adele stood nearby, staring angrily at her son. "Those creatures aren't hunting the other children from Cloud Chief. They're hunting *you*."

"Mom?"

"What, son?" Adele's voice was clipped.

"Ask Sali if that man smelled human or not."

Marcus called Sali into the kitchen so Aedan could question him about the scent. "I was talking to Ashe when we were in the checkout line, but I think I'd notice if somebody didn't smell human," Sali muttered.

He'd gotten the same treatment from his parents that Ashe had received; he was grounded for two weeks. Aedan listened carefully to Sali's words—he'd gone to the DeLuca home after getting a call from Adele on his cell phone. Ashe had thought to ask a good question.

Marcus sent Sali back to his room immediately and then followed Aedan as he walked out of the house. "I don't know, Aedan," Marcus sighed. "The boy was likely distracted, so I can't say for sure that he remembers with any certainty. It was a good thought, though. I hope those two agents can track this one down and prove he had nothing to do with any of this."

Thunder rumbled overhead and a few drops fell on both their heads as Marcus gazed up at a heavily overcast sky. Lightning briefly lit heavy clouds to the west.

"Rain moving in," Aedan observed, sniffing the air. The community was still shy around thunderstorms since the tornado the previous year. He and Nathan would be patrolling Cloud Chief in a storm.

"I've got an extra slicker if you need it," Marcus offered.

"I can get home for mine before it gets too wet," Aedan replied. "Thank you for the offer, though."

"No trouble. Call if you need any help—I think I can send out a wolf or two."

"Shouldn't need it, but we'll let you know." Aedan nodded at the Cloud Chief Packmaster and disappeared in a blur.

"Wish I could move that fast," Marcus sighed and walked inside his home.

"Dad, do you think we might see a tornado?" Edward stood at the front door of their mobile home, watching as the rain began to fall amid thunder and lightning.

"Son, I hope we don't; this house will fold up like a wet cardboard box," Steven Pendley replied. "And we'd better be in a storm shelter if that happens."

"Can we go look at the storm shelter? We haven't seen it yet," Edward bounced on his toes in excitement.

"How heavy is the rain?" Steven asked.

"It's making puddles in the field outside."

"Then let's wait. I hope we won't need to get in it tonight. Come away from the door, son. That lightning is getting closer."

"Dad, I know that Director Jennings said we'd probably move away at the end of summer, but what do you think our chances would be of staying here?" Edward closed the front door reluctantly—he'd enjoyed watching the lightning and the rain, unobstructed by rows of houses or city blocks filled with tall buildings.

The Oklahoma prairie was a new and welcome experience for him. He had no care for shopping or the need to be surrounded by crowds of people. The quiet appealed to him very much.

He also wanted to get to know Ashe and Sali better—they shared a friendship that he envied. If he could become good friends with them, who knew what the future might hold?

In all his life, Edward had no close friendships. He knew his father was trying to protect him, but pointed ears didn't seem to be a concern to the citizens of Cloud Chief. In fact, Luanne had told him that one of the residents became a white buffalo. Edward wanted to see someone who could turn into a buffalo. And Sali's wolf? That was amazing.

"I don't know that they'd allow it—this is a hidden refuge for these people," Steven replied. "Want cocoa?" Edward's father pulled a box of instant out of the pantry.

~

"My Queen, I would not have offered this to our previous monarch," Diamond lifted the sleeve of his silk shirt, revealing the single, square gold talisman beneath. It shone brightly in the torchlight surrounding

Friesianna, marked with runes denoting power in an ancient language none remembered.

Friesianna's crown was grasped in her left hand as she reached out for Diamond's talisman with her right. The Bright crown held power over the talismans and all four medallions could be called forth if there was great need.

Diamond failed to see six children as great need, but his Queen asked, therefore he answered. His brothers Emerald, Sapphire and Ruby waited behind him, ready to offer up their talismans as well.

Hilbah stood nearby, a triumphant gleam in his eyes as he watched the first of four gold power charms peel away from Diamond's flesh and float toward Friesianna's hand. The *Call* would go out within days.

"Wildrif is worth his weight in gold," Obediah Tanner chuckled, causing the scar running from the old werewolf's left eye down to his chin to pucker. Gray peppered Obediah's thick brown hair and he sported a rather large and bushy moustache that hid most of his mouth. Smoking a cigar and having a glass of whiskey, Obediah grinned at Lester, his second-in-command.

Obediah wasn't an officially recognized Packmaster, so Lester had to settle for being an unofficial Second. The Grand Master considered Obediah an outlaw; he just hadn't been able to pin any wrongdoing on the old wolf. All thanks to Wildrif, who was something of a clairvoyant.

Wildrif always knew when someone was coming for a surprise inspection of *Tanner's Wild Game Preserve*, located near Amarillo in the Texas Panhandle. Obediah was able to hide any contraband and the rare, endangered or exotic animals used to lure wealthy hunters to his land; Wildrif warned him days in advance in order to give his employer plenty of time to conceal everything.

"How much this time?" Lester raised a glass of whiskey to his boss.

"Three hundred thousand. I think we could get more if we turn those kids over," Obediah grinned. "A lot more."

"Are we still getting information regularly?"

"Yeah. Josiah won't say who his spy is, and I really don't care as long as we keep getting what we need on that community. Wildrif has trouble seeing past their boundary, but he sure knows what the Bright Ones are up to. No idea where the Dark Ones get the money to pay, but we don't care about that, do we?" Obediah sipped his whiskey.

"Nope. Boss, that's the easiest money we've ever made. No animals or contraband to smuggle, no politicians to pay to keep quiet—it's all information and simple to get."

"I thought about giving Wildrif a raise, but that might get his hopes up," Obediah continued, rattling ice cubes in his glass.

"Boss, I wouldn't have taken him on, looking the way he does," Lester pointed out. "Wildrif scares some of the others, what with two different colored eyes and all."

"He refuses to get haircuts, and that makes him look even wilder," Obediah agreed. "But he knows what he's talking about. Every time."

"At least he keeps himself clean—when you first got him, he smelled terrible."

"Kept in a cage somewhere down south," Obediah blew smoke rings in the air. "Don't know how he managed to get himself locked up like that. Unless he knew he'd end up here."

"Could be. You treat him good, boss."

"Yeah. Go offer to bring him a steak—he's earned it."

Ashe could hear rain drumming on the roof from two floors down. He'd checked the weather reports—just a thunderstorm with no tornadic activity reported. Blowing out a relieved sigh, Ashe sent an instant message to Sali.

His father hadn't forbidden email or instant messaging, after all. Likely hadn't thought about it—Aedan refused to use it, preferring his old cell phone. Ashe had only attempted to persuade his father to buy one of the newer, smart phones once.

Dude, I got two weeks, too. Sali's reply came swiftly—Marcus hadn't cut off Sali's electronic communication, either. *Man, this sucks,* Sali added.

Yeah, Ashe dutifully replied. They'd gone off the reservation; now they paid the price. *I'll send an email to Wynn and ask her to let Edward and the others know we can't see them for two weeks.*

Better you than me, dude. Sali never spoke civilly with Wynn or Dori, in any form of communication. Attempts at such met with cold and calculated insults and unmerciful teasing.

Can't we all just get along? Ashe mused through his keystrokes. It was an oft-moaned response to Sali's war with both girls.

Dude, Armageddon will happen before that does, Sali sniped back.

You may eat those words someday.

Not likely.

You eat everything else.

Hey, that's just mean. And not true. I don't eat beets.

I stand corrected.

Then stop implying that I eat everything.

I wasn't implying, I was inferring. I was arriving at a conclusion based on the evidence at hand.

I owe you a kick.

In two weeks, dude. Unless you want Billings to catch us.

Detention on top of grounding? No, thanks.

"The *Call* will go out in a few days. I want you to track those children when they leave the protected area to seek out the Bright race," Baltis instructed his Destroyers. Rend, Slash, Grind and Crush bowed before their King.

"What is your will in this?" Rend, eldest of the four, asked.

"Kill them. We have no use for them—I hear they have not

developed any talent as yet." Baltis examined his nails. Perhaps he would have a servant take care of them—they looked a bit ragged.

"We will have to drain power from our talismans to relocate—it will take four jumps from here," Rend informed Baltis.

"Then go tomorrow. That will give them time to recharge." The Destroyers wore the gold duplicates of the Bright talismans—all bearing the ancient text that none now recalled or were able to read.

It gave the Destroyers extra power to relocate, hopping from one place to another. Four hundred miles was the maximum any Destroyer could jump at one time. The talismans enabled them to make additional, difficult relocations.

Most Elemaiya capable of the feat could only perform one or two relocations before taking a rest. Baltis' crown helped him relocate farther and faster, but he used it only if his life were in danger.

"It will be as you say, my King," Rend bowed low and disappeared; Slash, Grind and Crush following closely behind.

Dude, I have to get in bed, Mom will be knocking on the door anytime, Ashe was still messaging Sali and it was after ten.

Me, too. See you at school. Sali shut down his computer before his mother caught him communicating with Ashe.

Ashe sighed and turned off his own machine, pushing his chair back and stretching a little before rising.

"I was hoping you'd stop soon, I've been waiting for more than one of your Earth hours," someone said behind him, making Ashe whirl around in terror. A very tall boy with sky-blue skin, wheat-colored hair and bright blue eyes sat on the end of Ashe's bed, smiling.

CHAPTER 9

"What the?" Ashe was about to turn to mist and flee.

"No, do not run away, I must speak with you," the blue being held out a hand in a calming gesture. "I have the room shielded; we may speak without fear of discovery."

"But," Ashe began to wonder if he'd fallen asleep and was now dreaming. Tugging on his short, slightly curly brown hair, Ashe stared at his visitor.

"I am of the Larentii race and am younger than you, although I am taller—my race is very tall. My name is Renegar. I ask that you remember it from this point forward—if I use it more than once my father will know. He has employed Nexus Echo while I am studying other worlds."

"But," Ashe repeated. He had an alien in his bedroom? How did that happen? And did he call himself Renegar? How had he gotten past the shields surrounding Cloud Chief?

"I asked Uncle for an unusual race to study. He handed over information on the Elemaiya," Renegar smiled, revealing white, even teeth that contrasted sharply with his blue skin. Renegar's face was evenly proportioned; his nose was perfect and his blue eyes twinkled with something akin to mischief.

"But," Ashe said a third time.

"You wonder how old I am and why I am here," Renegar went on. "I am nine years old and six inches taller than you, using your measurements, of course, and the Elemaiya are on a path toward destruction. That is why my uncle sent me in their direction—he says to study them at this time because they may not survive past the next six hundred years. Not as they are now, anyway."

"But that doesn't explain why you're in my bedroom," Ashe muttered, sitting down at his desk again.

"You should not fear for your safety; we Larentii are benign and are forbidden by law to interfere," Renegar said. "I will not stay long now, but I may come back to visit occasionally—while the Bright children remain within your village. You are a puzzle to me, Ashe Evans," Renegar added. "An unreadable one."

"What does that mean?" Ashe demanded helplessly.

"We Larentii know a great many things, even at such early stages of our lives," Renegar stood, showing Ashe that he was taller than Ashe's father. "We young ones know much of what was, but we must study what is and what is likely to be. Hence, my curiosity over the Elemaiya. I hope you do not mind if I fold in once in a while."

"Fold? How do you speak English?" Ashe eyed Renegar suspiciously.

"Folding space. And I speak most languages. Yours is a rather simple one. I hope that does not offend. Good night. Is that the proper term?" Renegar smiled again and disappeared, leaving Ashe to use a few swear words that he saved for special occasions.

Employing Sali's habit of venting frustration by kicking dirt clods along the road on his way to school, Ashe shrugged away a nearly sleepless night. Over and over, he pondered the appearance (and disappearance) of the one who called himself Renegar.

Ashe had almost convinced himself that the nine-year-old alien existed only in his imagination when Renegar and Sali joined him at nearly the same moment. Sali had walked through the field behind his home; Renegar appeared from nothing. Ashe had been so preoccupied he hadn't seen Sali wander to his side, and Renegar's sudden appearance startled him and made him jump.

"Sorry, didn't mean to scare you—you've got that *I'm on another planet look*," Sali said right away. Renegar smiled. Ashe stared from Sali to Renegar, realizing quickly that Sali didn't see the tall, blue-skinned Larentii youth at all.

"He cannot hear me either, as the others will not. You are the only one, Ashe Evans. I have decided to observe you at a normal school day."

Sali would think him crazy if he talked to empty air, so Ashe resorted to mindspeech. Everyone else could hear it, why not an alien? *It won't be a normal day if you're following me around,* Ashe grumped mentally. *And who says you can just hang around anyway? I've got enough problems as it is.*

Excellent, you have mindspeech. This is more exciting than anticipated, Renegar replied gleefully. *You may use my name in mindspeech; Nexus Echo will not activate unless it is spoken.*

Goody for us, Ashe wasn't excited in the least.

Is that slang? Oh, how marvelous!

Dude, pace yourself. It's not that special, Ashe replied. *And just what is Nexus Echo anyway?*

Nexus Echo is an invisible net, cast by one powerful enough, Renegar replied. *It will ripple if certain words are used, alerting the caster. I do not wish my father to appear if I use my name in the same location twice. You cannot use it either, or I will not be allowed to return and will face punishment. In addition, I will be prevented from leaving the Larentii homeworld for a specified period of time.*

"Dude, where the hell are you?" Sali waved a hand vigorously in Ashe's face.

"Don't know," Ashe muttered. "Never heard of the place before." Renegar grinned while Ashe kicked another dirt clod and continued toward school.

The day was terrible. Chad and Jeremy discovered Ashe and Sali's punishment and gloated over it outside Ashe's locker while Renegar looked on, silently observing.

None of the other students saw the tall, blue youth, but they flowed unconsciously around him like water anyway. Ashe shook his head at what must surely be a mystifying ability to shield and pretended to ignore Chad and Jeremy while a flush crept into his face. Renegar sent mindspeech after Ashe handed in a test for science class, telling Ashe what he should have added to a poorly answered question.

Thanks for the update, Ashe hissed mentally, employing as much cerebral sarcasm as he could muster.

Ah, I see you do not desire corrections, Renegar's mental voice floated back.

What was your first clue? Ashe jerked his backpack off the floor as soon as the bell rang.

Sali wasn't happy either when they walked toward home—he'd gotten the brunt of Chad and Jeremy's taunts at lunch—Ashe had stayed behind in Math, doing homework and reading through his English textbook, pointedly ignoring Renegar and skipping the midday meal. "Gotta go," Sali lifted a hand in a half-wave and cut across the field that led to his home.

"Yeah," Ashe muttered miserably and watched his friend walk away.

"What is grounded?" Renegar asked aloud as soon as Sali was away.

"Punishment," Ashe sighed and hefted his backpack to a more comfortable position.

"For which infraction?" Renegar's bright-blue eyes held curiosity and a bit of concern.

"For misting into Cordell and buying snacks for the other kids," Ashe replied. "Why don't you just know that? You knew the other things I was thinking last night."

"Those were standard reactive questions," Renegar smiled. "I can't read you as I can the others. If you recall, I named you unreadable."

"You said that," Ashe acknowledged. "I still don't know what that means."

"Larentii are adept at reading others' thoughts and actions; yours are unknown to me. That is why I returned today—to learn more if I could."

"How did you know to come looking for me, then?" Ashe stopped in the center of the gravel road and stared up at the tall, nine-year-old Larentii.

"I pulled the information from one of the half-Elemaiyan children —Edward, I believe his name is," Renegar said. "He thinks you are—in his words—*cool*. Although I failed at first to understand why he would employ such a term unless you were, indeed, cold."

"And now you understand it to be slang." Ashe started walking again.

"I was able to receive your approximate location from that one, and decided to pay a visit. As you see, you have become quite the subject matter for this lesson in the condition of dying races."

"Glad to be of service," Ashe muttered, his voice thick with sarcasm.

"What do you know of these children?" Renegar steered away from Ashe's remark.

"Not much. Philip and Elizabeth aren't easy to get along with. Edward I like—he could be a friend, I think. Luanne, well, she has something the others don't. They all seem calmer around her, even Philip, who's a little hyper and Elizabeth, who's smug and superior."

"Superior, meaning that is the manner in which she compares herself to others, and not her actual condition?" Renegar was trying to understand.

"Yes. Exactly," Ashe nodded. He was nearly home and wondered how inviting an invisible Larentii in might affect his grounding. "Are you hungry? I have popcorn or peanut butter and jelly."

"Ah. Well," Renegar looked uncomfortable for the first time. "We, ah, do not eat in the same manner you do."

"Sali doesn't eat in the same manner, either," Ashe pointed out. "He eats anything that isn't nailed down. His metabolism is so high I don't know how his mom deals with it."

"I meant," Renegar said, "that we do not eat food—not your

definition of it, anyway. Larentii absorb sunlight, mostly. It feeds us. Another energy source is acceptable but not particularly appetizing."

"Like broccoli?" Ashe asked, schooling his face. He was astounded that Renegar and his race survived by absorbing energy.

"Broccoli being a much less acceptable food?"

"To some," Ashe ducked his head to hide the grin.

"Then any other energy source is broccoli. I will refer to it as such when we converse."

"Do you want to come in the house or not?" Ashe asked.

"Of course. Thank you for inviting me."

Ashe didn't point out that Renegar had come in the night before uninvited. That would be rude. He punched in the code outside the garage door. Renegar followed him inside while Ashe closed the wide, steel door before punching in the second code to let himself into the kitchen.

"Your father is vampire," Renegar nodded, examining the kitchen curiously. "Most vampires are quite wary and tend to place as many thick walls about them as they can. Steel and concrete are preferable, I've discovered."

"You've studied vampires?"

"I have been quite close to several, had they but known," Renegar smiled. "Please, go ahead and have a snack. You will not offend me."

Ashe dumped his backpack on the kitchen island and set about making a peanut butter sandwich. Renegar watched in fascination as Ashe spread peanut butter across bread before folding it in half and biting into it. While he chewed, Ashe poured out a glass of milk to go with his sandwich.

"You do not have to eliminate waste, do you?" Renegar asked after Ashe swallowed his first bite.

"Dad always said it was because I got more vampire in me than anyone thought," Ashe said. "Mom was happy because she didn't have to change diapers. Sali hates it because he isn't the same."

"Hmmm," Renegar examined Ashe closely. "I still cannot get a reading, so I have no way to determine the truth in this case. I may have a hypothesis, but that will remain with me at this time."

"What is it?"

"I cannot say. It could be construed as interference and I will certainly not do that."

"Then why bring it up?" Ashe took another bite of his sandwich.

"If it offends, I apologize. With the Larentii, no subject is taboo. Is that the term, taboo? Meaning unacceptable?"

"Yes." Ashe drank milk as he watched Renegar process the information. Renegar's blue skin resembled a sunny, cloudless day. His eyes were a brighter shade of blue and they were focused elsewhere for a moment.

"Where do you go when you do that?" Ashe asked curiously.

"I am mentally searching for information. Somewhat as you do with the Internet, only much more accurate," Renegar's smile was bright.

"That must be a big time-saver," Ashe teased.

"Most certainly," the teasing went right past Renegar for a few seconds. "Oh, I see. You are teasing me. That makes us more familiar. Like friends."

"Hey, I never said that. And it's just awkward, having you following me at school. It's like I'm under a microscope."

"You do not feel this way with Salidar? Your werewolf friend?"

"No, but we've known each other for a long time."

"If that engenders trust and will alleviate your distress, then I will continue to follow you as time allows so you will become adjusted to my presence and cease feeling discomfort."

"Dude," Ashe held up a hand.

"You call me dude? A slang term? Almost a gesture of friendship? This is indeed a good day. I have not had any friends among other races until now." Renegar smiled brightly.

"Dude," Ashe stomped a foot and lowered his shoulder helplessly. He felt obligated to befriend the tall Larentii child now. "Come on, let's go downstairs," Ashe sighed as he punched in the third door code to the underground portion of the Evans home.

"You play with this?" Renegar handled the lime-green Frisbee with care, touching Sali's teeth marks reverently.

"You should try it," Ashe said, pulling up information for his History final on the computer.

"Might we go outside, then?"

"I'm not supposed to—grounded, you know," Ashe muttered. The day had been nice earlier and he wouldn't mind throwing a Frisbee around.

"I can shield both of us," Renegar offered.

"Is there a name I can call you so we won't affect that nexus thing you talked about?"

"A nickname?" Renegar almost went into raptures, his blue eyes glowing brighter than they normally did.

"Can we shorten yours or should we do something else?" Ashe turned away from his desktop, History forgotten for the moment.

"Hmmm, that might work. Call me Ren. That sounds the same as the bird's name, does it not?"

"Yes. You can be Ren. Come on, Ren, and that shield better be good or I'll be grounded for another two weeks."

"Not to worry, friend," Ren was smiling again as he and Ashe rushed up the stairs and into a sunny afternoon.

❧

"The fingerprint isn't in any database, Director." Vince Jordan handed the information on an electronic tablet to Bill Jennings.

"We don't have information on the killer in that way. Damn, this is frustrating," Bill muttered. "How are we going to tell if this man is after those kids? If it is a man. Do we have information on those Elemaiya, to see if their fingerprints are similar to those of humans?"

"The information is here," Vince tapped the tablet he'd set in front of the Director.

"You mean it's the same sort of lines and everything?" Bill shook his head at the information Vince had gathered. That information had been supplied, surprisingly, by one of their vampire agents, who'd gotten it from the Vampire Council.

"It appears to be so," Vince agreed. "But we know it isn't a vampire

—one of the murders took place during the day, and the two werewolves who are assisting our investigators insist that the scent they got wasn't a werewolf's. They'd have recognized it right away."

"Do we know for sure that the perpetrator—that English teacher in Cloud Chief, was the one responsible for those murders last year?"

"He admitted it under compulsion, according to our vampire sources."

"Then this is someone new. Vince, I'm beginning to think we need a magic wand to sort this out. If two of my best agents with the help they've got in the field can't come up with something, we're screwed."

"Director, the children are still safe, are they not? Perhaps we should consider our small victories."

"Yeah. Maybe you're right, Vince." Bill went back to the information on the tablet.

~

"Jason, I brought iced tea and sandwiches," Marcie Pruitt, Denise DeLuca's sister, handed over a thermos jug and a brown paper bag for the two werewolves. They'd set up a small rest tent, the striped cloth top flapping briskly in the late afternoon breeze.

Both Trace and Jason occupied comfortable lawn chairs beneath the high-topped cover while they kept an eye on Cloud Chief's guests. Jason Landers offered Marcie a brief grin before digging into the bag and handing a sandwich to Trace and then taking one for himself.

"This is mighty nice of you, Mrs. Pruitt," Jason said, pouring iced tea into the thermal mug he kept with him for coffee and such.

"Just call me Marcie. Dominic and I are divorced now." Marcie didn't like talking about her ex-husband, who was doing his worst and keeping her youngest son Jackson from calling or writing. Her oldest, Dustin, got around Dominic somehow and managed to keep his mother updated on everything, including his younger brother.

"Marcie, then," Jason said. "Would you like to sit? The kids seem pretty quiet today." Jason nodded in the distance, where Edward had a long-tailed kite in the sky and Bryce and Keith were tossing a football. The others were indoors.

"Maybe for a few minutes," Marcie agreed. "Denise tells me you know a lot about farming and growing vegetables. I think we have some sort of bug eating the tomato plants in the community garden."

"Then I'll have a look when the vamps come out to guard," Jason nodded.

"Good. Can I have a little of your tea? It's really warm today." Jason didn't hesitate to offer his cup and his lawn chair to Marcie.

"Dude, the phone is ringing," Ashe turned to mist in a blink, almost leaving Ren behind when he misted inside the house to answer the call.

"Mom?" Ashe said when he picked up. Caller ID identified his mother on the other end.

"Ashe, I was just checking to make sure you're home and safe."

"I'm home, Mom," Ashe replied, doing his best to keep the breathlessness out of his voice. Once Ren had understood the object of tossing a Frisbee, he'd become quite adept at it. The young Larentii now stood at Ashe's shoulder, having folded into the house carrying the Frisbee in his hands.

"Do you have homework?"

"Already did the Math, just have to study a little for the History final next week."

"Good. I'll be home in about an hour, hon. Let's have sandwiches tonight; I'm tired."

"Yeah. I'll make them so you can sit down when you get here," Ashe offered.

"That sounds good, honey. See you in a bit."

"Bye, Mom." Ashe hung up.

"Frisbee is quite entertaining. Perhaps we can do other things later," Ren reluctantly handed the Frisbee to Ashe. "I should go now, since your mother is coming home soon. I had a very good time, friend." Renegar disappeared.

"Must be nice to be able to do that," Ashe said and went to get a glass of water.

∾

"Wildrif, why do I have to depend upon a spy to get information on the seventh child? Those Dark Ones are offering half a million if we can get information on all seven of those kids. They'll hand us a million if our information leads to their capture." Obediah Tanner stared at his hired clairvoyant.

"You know I have difficulty seeing past those witch boundaries," Wildrif sniffed, his thin, nearly colorless hair floating about his face, one brown eye and one blue eye studying Obediah earnestly.

None knew Wildrif's true age and he wasn't planning to tell them. He also wasn't planning to tell Obediah that he couldn't see the seventh child, even while he was outside the witch's border. It was luck that their spy had learned of the child and of his beginnings, else they'd have never known of him and the Dark Elemaiya would be just as ignorant of the boy's existence as the Bright Ones. "And we are not talking capture, wise wolf," Wildrif bowed before Obediah.

Subtle flattery never failed to gain Obediah's attention, and Wildrif knew it well. "I know they desire the deaths of those children, and I have no concern for that. I know of many that are buried across the country already."

"You're tougher than I thought," Obediah chuckled, causing his thick moustache to bristle and the deep scar on his face to bounce. "Wildrif, with your information and what's coming in from Josiah's spy, we may be on our way to an easy million. You'll get a nice bonus if we hit pay dirt." Obediah laughed at his own weak joke.

∾

"What are you doing here?" Elizabeth, her hair styled neatly and dressed in jeans and three-inch heels, stared over the fence that marked Cloud Chief's boundary. Chad and Jeremy had walked up beside her, prompting Liz's angry question. She'd understood that both boys were grounded or under house arrest.

"Mom had to go into Cordell for groceries. We sneaked out. They can't watch us every second," Jeremy huffed. "Besides, you're supposed to be back there with the rest of the *empties*."

"I can sneak away too," Elizabeth's voice was cool and haughty as she pointedly refused to look at the two boys. "Just because you can turn into a werewolf or whatever doesn't mean you have the market cornered on cool and different."

Liz had a new secret, one she'd discovered after seeing that *boy* lift Luanne and her parents out of a burning house, appearing from nowhere to drop them into a field. Liz had questioned Luanne at length about it, and Luanne had finally admitted that it was like flying invisibly through the air.

Linda and Peter Jansen, Luanne's parents, hadn't remembered much at all concerning the incident, but Luanne had remembered after a time.

"So, where is the nearest city from here?" Liz asked. She was at a disadvantage—she had no idea where she was and hadn't bothered to study any maps before coming to Oklahoma.

"Cordell is a few miles west," Jeremy deliberately pointed in the wrong direction while Chad snickered softly.

"Liar," Liz muttered. "It doesn't matter. I can find it for myself." With that, she disappeared right before a stunned werewolf and shapeshifter, becoming mist swiftly and flying toward her temporary home in Cloud Chief. She'd make plans and stay in Cloud Chief —*for now*.

CHAPTER 10

"You think I'll risk getting into more trouble with Packmaster DeLuca right now?" Chad hissed at Jeremy, who suggested they tell his mother, Diane about Liz's disappearance. "Just keep it quiet. Who the hell cares that she can disappear? If she could do more than that, she would have done it while we were there. Trust me, we still have the upper hand—did you see the way she was looking at us? Man, if looks could kill," Chad chortled over Liz's impotent fury.

"And who dresses like that in the middle of nowhere?" Jeremy snickered. Liz's shoes were completely inappropriate for walking through grassy prairie.

"They're all worthless. Did you hear what Principal Billings said when Mrs. Rocklin asked if we should let them come to graduation?"

"That was epic," Jeremy agreed. "Why don't you send them to the human graduation in Cordell where they belong?" Jeremy puffed out his cheeks and lowered his voice, imitating Billings' booming speech. "Come on, Mom may be on her way back. We can't be caught out here." They'd begun walking toward the Booth home, half a mile away.

"Yeah. But this fall, we'll be far away from that meddling empty and the rest of these empty-lovers," Chad couldn't wait to get away from Cloud Chief. He'd gotten the news from Jeremy's father the night before that not only would Jeremy's car be sold to pay restitution for the burned home, but the money they'd planned to use to buy a second car for Chad's graduation gift would go to that cause as well. Chad was despising Ashe Evans more and more as time went on.

"When I think about what that stupid empty has cost us already," Jeremy's fists clenched furiously.

"If Billings had his way, there'd only be werewolves here," Chad said. "And none of this would have happened."

"Yeah."

~

"I heard from Denise that the Booths are selling Jeremy's car and using that money plus what they would have spent on Chad's car to pay for the damage done to the Jansen's mobile home," Adele told Ashe as he set a ham sandwich and a bowl of tomato soup in front of his mother. She'd taken her shoes off the moment she'd come through the door, telling Ashe she'd been on her feet all day.

"At least some things turn out right," Ashe blew out a sigh.

"Ashe, you're not saying you don't deserve your punishment, are you?" Adele studied Ashe's expression.

"No. Mom, I knew I could get in trouble and I did it anyway. I just thought we needed to do what we could to make those kids feel welcome after what Chump and Wormy did."

"They have proper names, hon."

"Yeah. I know." Ashe wasn't meeting his mother's eyes as he sat down to eat his own hastily prepared meal.

"Ashe," Adele pushed a few stray strands of hair behind an ear, "my mother used to say that no good deed went unpunished. What you did was a kind thought, and possibly a good deed, too, *but.*"

"I went off the reservation. Yeah. I get that," Ashe slurped a spoonful of soup after finishing his mother's thought. "What was my grandmother like? You never talk about her. Or my grandfather."

"Ashe," Adele lowered her eyes, staring at the sandwich on her plate.

"It's okay if you don't want to," Ashe shrugged and lifted his sandwich.

"No, honey, you deserve to know," Adele sighed. "Your grandmother—my mother, she was a Great Horned Owl. Your grandfather was a Cooper's hawk. Birds are rather rare in the shapeshifting world. Jonas O'Neill and I are the only two bird shifters in this part of the country. I was hoping that you might be one, too."

"Sorry, Mom," Ashe apologized quietly.

"Hon, with a vampire father, I was only dreaming," she reached out to ruffle Ashe's hair. "And now, we all know you got a little extra from the Elemaiya. I wish we knew more about them."

"Mom, they aren't my family. My family is right here."

"Yes we are, aren't we?" Adele smiled for the first time since she'd gotten home. "Hear that Aedan? Ashe's family is right here." Aedan walked through the door into the kitchen from the lower level.

"Where else would we be?" Aedan smiled slightly. "How's the penance coming?"

"Terrible." Ashe took another bite of his sandwich.

"Just what I wanted to hear," Aedan chuckled, this time. "The definition of penance to some is the confession of a sin, followed by punishment to make amends."

"Yeah, but most see it as self-punishment or abasement," Ashe pointed out. "Dictionary, you know."

"And this is certainly not self-imposed," Aedan sparred verbally with his son.

"In a way it is. I was just discussing with Mom that I knew what the consequences might be when I made the decision to go to Cordell. It was a calculated risk."

"Son, I should know better than to ever think you'd just go off without thinking about it first." Aedan sat down at the table and tucked more stray hair away from his wife's face.

"Is it bad? I didn't have time to look in the mirror today, it was so busy," Adele tidied her hair self-consciously. "And the chicken farm outside Dill City sent two trucks for chicken feed. They cleaned me out this afternoon and they didn't do very much to help load it up."

"Adele, I wish I could be there to help."

"I know, honey. But Ashe will be there to help in a couple of weeks, and maybe Sali too, if he wants."

"He wants to—he's already said so," Ashe said, brightening immediately. "And it doesn't hurt that he can spend some of his money on lunch at Betsy's."

Ashe didn't say that Sali was jealous because Marco would get to spend his summer in Dallas, working for Mr. Winkler. "Dad, have you heard anything else on Amy's murder—the cashier from the grocery store?"

"No, son. But it's a little too soon, yet. Have some patience—you've already helped more than anyone expected. And just so you won't worry, those two agents will have compulsion placed before they get away from the area."

"Is that necessary, Dad? I think they can keep secrets."

"We're not going to take chances." The finality of Aedan's tone informed Ashe that there would be no argument on the subject.

"How ticked off are Chad and Jeremy gonna be over having their cars taken away? I guess Chad's was just a hypothetical car at this point, but it's almost the same."

"If they bother you, go straight to the Principal or a teacher right away."

"Like Principal Billings would do anything." Ashe was back to depression.

"Ben Billings is contractually obligated to protect all the students, not just some of them," Adele said, lifting her plate and soup bowl off the table and carrying them to the dishwasher.

"Contractually obligated?" Ashe shook his head. "That's not the Principal I know. He was almost dancing a jig when he handed that note to me last year."

"Ashe," Aedan's voice held warning.

"All right. I'll go study for my History final." Ashe carried his dishes to the dishwasher and loaded them in before slumping toward the steps leading to his downstairs bedroom.

~

"I hate grounding him," Adele said once Ashe's bedroom door closed downstairs.

"It's like grounding an adult family member," Aedan nodded. "Hard to do and harder to enforce. I get the idea that Marcus wouldn't have been so harsh with Sali if he hadn't gone off with Ashe."

"What?" Adele stared at Aedan in alarm.

"I think he doesn't trust what Ashe can do, somehow."

"But he's gotten into those crime scenes because Ashe can do those things," Adele snapped, rising and hugging her arms tightly about her waist.

"He's ex-special ops, Adele. He can respect a weapon, but he doesn't have to trust it."

"You're calling our son a weapon, Aedan? Listen to yourself."

"Do you think for one moment that others wouldn't see him the same way? I spoke with Trace and Jason, Adele. They told me they've seen the way those two agents—Lawford and North—look at our son after he gets them into those crime scenes. That's why compulsion will be placed; Nathan and I have discussed it already. Their Director is retiring, and if he thinks to place our son in danger, he'll get a visit as well."

"Aedan, one day Ashe is going to be an adult and he's going to make up his own mind. Would it be so bad if he worked for the government like some vampires and werewolves do? I imagine they'd pay him well for his efforts."

"My love, that decision may be taken out of our hands."

"You mean the Council, don't you?"

"Or the Grand Master. He knows whatever William Winkler knows, you can bet on that."

"I hope you don't take this the wrong way, but I'd rather see him work for the Grand Master."

"I'm hoping the Council doesn't learn of his talents." It was Aedan's turn to rise and pace. "Radomir owes Ashe blood debt and has promised not to volunteer the information, but if it is requested, he will not only be compelled to give it, he will be punished for withholding it." Aedan referred to the Council Enforcer who'd come the previous year to investigate the murders in the Cloud Chief and Cordell area.

"I'll have nightmares, now," Adele moaned. "Tell me they won't take my boy away. He's so young. They can't—they won't," she didn't finish. The possibilities were too horrible for her to consider.

"Vampire law states that someone must be eighteen years of age before the Council may conscript. That age should be raised, in my opinion. Meanwhile, we will attempt to keep the boy from their sight as long as we can."

"He's not yet fourteen and already he's lost so much of his innocence, going off to those crime scenes. Ashe has been hunted and shot by that psychopathic teacher and those aberrations he associated with—and now the Council may take my child away? Turn him into something even I might not recognize?"

"I was an Enforcer. Was I so terrible when you met me?"

"You're different and you know it."

"Perhaps not. I have to go, love. Trace and Jason are waiting to be relieved."

Ashe floated over the five mobile homes lined up neatly in the pasture behind his home. His father was joined by Nathan Anderson as they walked toward the small tent Trace and Jason had erected to provide shade during warm afternoons.

Ashe, as mist, had zipped past the tent, finding Marcie Pruitt there, talking with Jason and Trace about the worms they were having trouble with in the vegetable garden. He'd heard Marcie ask both werewolves if they'd like to come to her home for dinner. Jason accepted, Trace didn't.

Figuring that his mother might check on him soon, Ashe swept through the nearly moonless night, misting through the roof of his home and then through the floor of the kitchen to get to his bedroom underneath. Sure enough, his mother was just about to knock on his door.

"Ashe, are you studying?" Adele asked through the solid wood of his bedroom door.

"Yeah." Ashe opened the door after becoming solid again. His computer showed a page depicting the Civil War in the background.

"If you want a snack before going to bed, let me know," Adele smiled at her son before closing the door again. Ashe knew she was checking to see if he were doing exactly what he had been doing—turning to mist and getting away from the house. Shivering a little over almost getting caught, Ashe sat down at the computer and began making notes on the Battle of Antietam.

"I overheard some discussion in Principal Billings' office this morning —I think the teachers are beginning to pick their favorite essays and argue their case," Cori set her tray down, brushed long blonde hair back one-handed and plopped down next to Ashe during lunch.

"Hear any names mentioned?" Sali looked up from his tray of spaghetti and meatballs to stare at Cori.

"Not really," Cori hedged, using a knife to quarter the large meatball a cafeteria worker had set atop a mound of spaghetti. "But Mrs. Rocklin and Mr. Dodd are arguing for the same paper. And I heard the word *him*, so it has to be one of the guys."

"Bet it's Rowdy," Sali muttered dispiritedly. Rowdy Hankins was a senior, an A student and had been accepted into Brown University. Word had it that one of the faculty there was a werewolf just as Rowdy was, and the Grand Master had cleared the way for the studious young wolf.

"Sali, don't get all depressed," Ashe said. "Want my roll?" He pushed his tray across the table toward Sali.

"Sure." Sali grabbed the yeast roll off Ashe's tray and added it to his own. "But a roll doesn't make up for a cell phone," Sali stuffed spaghetti in his mouth.

"Yeah." Ashe began to wind lengthy noodles around his fork. "Man, being grounded sucks rocks."

"Losing the essay contest sucks boulders," Sali offered.

"It sucks in Regolithic proportions," Ashe countered.

"You know, I'm not even going to ask what that means," Cori speared a quarter meatball and ate it. "Marco will be here around the time you two come off your prison sentence."

"*Nobody knows the trouble I've seen,*" Sali sang off-key.

"Maybe we can hook Mr. Thompson up to the bars of your jail cell and bust you out," Ashe laughed.

"Mr. Thompson in a harness? Are you kidding?" Sali grinned at the imagery. "I thought people hooked horses up for that."

"Well, there's no chance of getting Wynn or her mom, so you'll have to settle for a buffalo," Ashe ate another forkful of spaghetti.

"Cause the itty, bitty bat is in jail too," Sali said.

"Hey, now," Ashe pointed his fork at Sali.

"Remind me again whose fault it is that the werewolf and his bat sidekick are in the slammer?"

"Oh, yeah," Ashe said.

"I'd have done the same thing if I could," Cori said. "It was a nice gesture, Ashe. Too bad you got caught."

"Well, confessed," Sali said. "After that cashier at Jerry's got killed. We saw her that afternoon."

"That's what Daddy said," Cori nodded. "Amy always talked to us whenever we went in to buy anything."

"She talked to everybody. Knew everybody, too," Ashe agreed. "That may have gotten her killed."

"That gives me the shivers—that being so friendly gets you dead." Cori shook herself.

"How's Marco?" Ashe changed the subject.

"Ready to take on a werewolf and a shapeshifter," Cori glanced up in time to see Jeremy and Chad staring at Ashe.

"You're dead meat," Chad hissed at Ashe before Mr. Dodd began walking toward Ashe's table. Jeremy hauled Chad away before Mr. Dodd could catch any of the conversation.

"Everything all right here?" Mr. Dodd stood at the end of the cafeteria table, his eyes on Ashe and Cori.

"Yeah. Everything's fine," Ashe shrugged.

"All right." Mr. Dodd moved away to stop a food fight in its infancy between third-graders.

"I guess it's a good thing we're grounded right now. We might have a fight on our hands if we weren't," Sali said, turning to watch Chad and Jeremy sit at a table near the cafeteria windows.

"They're supposed to be grounded too," Cori said. "But Susan Wilkes said she saw them wandering around outside yesterday when Jeremy's mother went into Cordell to run errands."

"Not surprised," Ashe said.

"If they have no conscience about setting somebody's house on fire and nearly killing three people, you know they're not going to stay inside," Sali huffed. "Mom watches me like a hawk, now."

"My mom *is* a hawk, and she calls or knocks on my bedroom door every half hour," Ashe sighed gloomily, recalling how he'd almost been caught after misting out of the house the night before.

"I heard something else," Cori toyed with her fork.

"What's that?" Ashe and Sali both turned to the pretty, blonde senior.

"That your Aunt Marcie and Mr. Landers had dinner together last night."

"Yeah. I overheard Mom and Aunt Marcie talking about Jason," Sali said. "I think Aunt Marcie likes him a lot. Says he's a gentleman."

"You knew and you didn't tell anybody?" Cori snapped at Sali.

"Hey, now, panther-pants," Sali snorted. "Is it any of your business?"

"Don't call me that." Cori rose in a huff and stalked toward the tray drop.

"Sali, don't pull Cori into your feud with Wynn and Dori," Ashe warned. "Cori is my friend, too."

"Can't help it," Sali muttered, staring at his nearly empty plate. Ashe watched as Cori walked stiff-backed out of the cafeteria before turning back to Sali.

"That's Marco's girlfriend, in case you're forgetting," Ashe added softly.

~

"This is more amusing than I initially imagined," Renegar was busily crashing cars in one of Ashe's video games. "It is much better when I know I am not actually damaging anything."

"Like that's possible," Ashe leaned over and stabbed his controller violently, doing his best to compete with Renegar, who was the first real video game competition he'd had in a while.

"It is certainly possible with my kind—we are quite powerful," Ren was moving along with Ashe, trying just as hard to compete. "You are quite good at this—I thought it might be simple to defeat you."

"Thought you'd be bored, huh?" Ashe jerked his hand and more automobiles crashed.

"Truthfully, yes."

"I'm having fun, too. For the first time in a long time at this," Ashe admitted.

"I like having a friend outside my race," Ren chortled as he crashed several automobiles at once. "This demolition game is quite entertaining."

~

Elizabeth waited until her mother was out of the house before searching through Mary Ellen Frasier's purse for a credit card. Elizabeth's father was watching a baseball game on television and oblivious of his daughter's stealthy rustlings. There had to be a dress shop in Cordell—had to be—and Elizabeth was going there just as quickly as her mist would take her.

"Francis, where is Elizabeth?" Mary Ellen had arrived moments earlier and failed to find her daughter inside the house. Lizzie wasn't outside —there'd been no sign of her and those two *werewolves* were sitting beneath their tent, watching Edward, Keith and Bryce toss a football in the newly grown prairie grass surrounding their temporary housing. Francis grunted noncommittally before Mary Ellen's words registered, forcing him to look up from his baseball game.

"She's here somewhere—Lizzie never went out the door," Francis rose from his easy chair and cast a worried glance at his wife. "Did you check the windows?"

"All of them. Francis, go get those—men," Mary Ellen couldn't bring herself to say what Trace and Jason were a second time. "The windows and the back door are all locked. She had to walk out the front door." Hysteria found its way into Mary Ellen's words. Francis charged out the door as Mary Ellen screamed Elizabeth's name.

CHAPTER 11

"Got a hit on her mother's credit card here, at Janie's Dress Shop," Nick Lawford directed Trace and Marcus into the dress shop in question. Trace, Jason, Marcus and Micah had all sniffed around the Frasier's mobile home, detecting no fresh scent from Elizabeth.

Marcus asked Linda Jansen and Ramona Hill to sit with Mary Ellen; Micah Rocklin stayed in Cloud Chief to keep a close watch on Francis Frasier, who blamed the werewolf guards for allowing his daughter to escape.

Marcus contacted Agents Lawford and North, who'd started the wheels of investigation turning immediately. Mary Ellen's credit card was missing from her purse, and a quick check on recent charges led the agents and the accompanying werewolves straight to the only dress shop in the small town of Cordell.

"May I help you?" Jane Scott, owner of Janie's Dress Shop, didn't see men inside her business often. Jane, with salt and pepper gray hair, was stylishly dressed in a pale gray suit she sold in the store. She was folding T-shirts for a display when the four men walked inside her shop.

"Ma'am, have you seen this girl?" Agent Lawford held up a recent photograph of Elizabeth Frasier. Jane stopped folding for a moment and squinted at the picture.

"Just this afternoon," Jane nodded. "She spent six hundred dollars here, then stuffed all the clothes she bought inside one of the large tote bags we sell. And then she asked if I would call a taxi for her." Jane snorted at the idea that anyone would think Cordell might have a taxi service.

"When did she leave? Do you recall?" Lawford asked.

"Around four-thirty, maybe? Two more customers came in around the same time." Jane finished folding a turquoise T and patted it into place on a display table.

"Did you see which way she went?"

"North, I think. Why do you want to know?"

"Possible runaway, ma'am," Agent Lawford's voice was flat and unemotional. "Stole her mother's credit card and slipped out of the house."

"The credit card was stolen?" Jane seemed more concerned over that than a runaway teen.

"She may be in danger," Trace added, since the agents hadn't expressed the urgency of the situation.

"I'll check with the businesses north of here and ask if they saw her," Marcus walked out the door. Derik North frowned at Marcus' retreating back.

"I'll go with Marcus," Trace figured they'd gotten all the useful information they were going to get from the dress shop owner. His and Marcus' noses might tell them more than the agents were likely to get.

"If you think of any other information, let us know," Agent Lawford handed a business card to Jane. Jane blinked, open-mouthed, as the two agents rushed out the door. *Department of Homeland Security* was printed plainly across the top of Nick Lawford's card.

~

Ren had left two hours earlier and Ashe, unable to explain the discomfort he felt, nearly jumped when his mother knocked on his bedroom door before walking inside. She hadn't been home long; it was after seven and sunset was still more than an hour away.

"Honey, that was Marcus on the phone," Ashe's blue eyes met his mother's light-brown ones and he shivered.

Ashe crawled inside the agents' van fifteen minutes later. "Ashe, Elizabeth Frasier got away from us somehow, even though we can't get any fresh scent that shows she left the house. Went straight to Cordell and bought a bunch of clothes," Trace said as Ashe buckled in and Marcus closed the door.

"I was afraid of this," Ashe murmured.

"Afraid of what?" Marcus glared at Ashe from his seat in the center of the van.

"I can turn to mist and mindspeak, and I'm like them," Ashe jerked his head toward the row of mobile homes behind his house. "It makes sense that at least some of them might be able to do those things, too."

"This is a nightmare," Marcus growled and turned to face the front again.

"You think that girl turned to mist and got out that way?" Trace asked softly.

"It makes sense; that's how I got grounded," Ashe grumped unhappily.

"It sure does," Trace settled back in his seat. "Mrs. Pruitt is helping us guard the rest of those kids while we go to the last place the girl was seen."

The last place Elizabeth Frasier was seen ended up being a gas station and convenience store on the northern edge of Cordell. Agent North had stayed behind earlier to question the employees. They'd watched Elizabeth Frasier climb into a sports car with two young men after tossing her new tote bag into the back seat.

"The car was black, but the right front fender had gray primer paint on it and it hadn't been repainted yet," the owner of the service station said. "The girl came in askin' us if we'd drive her someplace, but we're not that stupid."

"Did you recognize the boys?" Ashe, Trace and Marcus walked up as Derik North asked the question.

"Nah. Probably some kids from Clinton or Elk City." The man might have been in his mid-fifties and had worked outdoors most of his life, Ashe decided as he watched the man. His face was the weathered brown of old leather and wrinkles fanned out from the corners of hazel eyes. Ashe was as tall as the man was, but his younger employees were slightly taller and in their early twenties.

"I don't suppose you got a tag number," Agent North asked hopefully.

"Nope."

"The last part was GVU. I didn't get the numbers before that," the youngest employee said. His brown eyes appeared more worried than his elder employer's did, while his close-cropped blond hair stood up like ripe wheat in a summer field.

"Oklahoma plates?" Nick Lawford asked.

"Yeah. Car was a sixty-eight Camaro. Looked like they were restoring it." Ashe nodded at the employee's description—Sali would have noticed what the car was, too.

"Run a check," Agent Lawford jerked his head at Derik North, who walked toward their van to make the call.

"Let's look around a little," Trace steered Ashe away from the questioning. Trace would sniff his way through the business while Ashe looked. Ashe trailed Trace as he followed Elizabeth's scent, ending up outside the women's bathroom. "Ever been inside a ladies' room?" Trace grinned at Ashe.

"When I was in the third grade," Ashe nodded. "Sali shoved me inside as a joke."

"This one might be cleaner than most gas station bathrooms," Trace shouldered his way through the door without knocking. Ashe held his breath until he realized there wasn't anyone inside. Releasing the air in his lungs as a grateful sigh, Ashe began to search the restroom.

"Tag from Janie's" Ashe poked the tag with the toe of his shoe—the small paper tag was lying next to the toilet in one of two stalls.

"I think she changed clothes first, then put on makeup at the sink and probably brushed her hair, so she had her purse with her," Trace agreed, sniffing around the Formica vanity and mirror.

"Find anything?" Agent North joined them in the small bathroom. Collecting the tag and a strand of long, dark hair from the sink that Ashe and Trace pointed out, the agent placed both in evidence bags.

"We've got the local authorities and Oklahoma Highway Patrol looking for the car," Nick Lawford said as soon as Ashe, Trace and Agent North came out of the restroom. "Owner says those boys filled up and paid cash, so no credit card records to tap and no security camera, either."

"Let's take the kid home and we can start looking for ourselves," Derik North suggested to his superior.

"Sounds as good as anything else," Nick Lawford agreed. Marcus, who'd stayed with Agent Lawford, hadn't said anything during the questioning, settling for listening and observing while the others talked.

"The owner knows something he isn't giving up," Marcus slid into the same seat he'd occupied before as the others loaded up and buckled in around him.

"I get that idea, too," Agent Lawford agreed.

"He frowned at the boy who told us what kind of car it was," Ashe said.

"Caught that, too, did you?" Agent Lawford spared a grin over the back of his seat for Ashe. "Kid, you're better than a lot of agents I know."

"Well, it makes sense that he may have seen those boys before," Ashe offered. "This isn't a regular hangout for tourists driving through, and there's another gas station only a little farther down the road, between here and the interstate. Their gas is more expensive, but you wouldn't know that unless you were familiar with Cordell."

"You think the kid may have friends or family here?" Derik North asked.

"Possible. I can bring Aedan or Nathan back after sunset and question the owner again," Marcus offered.

"Do it," Lawford said. The gravel drive surrounding the service station crunched beneath the van's wheels as the agent drove away from the service station.

~

"You didn't tell us you were running away." Nineteen-year-old Dale Sherman glared accusingly at Elizabeth, who sat in the back seat of his nearly restored 1968 Camaro.

His uncle had called Dale's cell, so he'd pulled over at a truck stop on I-40 East to answer. "Now Uncle Rick has police crawling all over his gas station."

"I said I'd pay," Elizabeth's haughtiness was beginning to wear on Dale's nerves. Dale's best friend Lex lifted his chin over the seat to stare at Elizabeth as well.

"Uh-uh. You get out here. They said you were fifteen, not eighteen, like you told us. You get out now. You can call your folks or get another ride. I'm not goin' to jail for you." Dale's pale-blue eyes sparked with anger; his brown hair stood up in spikes after he'd raked fingers through it in frustration.

Elizabeth glowered at the two boys—they'd jumped at the chance to make five hundred dollars—that's what Elizabeth offered them to drive her north. She didn't have an exact location; the seductive whisper that had come the moment she left Cloud Chief behind kept promising all sorts of things if she'd travel to North Dakota.

The term *Grassland* kept popping into her head, but that meant little to Elizabeth. She also didn't have five hundred dollars in her purse as she'd promised—but the voice was so persuasive Elizabeth would do anything to get where it asked her to go.

"One of those truckers would take you." Lex Snelson, worried that he'd be hauled off to jail with his best friend, urged Elizabeth to try other means to reach her destination.

He figured his description—not that different from Dale's (brown hair and blue eyes, they were distant cousins, after all), was already in the Highway Patrol's database, along with a description of Dale's

Camaro. Uncle Rick's new employee hadn't been warned to keep quiet before the cops showed up.

"I'm not that stupid," Elizabeth huffed. "You have to let me out, jerk." She lifted a spike-heeled foot and kicked the back of Lex's seat, ripping a hole in Dale's new upholstery. Dale cursed at the damage his passenger had caused as Lex opened his door and got out, pulling the passenger seat forward so Elizabeth could exit the vehicle.

Lex and Dale watched as Elizabeth walked unsteadily across the uneven truck stop parking lot in the heels she wore. Both struggled to hold onto car doors when the fierce blast of wind hit.

It swept Elizabeth off her feet and carried her ten feet into the air, pushing her along with the force of a tornado until she crashed through the thick, plate-glass window of the truck stop.

Dale's leg was nearly crushed in the door of his car as the wind slammed it shut. Lex had slid across the rough surface of the parking lot, ending up on his belly halfway between the Camaro and the building. Road burns covered his torso where the T-shirt he wore had been ripped away. Lex and Dale lifted their heads in horror as screams emanated from the building.

"You're saying it was the wind?" Agent Lawford stared at a grimacing Dale Sherman, whose leg was encased in a cast after x-rays at the hospital emergency room in Clinton determined it was broken.

Lex was being treated in a cubicle next door for his own injuries—the parking lot surface had claimed quite a bit of skin across his chest and belly. The girl was dead—from a head injury after flying through the thick, plate-glass window of Teddy's Truck Stop east of Clinton.

"Man, I saw her fly through the air when the gust hit, and then it threw me into the car and the door almost slammed shut on my leg," Dale whined.

"If your uncle had informed us immediately, this might have been prevented," Nick Lawford snapped and stalked out of the cubicle.

"How many other deaths were reported under similar circumstances?" Director Bill Jennings stared at his assistant, Vince Jordan.

"Seventeen, sir. That we know of." Vince tapped the tablet in his hand for a moment, pulling up information. "It appears that this race can somehow command the wind or other weather elements."

"I was afraid you'd say that."

"Sir, if they can do this, it makes me think that the other murders in the area may not be by the same ones—how much easier would it be to just kill them with a blast of wind rather than breaking necks or strangling somebody?"

"True. Are any other deaths of these children by strangulation or broken necks?"

"None, sir. Plenty of gunshots, drownings and other things, but nothing like that."

"Then we may have two murderers, or sets of murderers, in the area."

"Possible," Vince handed the tablet to Director Jennings so he could scroll through the gathered information.

Marcus had allowed Sali to come; he and Ashe stood in the backyard of Ashe's home and watched as the dark limousine carried Mary Ellen and Francis Frasier away from Cloud Chief, the driver moving slowly through foot-high prairie grass toward the gravel road and Cloud Chief's hidden entrance.

Ashe wished at that moment he didn't have exceptional hearing; he detected Mary Ellen's sobs as the car drove past.

"Son," Aedan's hand dropped gently onto Ashe's shoulder—the sun had set an hour earlier, bathing the Oklahoma prairie in twilight. Aedan and Nathan had already visited Elizabeth's grieving parents at Marcus' request. The human couple wouldn't remember where the supernatural community lay, or that it housed the unusual inhabitants that it did.

"Dad," Ashe's right arm slipped around his father's waist as the limo crunched onto the gravel road and rolled past.

⁓

"Ashe, do you want to go to work with me tomorrow?" Adele brushed Ashe's hair back from his forehead as he walked into the house a few minutes later. "It's Saturday and it'll be busy at the store. Your father said it was all right as long as you stayed inside the store with me."

"Yeah." Ashe nodded, his eyes downcast.

"Honey, you're only grounded one more week, and then you can play with Sali. School will be out, too, so you can help watch over Edward and the others."

"Mom, we need to find out if those kids can do anything that might get them killed. And they need to know not to leave Cloud Chief unless somebody's with them."

"I hope this has driven that lesson home, honey."

"It kind of has, Mom, but I still have the feeling that there's something going on with the rest of them that isn't affecting me, somehow."

Ashe wasn't about to bring up Renegar; the blue-skinned Larentii said that Ashe was unreadable. The other six half-Elemaiyan children had been easy enough for Ren to locate. It made sense that the Elemaiyan hunters might possess the same talent.

"We can't know that for sure. Why don't you read or watch TV for a while?"

"I think I'll read." Ashe hadn't read anything for fun all week. He walked through the middle door and clumped downstairs. Ren was waiting for him at the bottom.

"I'm very sorry," Ren seemed sad. "I could not tell you she'd escaped, but you did realize quickly that she gained her abilities."

"How did you find that out?" Ashe shouldered past the taller child as he walked toward his bedroom.

"I placed Nexus Echo on Salidar's father and on the agents, so I know about the investigations."

"You know who the murderer is." Ashe turned sharply to stare at the Larentii youth.

"Ashe, I am not allowed to interfere." Ren's contrition was evident.

"But you are interfering. With me." Ashe wiped away the tear he couldn't hold back. "You stand there and tell me you have information you can't give while I watch people die. Do you know how frustrated and helpless that makes me feel? Do you?" Ashe stalked through his bedroom door and slammed it behind him, leaving Ren standing in the hall outside, worried that he'd lost his friend.

"Ashe made a good suggestion, Aedan. He says we should find out if any of those other children might have shown some kind of ability," Adele told Aedan as he stopped at the house for a brief break before Adele went to bed.

"It isn't a bad idea, but how do we find these things out? I have no idea what the talents might be, so how do you ask or test for these things? We still don't know how Ashe discovered his talents or when. These children are older than he was when he developed them." Aedan shook his head in confusion.

"Ashe is always ahead of the curve, Aedan," Adele pointed out. "What if these others are ripe to develop these talents? Do we have any information from the Director or those agents regarding the average age these children are disappearing? Perhaps we shouldn't gauge the dead ones against the ones that are counted as missing? There are two sides in this; two sides that are hunting these children for two very different purposes, according to Mr. Winkler."

Had they known it, Ashe was in his bedroom surfing his computer, searching for the same information.

"Ren, you can't offer information, but will you tell me if I'm right?" Ashe hadn't spoken to the tall youth until then, but he hadn't chased Ren away when he'd appeared inside Ashe's bedroom.

"If you say what's true, I can confirm that," Ren nodded slightly.

"Good. What I'm seeing here is that the ones who disappeared, most of them anyway, came up missing around age fifteen or sixteen. That means their talents develop around that time. True?"

"Correct," Ren verified the information Ashe had gathered.

"Then how did I get mine before turning thirteen?" Ashe mumbled to himself.

"I cannot say, since I do not have an answer for that," Ren replied, although the question hadn't been aimed at him.

"Elizabeth was fifteen and a half; anyway that's what Luanne told us when we visited Wynn and Dori last week, so that fits," Ashe ignored Ren's statement, putting his musings together aloud. "Edward is already sixteen, so he may be able to do something and not even know it. Macy is seventeen, so same there. In fact, all of them are older than Elizabeth, so we may be sitting on a time bomb."

"Correct," Ren affirmed.

Jane Scott settled her cell phone on the kitchen counter after talking with a friend. Jane lived alone and after a long and trying day at the dress shop (would she have to cover for the charges made on a stolen credit card?), she settled for a microwaved dinner.

Doors carefully locked and the alarm set, Jane waited for her meal to heat. Locked doors and an alarm failed to prevent the burly male from leaping through the picture window in Jane's living room.

Jane screamed and reached for her cell as the alarm blared and a neighbor rushed toward Jane's home from next door, a loaded shotgun in his hands. The intruder clapped a hand over Jane's mouth and dragged the struggling woman toward her garage.

"How can this be a coincidence?" Marcus stared at Agent Lawford. "We're in her store this afternoon and tonight she's abducted? I don't doubt we'd be dealing with a body now if she hadn't had an alarm system and a neighbor who came running with a gun."

"I agree with Marcus," Aedan nodded at the Cloud Chief Packmaster. "The kidnapper had no desire for discovery so he took the woman away in her own vehicle. It is a shame it was dark and the neighbor didn't get a good description."

"Agreed," Nick Lawford said. "The local sheriff has his employees searching, but so far there has been nothing. We have a search helicopter en route from Oklahoma City, but the woman may be dead before it arrives. Mr. Evans, will you allow Ashe to help with this?"

Nick Lawford was begging that Ashe might help prevent Jane Scott's murder. He felt responsible, somehow, for sending the killer in her direction. Obviously, someone was keeping a very close watch on local events.

"You have a description of the vehicle and which direction it was heading?"

"Yes."

"Then we'll try."

Before Agent Lawford was prepared, Aedan lifted the tall black agent with one arm about his waist and rushed toward the Evans home so quickly Marcus almost missed the movement.

Ashe jerked in his seat when his father knocked on the bedroom door. Ren was still sitting on the end of Ashe's bed while Ashe did his best to locate more information regarding the missing children on his computer.

"Ashe, we need your help, son," Aedan walked inside Ashe's room with Agent Lawford right behind. Knowing Ren was shielding himself from visitors; Ashe stood and nodded silently at his father.

I will come with you. Do not fear, they will never know, Ren sent mindspeech to Ashe.

Understood, Ashe returned without betraying his silent conversation to his father or the agent.

"We need your invisibility trick, son," Agent Lawford said. "We're looking for a red Buick Regal, heading southwest out of Cordell."

"I can do that," Ashe said. Without another word, Ashe gathered his father, Nick Lawford and a tall Larentii child in his mist. Ren exclaimed happily as they shot through two levels of the Evans home and straight into the night sky.

~

It hadn't taken much to knock the woman unconscious. She slumped in the passenger seat, oblivious of her surroundings as her stolen car sped through the twisting roads leading to Lake Altus.

The driver couldn't help but curse softly and angrily at what he'd learned from Jane Scott. The card she'd handed over almost made him kill her immediately—*Homeland Security* was printed plainly across the top with a seasoned agent's name listed below. He'd had to travel stealthily through Cordell and the surrounding communities since he'd killed the cashier from the local supermarket.

Too many things didn't make sense anymore, and now he'd be blamed for the girl's death east of Clinton, although he'd been nowhere near. The only information he'd gotten was that she'd suffered a brain injury. This bitch, though, and anyone else who thought to stand between him and his objective, well, they'd die too.

Shoving the car into park as he slid to a stop at the boat ramp, he carefully exited the vehicle, taking care not to touch any part of it with exposed skin. He flexed large hands encased in gloves before reaching inside the car and placing it in gear. Walking away swiftly, he heard the satisfying splash as the car hit the lake and floated in. Eventually the engine died as it was drowned in water.

~

Going down, Ashe shouted to his passengers when he spotted the top of the red car as it slowly sank into Lake Altus. The car was nearly submerged and Ashe, hoping he wasn't too late already, plunged his mist through the roof of the vehicle with no thought for himself or his passengers.

Jane's head was beneath the lake's surface and Ashe cried out in fear and despair, even as he lifted her limp body inside his mist and sped away. He was flying toward Clinton Regional Hospital as fast as he could go, terrified the woman might already be dead.

"We'll have to medi-flight her to Oklahoma City," the emergency room physician informed Aedan and Agent North.

Ashe and Ren sat in the waiting room while his father and Agent North talked to the doctor right outside. Ashe heard every word as it was explained that the head wound and near drowning might have serious consequences and Jane Scott could have permanent damage—if she woke at all.

"I'll notify Oklahoma City officials and she'll have a guard outside her room," Agent North pulled his cell from a pocket to make the call.

I have never experienced anything so exciting in my life, Ren sounded jubilant inside Ashe's mind.

Dude, she could die or suffer brain damage. Don't you care about that?

I see that you do. My father says that we cannot involve ourselves in the brief lives of mortals.

I think your father is wrong. A life is a life. I don't care how long it lasts or doesn't last. A really good person might live a very short life, while a terrible jerk could live forever. Ashe rose to pace inside the small hospital waiting room. A television mumbled in the corner, but Ashe and Ren ignored it while they waited and talked.

Ah. Ren didn't elaborate.

"Ashe," Aedan stood in the doorway. "Son, Agent Lawford is going to wait for the helicopter and escort the woman to Oklahoma City. He thanks you for your efforts. We might not have located her otherwise."

"Yeah." Ashe blew out a sigh as he walked toward his father. "Ready to go home?"

"Your mother is on her way. We'll drive home in a more conventional manner. I know it doesn't frighten you to travel the way you do, but I'm not used to it and not likely to ever get that way."

"Sorry, Dad." Ashe flopped onto a plastic chair and hung his head, his hands draped limply over his knees. He hadn't thought about his passengers as he'd blazed through the night, and the dive through the top of a car and into darkened lake water had to be frightening. He'd been focused on one thing and one thing only—saving a life. Ren had listened to Aedan's words carefully and then watched Ashe's reaction with interest.

"Ashe, there's no reason to feel shame. That's not what I meant. It's just that I'm usually going somewhere under my own power. This is different from anything I've ever known and I have to get used to it."

Ashe hunched thin shoulders at his father's comment. He knew he was different; nobody had to tell him that. *He doesn't like relinquishing control,* Ren silently offered.

I'm the cuckoo's child, Ashe muttered mentally. *My parents have no idea what was dropped into their nest to raise. And the sad thing is, I don't know what I am, either. Just like Elizabeth, who died this afternoon. Maybe that doesn't bother you or your race, Ren, but it sure as heck bothers me.*

I was born knowing what I am. I am attempting to understand what it would be like if that were not true.

Let me know when you discover how frustrating it is. Aedan watched as his son rose abruptly from his seat and began pacing again.

"Son, it's nothing to be upset over. You did a good deed tonight. The best of deeds, perhaps. Fretting will not solve anything."

"Yeah? Tell that to Elizabeth Frasier." Furious in the space of a moment, Ashe turned to mist and blazed toward his Cloud Chief home, leaving a puzzled Larentii child and a cursing father behind.

CHAPTER 12

"Adele, I upset him—more than he was already. Somehow, he feels responsible for that girl's death. And then I may as well have called him a freak." Aedan spoke as he drove his SUV home after Adele had arrived at the hospital.

"We can't allow this kind of behavior. I don't care if he did go straight home." Adele called the house as soon as she'd learned that Ashe had disappeared. Ashe had sullenly answered the phone.

"Then we will determine his punishment and let him know what it is when this grounding period is over."

"All right. Aedan, what are we going to do?"

"We'll think on it for the next few days."

"Baltis has managed to kill this one." Friesianna handed the girl's chip to Hilbah. "Did you realize how close his Destroyers might be?"

"My Queen, something obscures my sight in that area. Yes, I felt the Destroyers as soon as they attacked, but my vision came much too late." Hilbah wanted to cower before Friesianna, but forced himself to remain upright.

"Call Diamond and his brothers. You will accompany Diamond and another of my Jewels. You will personally escort the remaining children to me."

"As you wish it, my Queen." Hilbah bowed respectfully and quite low, backing away from Friesianna's cold glare.

~

"Dude, what were you thinking?" Sali stared at Ashe during lunch the following Monday. "You get even more punishment?"

"Mom and Dad won't even say what it is. They'll tell me Friday when the grounding is over." Ashe pushed meatloaf around his lunch tray.

"This is the worst," Sali mumbled hopelessly. "You know what Friday is, too—last day of school. Awards Assembly is Friday night, dude."

"Yeah. And we still won't get a cell phone." The winner of the essay contest was always announced at the end of the assembly. All of Cloud Chief's parents attended, while the night was guarded by werewolves who had no children attending school. At least until the Awards Assembly was over. Ashe shoved his lunch tray toward Sali, who gladly accepted it and dug in.

Throughout the last week of school, amid finals and anxious, last minute studying, rumors leapt from student to student concerning who might win the essay contest.

Many students argued that Rowdy Hankins would win. Ashe knew Cori had started that rumor after hearing what she had in Principal Billings' office. Ashe slumped through his exams. Elizabeth Frasier's death and Jane Scott's kidnapping weighed on his shoulders more than additional punishment. He'd asked about Jane Scott's condition, but his parents refused to tell him anything.

No information could be found on the Internet, either, so he hoped she was still alive. Ren had also failed to appear during the week, making Ashe wonder if the blue-skinned youth might be gone for good. Despite Ren's attitude toward mortals, Ashe realized he missed the strange Larentii youth.

"It's over." Sali heaved a grateful sigh as they handed in History papers and textbooks on Friday, May twenty-second.

"Until next fall," Ashe pointed out.

"You had to point that out, didn't you? What do they say about the bearer of bad news?" Sali poked at Ashe.

"Are you referring to killing the messenger?"

"Seems a little harsh," Sali said, jumping away when Ashe attempted to flip Sali's ear.

"You brought it up."

"Sure—*ridicule* the messenger."

"A more fitting punishment, don't you think?"

"Depends on the level of ridicule. Insulting your shoes isn't as bad as trashing your mama."

"Hey, now." Ashe pointed a finger at Sali.

"See?" Sali said. "Definite levels of ridicule. You don't care if I say your shoes suck. The bat would fly into my oatmeal and do a little bat dance if I insulted your mom."

"Or worse. I could put little bat prints on your underwear and make sure all of it hung from the school flagpole."

"You're not out the door, yet," Principal Billings' voice growled behind them. "I've given summer detention before." Ashe gaped at Sali while Sali turned a shocked stare toward Ashe. Both boys walked toward Cloud Chief Combined's double-doored entrance as quickly as possible.

Ashe spared a glance for Sali as he, Aedan and Adele found seats across the temporary aisle in the school cafeteria. Tables had been cleared away and folding chairs had been lined up in neat rows to accommodate students and parents.

As usual, the junior high class awards went to ninth graders, while the advanced awards were handed to senior students. And then it was time to announce the winners of the essay contest.

An expectant hush fell as Principal Billings strode stiffly and purposely to the podium to make the announcement. Tapping three sealed envelopes against the oak surface of the podium, Principal Billings scanned the crowd. If Ashe hadn't known better, he'd have said the sturdily built werewolf was furious.

"As you all know, each instructor has an equal vote in the essay contest," Principal Billings began, sounding very much as if he regretted that fact. "The winners are as follows: Third place and one hundred dollars goes to Emily Jackson. Ms. Jackson, if you'll come forward, please."

The crowd clapped while Emily's eleventh-grade classmates cheered. Emily, a pretty werewolf, blushed as she accepted the envelope and congratulations from the Principal. When she was seated again, Principal Billings cleared his throat and frowned. "Second Place and three hundred dollars goes to," he hesitated as if unwilling to say the name, "Rowdy Hankins." Many students gasped and whispers swept through the room—they'd all expected Rowdy to receive first prize.

Wow, Sali mouthed at Ashe. A dark horse would take first place for the first time in years.

Rowdy accepted his envelope with a wide smile, while Principal Billings congratulated him effusively and patted Rowdy's shoulder. Then, Billings cleared his throat a second time.

"Now, for the first-place winner. I must say that this was a hotly contested race between first and second place, with one eventually triumphing over the other." Ashe could tell from the Principal's sour expression that he hadn't voted for the first-place winner. "First place and five hundred dollars," Principal Billings announced as if he were delivering a eulogy at a funeral, "goes to Ashe Evans."

Sali stood and pumped his fist in the air, shouting, "Woot, woot," Cori, Dori and Wynn were clapping and screaming Ashe's name and Ashe's other classmates were shouting their support. All while Ashe remained in his seat, unmoving and completely stunned.

"Stand up, son," Aedan whispered, knowing Ashe would hear. Ashe never remembered the walk to the podium or Billings' begrudged congratulations. He was the second youngest student ever to win the contest. The youngest had been Randy Smith, and Billings had despised him, too.

Sali held a hand up beside his ear, imitating a cell phone there. Ashe nodded numbly as he sat down beside his parents again. A few last announcements were made about the fall semester, a few encouraging remarks were given and the assembly was over.

"Hold on," Aedan clapped a hand on Ashe's shoulder as everyone else exited the school cafeteria, all talking and laughing. Only graduation was left and then the summer would be theirs.

"Ashe, your punishment is this," Aedan said while Ashe's mother looked on. The cafeteria was now empty—Ashe could hear the noise from the crowd as it filtered in from the hallway outside. "You may not use that money to purchase a cell phone. You will wait until you turn fifteen as we originally planned. We won't tell you what to do with the prize money otherwise."

Ashe stared at his father as if he'd been struck by lightning. He and Sali had hoped and prayed to win the contest, just to get a cell. That option had been wiped away in the space of a blink with only few words from his father.

"Then I know what I want to do with it." Ashe rose stiffly from his chair and walked toward the door. Aedan spared a glance at Adele before following his son into the hall.

"Cori, this is yours. To help out when you go to college this fall." Ashe held the envelope out to Cori while Aedan and Adele walked up. Adele stifled a gasp—Ashe was giving the money away.

"Ashe," Cori shook her head, her pretty, blonde hair swinging.

"Cori, I want you to take it. As a graduation present." Ashe grabbed Cori's hand and stuffed the envelope into it. "I hope you get something really nice with it." Ashe walked away swiftly before a stunned Cori could hand the envelope back.

"Mr. Evans, I can't take this. Ashe worked so hard on his essay,"

Cori's green eyes were worried as she extended the envelope to Aedan.

"Cori, keep it. We just told him he could do what he wanted with the money, except buy a cell phone. This is what he decided." Aedan moved so smoothly around Cori she almost didn't see it.

"Congratulations, Cori. I hope you enjoy college," Adele gave Cori a tremulous smile and followed her husband down the hall.

∾

"Aedan, he'll never try to win that contest again."

Ashe had gone straight to his room and shut the door the moment they'd arrived at home. Adele's arms were crossed tightly over her midriff and she was close to tears. She thought, as had Aedan, that Ashe would spend the money on books or electronics. Instead, he'd gone straight to Cori and handed the money to her.

He hadn't spoken a word on the short drive home, and neither parent missed the lost look on Ashe's face. They hadn't missed Billings' attitude, either—the Principal had waged war against Ashe's winning the prize and handed it over with anger and reluctance. Now, his own parents had taken the reward for Ashe's hard work and turned it into a punishment. What should have been triumph had metamorphosed into crushing defeat.

"When they notified us on Wednesday that Ashe had won, I thought this would be a fitting punishment. I don't know what to do, now." Aedan rubbed the back of his neck uncomfortably.

∾

"I have no platitudes." Ren appeared and sat on the end of Ashe's bed as he usually did.

"I'd like to be alone now, if you don't mind." Ashe rubbed wetness from his face before turning around to look at Ren.

"Understood. Are we still friends?"

"Yeah." Ashe turned to face his computer again.

"I'll see you soon, then." Ren disappeared; Ashe turned to make sure.

Dude, what happened? Sali instant messaged Ashe.

Not now, Sali.

Never mind, I just heard from Hayes, who heard from Dori, who talked to Cori.

Rumor mill, Sali? How unlike you. Signing off, now. Ashe shut down his computer with a sigh.

Josiah mailed the envelope reluctantly. He should never have promised half the money to his spy. A third or a fourth, maybe. But all the spy had to do was talk to the right ones here and there and information was given freely. Josiah dumped the payment into the mailbox with a sigh and turned to walk down the cracked and broken sidewalk in Amarillo.

At the age of one hundred fifty-four, Josiah wanted to retire. *Soon.* His hair was still a dark brown with no gray, but another thirty years and that would no longer be true.

Dark-brown eyes scanned the parking lots of local businesses on the north side of Amarillo as he walked toward his car. Obediah never suspected that Josiah and his handpicked spy were acting as double agents, selling information to him and to the Bright Elemaiya. Obediah kept the Dark Ones informed while Josiah and his associate handed nearly the same information to the Bright side.

Wildrif had given Josiah the idea in the beginning, in exchange for a working cell phone. With the money coming in from both sides of the fence, Josiah didn't mind paying Wildrif's phone charges every month.

Josiah had no idea what Wildrif might want with a cell phone and didn't really care. But if Obediah discovered that his clairvoyant and his top spy were selling information to the other side, neither Josiah nor Wildrif had any illusions as to what might happen afterward.

The Cloud Chief spy's name had always been hidden from Obediah, although Josiah felt that Wildrif somehow knew. Wildrif knew just about anything if he wanted to know it. Shaking his head as he walked down the darkened sidewalk, Josiah's keen eyes raked the street, searching for the car he'd parked two blocks away.

~

"Ashe, will you carry these boxes out for Mrs. Wilson?" Adele was already frazzled and it wasn't even lunchtime. Saturdays at Cordell Feed and Seed usually were busy during spring planting season.

Ashe lifted the box of tender plants his mother had carefully packed for one of their regular customers—an elderly woman who still insisted on doing her own gardening.

Even so, Mrs. Wilson, a widow for more than ten years, still carried herself upright and dressed nicely for her weekly visits to Cordell to do her shopping. She'd already been to the grocery store and carefully explained to Ashe what she'd purchased there as he carried her box of plants to an old Cadillac parked nearby.

Adele spared a glance at Ashe as he pushed the door open with an elbow and held it while Mrs. Wilson slowly made her way to the sidewalk outside the store. Ashe had barely spoken all day, and he'd been completely silent over breakfast that morning. Sighing in frustration, Adele turned to a customer who needed help in the fertilizer aisle.

~

"Where's Ashe? I was hoping we could play Frisbee again," Edward asked Sali, who'd brought a jug of ice water for Trace and Trajan. The werewolves stood guard as usual outside the temporary housing behind Ashe's home. Edward shaded hazel eyes from bright sunlight as he waited for Sali's answer.

"His parents own Cordell Feed and Seed, so he's helping his mother at the store," Sali handed the jug to a waiting Jason. Trace had gone to walk the perimeter surrounding the five remaining mobile homes—Luanne and her parents were packing up at Old Harold's house to move into the home recently vacated by the Frasiers, while the O'Neills and the Thompsons had gone to help.

"Really? I wish I could help. That sounds awesome." Edward's words were wistful.

"Maybe some other time, young 'un," Jason smiled at Edward. Jason and Trace had taken to Edward. Luanne, Macy and even Keith and Bryce talked to the werewolves often, but Philip remained sullen and generally uncommunicative.

"Maybe you can go with us, sometime," Sali said. "I would have gone to help but Mom made me stay home and clean my room today."

"Kiddo, wherever you go, you have to be protected. Don't count on going into Cordell with Sali and Ashe," Jason told Edward gently.

"I know. Lizzie's dead." Edward ducked his head and toed a clump of grass uncomfortably.

"Yeah." Sali agreed. "Edward, don't leave Cloud Chief unless somebody is with you. Promise?"

"I promise." Edward shivered in the warm Oklahoma air. His father hadn't given complete details on how Elizabeth Frasier had died; just that she'd been killed, somehow.

That was incentive enough for Edward to remain where he was unless accompanied by an adult and a strong one at that. Ashe's father, Aedan, came to mind. After all, Edward had seen the chunk of granite Aedan had casually snapped off the Frasier's kitchen counter. He'd put his hands experimentally on his kitchen counter, but it hadn't budged a millimeter.

"How strong do you think Ashe's dad really is?" Edward asked to fill the silence.

"All vampires are strong," Jason said. "I once heard that a single vampire killed twenty werewolves, but I wasn't there so I can't say whether it's true or not. And boy, werewolves are damn strong. Don't ever forget that. Some shifters, too. You're here for a reason—so we can protect you until those people stop hunting you. Don't ever think for a minute that either side will allow you to live your own life. If they tell you that, it's a lie." Jason got up and went to relieve Trace, who'd finished another complete round and was heading for the tent to get a drink.

~

"Denise, I don't know what to do. We've managed to crush him, when all we intended to do was take the possibility of a cell phone away." Ashe was minding the store while Adele shut herself inside the tiny office to eat lunch and call Denise. Sali had been scheduled to come to Cordell and work with Ashe at the store, but Adele knew Ashe would be too embarrassed to work with his friend this quickly.

"His birthday is coming up. What else did he want?"

"We were planning to buy a tablet of some kind. He could download books that way and not have to leave Cloud Chief to buy them," Adele sighed. "And Aedan and I know what happened to the Frasier girl. One witness said it was like huge, invisible hands lifted her off the ground and tossed her through that window. Ashe is in so much danger and he doesn't even realize it."

"Adele, how long do you think he can stay behind this boundary, or in the presence of someone else? He's growing, just like Sali and the others. Marco was driving at age sixteen, and leaving the community behind regularly. The others will, too, just as soon as they're able."

"But Sharon and Jonas keep an eye on Wynn. I don't think she'll have the freedom the others do—she's just too rare."

"True. Can you imagine what might happen if humans discovered a real unicorn?"

"There are some who wouldn't rest until she was captured, I know that much," Adele replied. "And it could be the same with Ashe. He has talent that is more valuable than gold. His life may be in danger from more than the Elemaiya." Adele didn't voice her fears over the Vampire Council.

"Yeah. Marcus says the same, but he won't elaborate."

"Just don't ask about it, Denise. Ashe has enough to worry about as it is."

"Wouldn't think of it. If you need help with Ashe's birthday party, just ask." Ashe's birthday was June twenty-second, barely a month away. "I can make punch or bring snacks."

"I'll call you later, after Aedan and I decide what we want to do," Adele said. "I need to get back to the store—Ashe refused lunch but I'll send him to the kitchen anyway. Maybe he'll make a sandwich for himself. If Mr. Winkler hadn't installed the security cameras last year, I wouldn't have left him out in the store by himself." Adele glanced up at the monitor over her desk; Ashe was ringing up a customer who'd purchased seed packets.

Denise agreed and hung up.

~

"Honey, go get a sandwich. You can eat in my office and phone Sali if you want," Adele said as she walked back into the store. Ashe glanced at his mother's face—it appeared pale and worried.

"I'll go phone Sali." Ashe moved toward the back of the store where the kitchen and Adele's office were.

"Make a sandwich, hon. You're growing again." Ashe didn't reply, he merely tossed up a hand in acknowledgment and kept walking.

"Sali, I don't want to talk about it." Ashe bit into the half sandwich he'd made for himself. The store had been busy from the moment they'd opened, and he was hungry. Sali was asking for details on *the cell-phone humiliation*, as he'd dubbed the incident.

"You just gave the money away? Ashe, you could have gotten all kinds of stuff with that. We could have bought new video games. Or books, even." Sali didn't like to read and never made a secret of that fact, so the books suggestion was an afterthought.

"Sali, Cori is going to college. She needs things, too. More important things than video games."

"Dude, did you have to give it all away?" Sali whined.

"I didn't need it," Ashe replied tersely. "Look, I'm eating lunch. Can't talk with my mouth full, dude. Bye." Ashe hung up and bit savagely into his ham sandwich.

Glancing at the security monitor over his mother's desk, he watched as a man walked through the door. The monitor that Mr. Winkler's security company installed a year earlier displayed six separate images from cameras located throughout the store. One image showed his mother in an aisle, helping a customer with weed killer.

The man who'd come in wandered out of the camera's view, so Ashe kept a watch on his mother as he ate. Adele rang up the customer who quickly left the store, purchase in hand. Now a lull had come; no other customers were inside the store except for the man who was wandering aimlessly through the aisles. Ashe's skin began to itch.

∾

"They are wary, wise wolf, after the girl was killed." Wildrif dipped his head respectfully to Obediah Tanner.

"Then how do we get to the others?" Obediah's wolves hadn't been in on the girl's killing, so his reward money was diminishing. Three of his were watching the boundary at a safe enough distance that the Cloud Chief Pack wouldn't notice or scent them. Somehow, the girl had managed to get past Obediah's guards.

"Hire a rogue witch or warlock," Wildrif suggested. "A strong one, to take down the boundary. And if the one we find has some friends, hire them, too. Should be easy enough to get those kids out, once the boundary comes down. And if they die, well, there's no real way to connect them to you, is there?"

"You know where to find somebody?" Obediah's interest was piqued instantly.

"I believe I can find some who are willing," a slow smile spread across Wildrif's face.

Mom! It was all Ashe had time to shout mentally before the man had Adele by the throat, demanding information on children hidden in the area. Blazingly angry at the attack on his mother, Ashe was mist and through the office wall in a blink.

CHAPTER 13

"Marcus, I only know he had dark hair and green eyes. That's all I really saw before he grabbed me by the throat." Adele was rubbing her neck—bruises had appeared from the cruel grip of her assailant. "He was asking about hidden children."

Adele gratefully accepted the glass of water Ashe held out. "Ashe might be able to tell you more; I'd be dead if he hadn't turned me to mist. We both watched that man go crazy after we disappeared. You see what he did," Adele's voice was raspy as she nodded toward the aisle that had nearly been destroyed.

The assailant had gone crazy, sweeping everything from the shelves surrounding him in demented anger and cursing loudly as he did so. He'd then rushed from the store and raced down the street, disappearing in seconds.

"I'm calling Agents Lawford and North," Marcus stepped away to make the call. Ashe had sent mindspeech to Marcus and Jason first thing, after the assailant had run from the store. Marcus, whose small locksmith office was only a few blocks away, arrived in record time.

Adele was coughing again and attempting to drink the water Ashe had gotten for her as Marcus punched numbers on his cell. Ashe's head jerked up as the bell over the door rang. Jason Landers, the old werewolf, had arrived.

~

"Winkler is sending up two more to help, and Marcie and I can run the store. I don't think Adele should come back to work until we have this well in hand," Jason said, dropping a hand on Ashe's shoulders. "Ashe shouldn't be here, either, I don't think." Jason had arrived at Cordell Feed and Seed quickly, driving the distance from Cloud Chief to Cordell in a matter of minutes.

"But Mr. Landers," Ashe worried his lower lip while studying the old werewolf's grim and determined expression.

"Ashe, that one was looking for hidden children. You're on that list, or near enough. I know you saved your mom, but that doesn't mean he won't be back and with even more malice on his mind. Mr. Winkler is coming up for the day tomorrow, with Roger and Toby. He'll take a look at those images in your security system, Mrs. Evans. Mr. Jennings may come, too. Winkler said he was going to call the Director right away."

"In the meantime, I'll have Micah and somebody else stay here at the store tonight," Marcus had left a brief message on Agent Lawford's phone before hanging up—the agent hadn't answered the call. Ashe moved to his mother's side and wrapped his arms around her shoulders.

"Honey, we'll be all right," Adele patted Ashe's arms. "You got both of us out of harm's way."

~

"I have a jet ready to go now," Director Jennings informed William Winkler. "Derik North called me earlier. Said that Nick Lawford didn't come back from breakfast this morning. Now, I don't think you know Nick as well as I do, but there's no way he'd just disappear, and no way he'd forget to answer his phone or return a call. Something has happened to one of my best agents, Winkler. The question is; did the killer get information from him before he died."

"You're sure he's dead."

"Unless he was overpowered somehow and confined. With this killer, that would be highly unusual. He likes to kill. I'm sure if he were aware that Jane Scott survived, even if she's in a coma, then he'd be working to finish the job."

"I agree with that," Winkler said. "Two Cloud Chief wolves are staying at the Evans' store tonight, but I've asked Jason to transfer the recorded images to me by computer. I'll have a look at what the security system shows us. This may be our best bet on identifying this man. Jason says that Adele and Ashe agree that the man has dark hair and green eyes, but Ashe says the man has a scar on his upper lip, slightly off-center."

"Off-center, you say?" Director Jennings was immediately interested.

"Something you know, Director?" Winkler recognized the Director's attentiveness.

"Can't say for sure at this point. Just a suspicion at the moment. I'll work on that while I fly to Oklahoma. Expect me there around eight tonight."

"I'll be there; my private jet is fueling up right now." Winkler hung up.

~

"Agent Lawford is missing?" Ashe wanted to shiver. He'd liked the tall agent, who seemed both confident and competent. Agent North had met with Marcus in Cordell and now he, Marcus and Mr. Winkler were sitting in Ashe's kitchen with Ashe and his mother, while Denise DeLuca handed out soft drinks and glasses of sweetened tea.

Sali had come with Denise, and he and Ashe sat together at the kitchen table. In half an hour, Aedan would wake and he and Nathan would be informed of the day's events. Ashe didn't look forward to seeing how angry his father might become when he learned Adele had been attacked.

"But if Mr. Lawford was already missing, and that man wanted information from Mom, doesn't that mean that Agent Lawford didn't tell him anything?" Ashe worked to keep the quaver out of his voice.

After all, Agent Lawford should be alive. Might still *be* alive; Ashe hoped he was, anyway. "Mr. Winkler, that man hauled Jane Scott to Lake Altus to dump her. Do you think he'd go back there again? Since nobody has reported that she was found there?" Ashe turned imploring eyes to the Dallas Packmaster.

"Kid, I'll send Trace and Jason out right away. I'll let them sniff around and see if they can find anything." Winkler slipped his cell from a pocket and made the call. In minutes, Jason and Trace were on their way, after Derik North described where Jane Scott's car had been dumped in the water.

"If there's anything out there, they'll find it," Winkler nodded at Ashe.

"Thank you, Mr. Winkler," Ashe loosed the breath he'd unconsciously been holding. He'd expected resistance from Marcus and the others, and from the look on Marcus' face, that's exactly what would have happened if Winkler hadn't spoken up right away.

"Not a problem; they were pacing like caged wolves anyway, and since Roger and Toby took over watching those kids for a while, they needed something to do," Winkler grinned briefly at Ashe.

Renegar chose that moment to appear in a corner of Ashe's kitchen, nearly causing Ashe to jerk in his seat. Sali lifted an eyebrow at Ashe anyway; he'd felt the slight twitch. Renegar gave the slightest nod in Ashe's direction.

You're still telling me when I'm right? Ashe guessed.

Correct.

We need to hurry, don't we? Ashe sent.

Correct.

"Mr. Winkler, ask them to hurry," Ashe stood, his eyes and his voice begging the Dallas Packmaster to move faster. Somehow, the situation was critical and a life likely hung in the balance.

Winkler pulled out his cell a second time. "Step on it," he barked into the phone when Trace answered.

"Will do, boss," came in clearly to Ashe's enhanced hearing.

"Mom, can I go outside for a little while?" Ashe asked.

"Sali, go with him," Denise nodded to Sali, who rose immediately from his chair. He and Ashe walked quietly through the door leading into the garage, and since it was open already, they wandered into a calm, Oklahoma evening. The sun was setting in blues, oranges and purples just above the horizon as Ashe lifted Sali into his mist and went straight to the roof of his house.

This is quite fine, Renegar settled on Ashe's left, whereas Sali had sat down on the right.

I'm glad you came, friend, Ashe said as all three watched the sun sink, leaving the prairie in twilight. Aedan would be up quickly and Ashe wanted the adults to handle the information dispersal without his presence.

I'm glad I came as well. Beauty is recognized by all races, did you know? Ren never turned to look at Ashe, keeping his eyes on the vanishing colors above the horizon.

Good to know, Ashe replied.

"Do you think Agent Lawford is still alive?" Sali ventured to ask, completely unaware of Renegar's presence.

"I sure hope so," Ashe replied softly.

Jason and Trace had both turned to wolf after parking their SUV in a picnic area near the lake's edge and leaving their clothing inside the vehicle. They'd have a much better chance at finding anything by tracking it in that manner, although both held good scenting ability while human.

Trace found the scent first—he and Jason had a good whiff of the man from Cordell Feed and Seed. The culprit had allowed his anger to prevail and he'd left scent all over seed packets and gardening tools after swiping those items off shelves surrounding the cash register.

Silently tracking now, both wolves began racing after the scent—the man had dragged Nick Lawford after a while and the agent's scent was strong, along with that of his blood. Jason and Trace could think clearly while in wolf form, and they were fervently hoping they'd find a live agent at the end of their trail.

~

Edward is peering out his window, Ren informed Ashe as the last bit of light and color disappeared in the west. Stars were now twinkling overhead, their tiny illuminations littering the deep blue of a night sky, far away from the interference of artificial light.

"Son," Aedan's voice floated up from the ground. "The wolves have found Agent Lawford, but he's unconscious and chained to a tree. They need you to get him out of there."

"I'll go with him." Winkler was already prepared to go.

"I'll come as well. Son, forget what I said before. Do what you have to do," Aedan said after Ashe misted Sali from their rooftop perch.

"All right." Ashe turned Ren, Winkler and his father to mist and rushed toward Lake Altus.

~

"Ashe, if you can't get him out, I'll cut the chains." Aedan was prepared to use his vampire claws to release Nick Lawford, whose unconsciousness was due to a severe head wound. Ashe drew in a shaky breath—the agent's body was slumped against the tree trunk, his head wound covered in thick, clotted blood.

"I'd prefer not to do that," Winkler said enigmatically. "And we need to stake out this spot. There's a good chance the attacker will return, hoping to get information."

"He'll die," Aedan muttered grimly.

"No, we need him alive," Winkler disagreed.

While his father and the Dallas Packmaster argued and Trace and Jason remained silent, Ashe turned to mist and turned the unconscious agent to mist as well, pulling Nick Lawford out of his shackles easily. *Who's coming with me to the hospital?* Ashe sent.

"I'll come," Winkler volunteered. "Aedan, I know the perpetrator attacked your wife. If he shows up, please practice restraint." Ashe gathered Ren and Winkler inside his mist after that and rushed toward Clinton Regional Hospital.

~

"I'm ten minutes away," Director Bill Jennings was on the phone with Winkler, who paced in the same waiting room Ashe had sat in only a few days earlier.

Seated in the same chair as before, Ashe watched while Winkler talked on his cell and paced restlessly, explaining to Mr. Jennings the circumstances surrounding Nick Lawford's discovery. Ren sat next to Ashe, just as he had before, and the two were carrying on a private conversation of their own.

Concussion, possible brain damage, in addition to the skull fracture, the physician says. The blow to the head was too hard, he also says. That explains the agent's unconsciousness. He might have died had he remained where he was. Ren explained what was happening inside the emergency room as a physician and the staff worked on Nick Lawford. *They will perform scans and electronic monitoring, to assess the damage.*

I hope he's okay. Ashe huddled in his chair, fearful for the wounded agent.

We must wait to see, Ren replied.

"The Director will be here in a few minutes," Winkler settled his tall frame effortlessly into the vacant chair beside Ashe. Somehow, Ren always managed to direct people away from his presence and Ashe wondered how the tall, blue-skinned youth was able to do it. Now, Ashe sat wedged between a Larentii and a werewolf inside a hospital waiting room. Winkler had already sent a text to Aedan, informing him that they'd arrived safely and that Ashe was guarded.

"How is he?" Bill Jennings, Director of the Joint NSA/Homeland

Security Department asked the moment he and two agents posing as bodyguards stepped inside the waiting room.

"Still waiting for the doctor," Winkler replied, standing up and extending a hand to the Director. Bill Jennings shook briefly, nodded and smiled at Ashe and sat down with Winkler while his bodyguards took up positions on either side of the door. Ashe had no doubt that the agents had guns hidden somewhere; they had that look about them. Agent Lawford and Derik North always did, although Ashe had never seen their weapons.

"Did that man take Mr. Lawford's gun?" Ashe thought to ask.

"Yes. It wasn't on him when we placed him on the gurney," Winkler nodded to Ashe.

"Not good," Ashe muttered, crossing arms over his chest defensively.

"No. Not good at all, since the perpetrator now has another method of committing murder at his disposal," Director Jennings acknowledged. "Sadly, we have our suspicions as to who it might be and that isn't good news."

"But he didn't kill Elizabeth Frasier, did he?"

"No. It would be convenient if this one was the only one we had to worry about, but he doesn't possess the power needed to do what was done to that poor girl."

"Yeah. I got that idea, too."

The bodyguards shifted when the doctor walked in, but relaxed immediately when they saw who it was. "Mr. Lawford is resting comfortably at the moment, but we are monitoring him continuously," the physician, dressed in traditional blue scrubs, informed Winkler.

"How quickly can he be moved?" Director Jennings asked as he rose from his seat. Winkler was already standing.

"Perhaps tomorrow," the doctor replied, eyeing the Director suspiciously.

"This is Bill Jennings, Director of the Joint NSA and Homeland Security Department," Winkler introduced the Director. "Nick Lawford is one of his agents."

"I recognize you now," the doctor shook hands with Bill. "Let us know when you want your agent transferred, and I'll make arrangements."

"Thank you. Nick and I are friends from way back, so I want him to pull through this. What can you tell us about his condition?" Bill searched the physician's face for any clues regarding Agent Lawford's actual circumstances.

"Can't say for sure at the moment," the doctor shook his head. Ashe noticed his nametag read Like. This was Doctor *Like*? Ashe forcefully pressed his lips together to keep a smile from surfacing. "My name is Melvin Like, in case you need to get in touch," the doctor handed a card to Director Jennings. Ashe turned his head and worked to squash the snicker.

Why do you find this humorous? Ren, who'd remained silent for several minutes, chose that moment to ask a question.

His name, Ashe coughed to cover the laugh that bubbled to the surface.

Ah. Like. Adverb, preposition, adjective, noun, Ren went through a list of potential uses for the physician's last name.

How do you say it if you don't like him? Ashe coughed a second time while a slow smile spread across Ren's face until it became a full-blown grin.

Yes—should you say you dislike Like? I like that, Ren's mental wisecrack almost forced Ashe from his chair as he stifled laughter.

"Is he all right?" The doctor was now staring at Ashe.

"He's fine." Winkler hauled Ashe upright by his shirt collar, setting him on his feet easily. Ashe schooled his face, forcing a blank expression. Ren gave a gleeful, mental snort at Ashe's predicament.

"One of my agents will remain here. Please inform him when Agent Lawford is moved from the emergency room. I want a guard placed nearby for protection." Bill nodded to the doctor. Winkler shoved Ashe toward the door and they swept out, one of the guards falling in at the rear of the procession.

"Kid, I almost laughed, too," Winkler grinned at Ashe as they followed Director Jennings to a black Lincoln Towne Car parked in the hospital's small parking lot. Ashe sat in the front passenger seat while Winkler drove, since the Dallas Packmaster was more familiar with the area than Director Jennings' bodyguard.

"I never can spot the entrance," Bill muttered as Winkler drove through the small gate into the community of Cloud Chief.

"Meant to be that way. Only the ones with a little extra can see it," Winkler said, slowing down to drive over the graveled road that ran through the hidden community.

"Dad's home," Ashe whispered as Winkler drove into the Evans' driveway and parked. Aedan was outside the house, talking with Nathan, Marcus and Adele.

"Bad news, Mr. Winkler," Aedan sighed as Winkler stepped out of the vehicle. "We almost had the culprit, until he got in a couple of shots." Aedan handed two bullets to the Dallas Packmaster. "He hit me twice, knocking me down. Managed to get in his car and drive away while I was picking bullets out of my chest."

"Dad!" Ashe rushed to his father's side. "You okay?"

"I'm fine, son. That gun carried a bit of a kick; otherwise, I'd have been on him. Trace and Jason did their best, but even they can't catch a speeding car."

"These are from Agent Lawford's nine millimeter," Director Jennings carefully examined the bullets Winkler handed to him. "May we come in to discuss our fugitive?" Bill asked politely.

Ashe was sent to his room while the adults remained upstairs. Adele was serving drinks and snacks as Ashe clumped downstairs. *Ashe?* An unfamiliar voice sounded in Ashe's mind, causing him to halt at the base of the stairs.

Who? Ashe sent out.

It's me—Edward. I just found out yesterday I could do this. We didn't start looking until Mr. DeLuca asked us, and then we started trying. Luanne has mindspeech, too. Macy and Keith don't—not that we could tell, anyway, and Philip is just too stubborn to try. Ashe, what is going on? Did they catch whoever killed Lizzie?

We tried, Edward. But he got away. Ashe was afraid to tell Edward that there was more than one killer on the loose. Edward sounded frightened, and Ashe didn't want to scare the older teen more than he was already. Ashe continued walking toward his bedroom, finding Ren sitting on the bed once he was inside.

Have you tried to do anything else? Like shapeshift? Ashe asked, attempting to calm Edward down.

We don't know how to do anything like that. Keith mentioned it since you can do it, but we have no idea what we're doing.

I'm pretty sure Elizabeth could turn to mist—that's how she got away from Cloud Chief without the wolves knowing. She should have told someone. Maybe you guys could have talked her out of leaving. Ashe was still upset over her death, although Elizabeth hadn't been the easiest person to deal with.

Luanne blames herself. She stayed home that day instead of coming to visit. I don't know how Luanne does it, but everybody feels better around her. Ashe agreed with Edward—he'd noticed the same thing about Luanne.

Luanne? Ashe included Edward in his sending to the teen girl.

Ashe? You can do this too? Luanne was surprised.

Yeah. Luanne, don't blame yourself for Elizabeth's death. It's not your fault. You, too, Edward. We have some of the best and strongest people here in Cloud Chief, and a mister can get right past all of them. Ashe realized he should take his own advice.

What's a mister? Edward asked.

Hold on, I'll be right there, Ashe sent and cut off communication. "I'm going to visit Edward," Ashe informed Ren. "Want to come?"

"Of course. I've been listening to your conversation through Edward. I can't hear your mindspeech unless you direct it to me. Part of the unreadable thing, you know."

"Want me to mist you, or do you want to get yourself there?"

"Please, take me as mist. I may never get the opportunity again, once this period of study is over." Ren stood, prepared to go with Ashe. Ashe obliged and in seconds, he was inside Edward's bedroom. Luanne was there with Edward, waiting.

"Wow," Edward's mouth was almost a perfect O as Ashe appeared from nothing.

"I turn to mist and get around that way," Ashe admitted. "See?" He went invisible again, causing Luanne to gasp.

"You mean Liz found out she could do that, and used it to leave us?" Luanne was upset.

"I'm pretty sure," Ashe said.

Correct, Ren silently supplied.

"In fact, I'm sure of it," Ashe added. "Did they tell you she went to a dress shop in Cordell first, before asking someone to drive her out of town? She would have been better off misting to her destination, but she probably didn't know enough about it to realize that."

Correct.

"So, if you get the urge to leave Cloud Chief, make sure you tell somebody. We're not dealing with amateurs that want to kill us," Ashe went on. "These people have one goal in mind, never forget that. They want us dead."

Correct.

~

"This is the one we're chasing now." Bill Jennings handed over photographs to Marcus, Winkler, Aedan and Nathan. "I don't know what the boy's mother told him about his father, but this one went as bad as it is possible to go."

Depicted in the photographs was a dark-haired man with green eyes and a scar on his upper lip. "If Ashe hadn't reported the scar, it never would have occurred to me that this one might be here, committing these crimes. We've all believed he was far away and no longer cared what happened to his son."

"You don't believe the boy has any idea?" Winkler lifted his gaze to the Director.

"Doubt it. I have no idea what he thinks at this point." Bill's white hair shone in the light of the pendant lamp that hung over the kitchen table.

"Are you going to tell him—and his mother?" Marcus asked.

"I'd prefer not to, at this point. We won't, either, unless we have no choice. He walked away from her and into a life of crime, leaving his son behind. It will only terrify the family more if they learn of this new threat."

"I agree," Aedan nodded. "The others shouldn't know, either. Ashe knows not to say anything—he wants to protect those children as much as any of us. I'll have a talk with him anyway, just as a precaution."

"Good. Alex and I have hotel reservations in Clinton. The hotel isn't far from the hospital, and we'll escort Agent Lawford to Oklahoma City tomorrow as quickly as it can be arranged. We'll make sure he's placed in the same hospital as the Scott woman, so my agents can easily guard both rooms."

"Want a wolf or two to help?" Winkler asked. "Marcus can send one of his tonight, and I'll get some of mine up here tomorrow, if you want."

"Do it," Bill sighed. "I hate to impose, but we've all seen what this one is capable of doing." He stuffed the photographs inside a folder and handed them off to his agent bodyguard.

"I'll get Ben Billings," Marcus dialed his cell and spoke rapidly to Principal Billings when the older werewolf answered the phone.

CHAPTER 14

"*D*ad, there's no way I'd say anything about that man. They have enough to worry about as it is." Aedan hadn't given Ashe the name of the hunted man, just that he had connections to one of the families and warned Ashe not to say anything to anyone about it. "But there's something you need to know—you, Mr. Winkler and Marcus," Ashe blinked at his father. "Edward sent mindspeech to me a little while ago. He says he and Luanne both have it, but he said that Macy and Keith don't seem to. They can't get Philip to even try."

"That could be a good and a bad thing," Aedan said softly. "What if those creatures attempt to contact them? Try to convince them to leave, as the girl did."

"They've never tried to contact me. Or if they did, it didn't get past the barrier. Why would they try with the others?"

"I don't know. We'll think on this and I'll have a talk with Mr. Winkler. It's past your bedtime, now. Get in bed, son, and we'll sort this out later."

"All right. Dad, I'm glad those bullets didn't hurt you."

"Bullets always hurt, but they generally don't kill a vampire. Getting them out is sometimes more painful than getting them to begin with. Goodnight, son, and don't worry about this." Aedan rose

156

from his seat on Ashe's bed. "Mr. Winkler says you can talk to him tomorrow—he has questions, I think." Aedan walked out of Ashe's bedroom, closing the door carefully behind him.

~

"You going to the graduation tonight?" Sali flopped onto a lawn chair beside Ashe.

"Yeah. Cori's graduating. Of course I'm going. Why wouldn't I?" Ashe shook his head at Sali's indifference.

"Marco called last night. He'll be here, too."

"Does this mean you'll come with me? Mom and Dad are coming; Mr. Thompson offered to help guard the perimeter since Nathan and Dad will be at the graduation. Trace and those new werewolves, Roger and Toby, will help Mr. Thompson. Jason and Marcie will run the store for Mom until they catch the guy who attacked us." Ashe and Sali sat outside in lawn chairs on the south side of Ashe's house. Aedan had built a small deck there that led into Adele's solarium.

"Mom says that Aunt Marcie really likes Jason."

"I like Jason, too."

"Yeah, but I think Aunt Marcie might like to marry Jason."

"Really?" Ashe stared at Sali. "You think so? That's outstanding."

"She gets to pick this time. She didn't with Uncle Dominic. We might not see cousin Jackson or cousin Dustin again," Sali muttered. "They had to stay in Phoenix with Uncle Dom."

"That sucks," Ashe nodded.

"Well, we didn't see much of them before. Jack's a year older than I am, and Dusty's five years older. Uncle Dom didn't like it if Aunt Marcie wanted to visit us."

"He sounds like a jerk," Ashe said.

"He is. Dad never liked him, and having two Packmasters in the house can be a little tense."

"Are you coming to graduation or not?" Ashe changed the subject, going back to the scheduled ceremony.

"Yeah. I'll come. Let's sit in the back."

"But I want to see Cori. Mom said I could borrow the camcorder and record it. Besides, she worked really hard on her speech." Ashe didn't blink when Ren appeared and sat down on the wide boards of the deck, silently joining the two boys. He did blink, however, when Elizabeth Frasier's ghost floated in and settled nearby.

"You didn't see her? Man, she was right there beside you," Ashe paced inside his bedroom later, after Sali had gone home for an early dinner. Most of the community was preparing to attend the graduation later. Ren sat cross-legged on Ashe's bed, his tall frame leaning against the wall behind the bed. He'd taken up the habit after seeing Ashe and Sali do the same.

"We, as a rule, do not have the talent to see spirits," Ren offered. "A talented few among the many races that populate the universes can. Sadly, I am not one of them."

"So I can see ghosts. You don't think I'm crazy, do you?"

"No. I do have the talent for detecting lies. You are not offering an untruth."

"Good. At least I don't have to defend myself to you."

"You would not, anyway. You are trustworthy, Ashe Evans."

"I'm not telling anybody else. Sali couldn't see her, and he stared right at her several times. What's she doing here, anyway?"

"Many tales abound regarding the reasons spirits stay in one place or another. As I have not been able to question any of them directly, I have doubts concerning those tales." Ren's bright blue eyes were thoughtful as he seriously considered Ashe's question.

"At least she left after a while," Ashe blew out a breath. "That was a little creepy, though. And she just kept staring at me." Ashe shivered at the memory. Elizabeth's appearance had rattled him greatly and he'd barely been able to stay focused on Sali's conversation.

"Friend, do not take responsibility for her death," Ren said. "Only she bears that burden. If she stares at you, perhaps she hopes that you might help her in some way."

"If I can, but how can I know that for sure? It's not like we can have a conversation," Ashe muttered.

"Again, I have no experience in this area, so I cannot offer advice."

~

"Kid, I don't expect this to end pretty," William Winkler sighed, taking a seat beside Ashe in the school cafeteria. Ashe, camcorder in hand, sat near the front on an aisle seat so he could get images of Cori when she marched in. He'd come early, just to get a good seat.

"How do you think it might end?" Ashe turned a curious gaze on the Dallas Packmaster.

"I'm hoping for no more deaths or attacks, but I think that may be unrealistic."

"Yeah," Ashe huddled into his seat.

"Kid, none of this is your fault. If anybody should take the blame, then Director Jennings and I should take it."

"But I should have guessed sooner that they might develop their abilities."

"Ashe," Winkler patted Ashe's shoulders, "we all think we should have known things after the fact. A good friend called that hindsight once, and asked me if I had eyes on my ass."

Ashe snickered at Winkler's description before schooling his face —Mr. and Mrs. Booth had come in to sit across the aisle. Usually the parents were ushered inside first, ahead of the graduating seniors. Ashe wondered why Diane and Neil Booth weren't waiting for that.

For a short while, he'd forgotten that Chad and Jeremy were graduating with Cori. Mr. and Mrs. Booth's appearance reminded him of that fact. At least Chump and Wormy couldn't give a speech and bore everybody; it was part of their punishment. Ashe felt sorry for Mr. and Mrs. Booth. They seemed like nice people. Perhaps a cuckoo had laid an egg in their nest, too.

"Hey, Ashe," Marco walked in, carrying a digital camera and smiling hugely.

"Marco!" Ashe grinned at Sali's older brother. "How's college?"

"Tough. Tougher than high school," Marco acknowledged before turning to Winkler. "Hello, Mr. Winkler."

Is that lipstick on your cheek? Ashe snickered mentally to Marco.

"Maybe. Depends on who's asking," Marco chuckled aloud.

"Are you two having a private conversation?" Winkler stood to allow Marco to move past him and sit down.

"Apparently I'm wearing some of Cori's lipstick," Marco grinned at the Dallas Packmaster.

"Good," Winkler laughed.

"Ashe, this is a new camera and I haven't figured it out, yet. Sali told me to give it to you to set up for me." Marco handed the camera to Ashe. It was a digital SLR and Ashe admired it as he handled it carefully, going through electronic settings quickly, setting up for auto focus and digital displays.

"Here," Ashe handed it back in a matter of seconds. "All you have to do is point and press the button now," he grinned at Marco. "Nice camera," he added.

"You've done this before?" Winkler lifted an eyebrow at Ashe.

"Nope." Ashe shrugged.

"Sali says Ashe never looks at the instructions for video games either. He was born knowing how they work, I guess," Marco supplied. "And he knows all the shortcuts, too."

"I just do," Ashe shrugged again.

"Kid, come see me when you're ready to graduate," Winkler said seriously. The community began filtering in quickly, so they turned their attention to the impending ceremony.

"No, we wait until Mom and Dad are asleep," Jeremy hissed. "Mom keeps her car keys on the counter beside the door. We can sneak out our bedroom window and go to Clinton. Somebody will buy beer for us, if we have the proper persuasion." Jeremy lifted the folded cash from his pants pocket.

"Put that back. You want somebody to see?" Chad hissed. "Are you sure the distraction will work? Can we even trust that kid?"

"I think he wouldn't mind causing a little chaos," Jeremy smiled grimly. "And we can drive out of here while the guards are busy elsewhere. They may even think Mom or Dad went somewhere, if they find the car gone afterward."

Jeremy and Chad had chosen the English classroom to dress in their graduation robes. At least their punishment had one up side—they didn't have to give a speech before receiving their diplomas.

"I'm glad we found that walkie-talkie after Lizzie left us," Chad grinned. "Who knew two of those empties would help get us what we want?"

"I'm glad Mom's not here to tell us not to speak ill of the dead," Jeremy laughed.

~

Philip was angry. As angry as he'd ever been. Those two boys had burned down Luanne's house and they'd only been grounded for it. Sure, everybody called it house arrest, but he knew they'd found ways around their punishment.

Then they'd had the nerve to contact him on Elizabeth's walkie-talkie, asking him to sneak out to find a box of fireworks they'd stashed somewhere and set them off while the night guards weren't looking.

Philip wasn't the only one who'd been observing the guards, once he knew what to look for and once he'd learned what he could become if he just concentrated a little. He'd lifted himself up after changing the first time, placing paws on his bathroom sink to see that he'd transformed into a mountain lion.

He wasn't going to tell his mother or anyone else about this. It was a secret that might become useful when all was said and done. Now, he was waiting patiently for those two arsonists to contact him again by walkie-talkie, and he'd be out his window as a large cat, racing to the fireworks. Only he didn't intend for things to turn out exactly as those boys wanted.

∾

Six students were in Cori's graduating class, and since Chad and Jeremy weren't giving a speech, that portion of the ceremony went quickly. Ashe recorded Cori walking in and sitting down, and then recorded a beaming Nathan and Lavonna Anderson as they watched their oldest daughter rise to give her speech. Marco, too, was snapping digital photographs as quickly as his camera would record them.

Shuffling notecards on the podium, Cori cleared her throat as Mr. Dodd adjusted the microphone for her. "I'm not giving the speech I originally planned to give," she announced as soon as Cloud Chief's History teacher stepped away. "Instead, I'm giving a speech about being unselfish." Ashe blinked in surprise at Cori's revelation.

"I told a friend that I wanted to win the essay contest, because I wanted to fix up my dorm room at college," Cori gazed around the crowd. "And when that friend won the contest instead, well, he gave the money to me. I didn't deserve it. I hadn't done anything to get it. But it was handed to me anyway. At first, I made all sorts of plans. I was going to buy a matching comforter and window curtains. Or a mini fridge. So many things went through my mind as I mentally spent that money. But I felt bad that I was getting what I wanted and my friend wasn't. Then I started thinking what I might do with the money instead. Thinking about better things. Unselfish things. Today, I donated all that money to a charity that helps find missing children. Ashe, I hope that's okay with you." Cori wiped her cheeks as every person inside the school cafeteria rose and cheered.

Ashe, his mouth open and the camcorder pointed at his feet, nodded wordlessly at Cori. She offered him a trembling smile and accepted her diploma from Principal Billings.

∾

"We're going to Clinton. Do you think your parents will let you come?" Cori stood in front of Ashe later, Marco right behind her. It was tradition that the graduating seniors went out for dinner in nearby Clinton after the ceremony, and then to a bowling alley to celebrate following that.

"Doubt it," Ashe muttered, lowering his eyes. Sali stood at Ashe's shoulder, a hopeful gleam in his eyes. It was a coup for anyone below senior level to be invited along.

"Marco, can I have your promise that he'll be safely guarded?" Aedan had come up silently behind Ashe.

"Absolutely," Marco nodded solemnly.

"We will, Mr. Evans," Cori was promising, too.

"I'm buying," Winkler handed a wad of cash to Marco. "Get what you want and bowl as long as they keep the doors open," the older werewolf grinned.

"I can go?" Ashe stared at his father in shock.

"Go have a good time, son. Just stay out of trouble." Aedan patted Ashe's shoulder.

"Come on, tapeworm," Marco crooked an elbow around Sali's neck. "I know you're hungry." Sali whooped as they walked through the corridor of Cloud Chief Combined.

Chad and Jeremy had to wait until nearly ten, but Diane and Neil Booth finally went to bed. They'd agreed to allow the boys to stay up and watch a late movie on television. As soon as their bedroom door was closed, Chad was on the stolen walkie-talkie, contacting Philip Raymond.

"What the?" Nathan had just relieved Roger and Toby, two of William Winkler's Pack, in order to help Aedan guard the community. Nathan

stared at the night sky as the first bottle rocket went up and exploded nearly a quarter of a mile away.

"Let's go," Aedan muttered grimly and both vampires swept away, faster than a human eye might follow.

~

"That's our cue," Jeremy snickered as he and Chad stood in the front yard, watching as fountains of fireworks burst in the night sky. Both ran for Diane Booth's small import. Jeremy slid into the driver's seat and started the car quickly.

When Chad was buckled in on the passenger side, Jeremy pulled away, driving toward the entrance to Cloud Chief as quickly and silently as he could. Less than two minutes later, Neil Booth and his wife were in the front yard, discovering that Diane's car was missing (along with both boys) and that someone was setting off fireworks in Cloud Chief.

"That's over the O'Neill's pasture," Neil muttered grimly. "Probably kids, but the grass may be dry enough for it to catch. Get in my truck, Diane. We'll help the O'Neills first and worry about those boys later. They're probably heading toward Clinton right now."

"Halfway there is more like it," Diane said. "Let's go. If that pasture catches on fire, we'll have to get the lambs out."

~

Philip had carefully planned the raid. His backpack fit well enough even after he changed to mountain lion, and it was simple enough to sneak out of the house and race away as an animal, until he arrived at the designated pasture.

Macy and Luanne had gone on and on about the lambs and calves in the O'Neill's pastures, and had visited with Dori and Wynn several times. Well, if he were lucky, he'd take some of those stupid animals out with the fireworks and draw everyone's attention away from what he intended to do.

Kneeling beneath the window of Chad and Jeremy's shared bedroom, Philip cut the screen with a pocketknife and then pulled the small bottle of gasoline from his backpack. He'd siphoned away a small amount of fuel from a resident's car they'd left parked outside their garage.

Uncapping the bottle, Philip stuffed a piece of cloth inside it and then pulled out the book of matches he'd found in his mother's things. She'd quit smoking but still had a few things left over, including matchbooks from restaurants they'd visited before their lives were turned upside down.

The gasoline-soaked cloth caught fire quickly. Stuffing the bottle inside the screen, Philip pulled his backpack on again, turned back to mountain lion and ran.

~

"I'm just thankful it didn't start a fire," Marcus stated flatly. Aedan and Nathan were examining the ground where the fireworks originated, hoping to find tracks.

"Do you smell that, Aedan?" Nathan looked up at Cloud Chief's other vampire.

"Smells animal," Aedan agreed. "Marcus, can you tell us what this scent is?"

Marcus walked over to the two vampires and drew in a breath. "Mountain lion," he declared right away. "And it's fresh."

"You think it might have been after the lambs or calves and was scared away by the fireworks?" Aedan offered Marcus a puzzled glance.

"I've heard of mountain lions in Oklahoma, but usually they're reported elsewhere. Jonas!" Marcus called. "We may have a real predator here. Have you had any livestock come up missing?"

Jonas O'Neill, followed by his wife Sharon, was walking the field, just to make sure no sparks lay in the grass to start a fire. The sheep and lambs were cowering in a far corner of the field, still frightened from the loud noise of the unexpected fireworks display. Jonas immediately joined Marcus.

"What did you find?" Jonas asked.

"Mountain lion," Marcus replied. "Have you lost anything?"

"No, everything's accounted for."

"Then we may have a hunt if more tracks show up. I don't want anything threatening the livestock," Marcus said.

"What did you find?" Amos Thompson joined the others. He'd come to help with the animals if needed.

"Mountain lion scent," Jonas sighed. "You should keep an eye on your poultry, Amos."

"I will. They're all locked inside the chicken house right now, but we'll watch." Amos nodded at Jonas.

"Aedan, I smell smoke," Nathan said.

"Yes. I smell it too," Aedan turned toward the scent. "Look. Isn't that smoke near the Booth home?" An orange explosion lit the night sky, with a loud boom following close behind.

"Neil!" Diane Booth shouted. She'd been talking with Adele Evans and Denise DeLuca in a corner of the field, only now realizing that her home was ablaze.

"Get the pumper truck!" Marcus shouted. Aedan and Nathan had already disappeared; running toward the Booth home faster than the others could imagine getting there.

CHAPTER 15

This looks intriguing, Ren sent to Ashe. He'd shown up at the bowling alley and seemed content to watch Sali, Ashe, Cori and Marco bowl.

You should try it, it's fun, Ashe returned.

You know I cannot reveal myself. That could become interference. Aside, of course, from frightening your friends.

Too bad you can't disguise yourself as me. I could turn to mist and watch you bowl, Ashe ducked his head to hide a grin.

I can do that, Ren said. *That will work quite fine.*

You're kidding? Really? How can we do this?

Follow me. Tell the others you are going to get a drink of water, Ren rose from an empty seat. Again, no other had taken it, choosing other seats instead. Ashe found himself wishing for that trick more and more.

"I need a drink of water," Ashe tapped Sali on the shoulder. Sali nodded before turning back to watch Marco toss a ball down the lane. Ashe followed Ren, who was making his way toward the water fountain located just outside the restrooms.

"Turn to mist, I have us shielded," Ren said, once they reached the tiny hall outside the restrooms. Ashe blinked at the tall, blue youth before going to mist. He watched in astonishment as Ren altered his appearance, becoming Ashe's identical twin. "Now, I bowl," Ren chuckled mischievously before turning and walking toward Sali and the others.

"I have achieved my objective," Ren laughed and clapped after throwing a strike on his third attempt. Ashe, hovering above Ren's head, sent mindspeech.

Dude, you have to talk like me, too, Ashe reminded the Larentii boy.

"Dude, that was awesome," Ren (as Ashe) said as he grinned at Sali, who rose to bowl next. Ren went one further and high-fived Sali. If Ashe had been solid, he would have laughed aloud at Ren's antics. Not only did the Larentii sound like him, he was now acting like him. Ren didn't hear Marco's cell phone ringing, but Ashe did.

"It's Mr. Winkler," Marco pulled the cell from his pocket. "Mr. Winkler?" A note of surprise was in Marco's voice, since it was only a few minutes past midnight. They weren't late. Ashe maneuvered his mist until he hovered over Marco's head so he could hear both sides of the conversation.

"Marco, have you seen Chad and Jeremy?" Winkler asked.

"No, sir. Aren't they supposed to be at home? I thought they were under house arrest."

"They are. But they managed to sneak away and take Mrs. Booth's car. After they left, the Booth home burned to the ground."

"Do you want us to come back?" Marco was standing in a moment, bowling forgotten.

"I think it's for the best. We may need your help tracking those two."

"We'll be there in half an hour," Marco replied and ended the call. "Come on, everybody. Chad and Jeremy are missing and it looks like they burned their house down behind them."

Pierce Ingram changed the bandage on his arm as he sat in the convenience store parking lot outside Clinton. His motorcycle was already gassed up—he'd taken cash from Nick Lawford's wallet when he'd knocked the agent out. He'd chained the agent to a tree, determined to get information from Nick before killing him.

Pierce had returned to Lake Altus to accomplish those things when he discovered the agent gone. Whatever had chased him afterward wasn't a normal man. Pierce had the evidence to prove it— two very deep gouges in his left upper arm.

If he hadn't turned around and fired the agent's pistol, he'd have been taken down. Pierce grimaced as he slapped a fresh bandage over the wounds. Pierce Ingram wasn't his real name. It was the name on his current ID, though. He'd gone through several incarnations since coming to Oklahoma. So many, in fact, during his lifetime that he hardly remembered his real name any longer.

"Mister, how'd you like to make a few buck," two youths now stood beside Pierce's motorcycle.

"How?" Pierce lifted an eyebrow in their direction. The agent he'd captured hadn't carried much cash and Pierce spent most of that on food, gas and bandages.

"Fifty bucks, if you buy a case of beer for us," one of the boys replied.

"Show me the money first," Pierce growled. The two boys looked at each other and grinned.

Ten minutes later, Pierce handed the case of beer over to the boys and slid onto his motorcycle. He watched silently as the boys loaded the beer into the small import they were driving. Pierce was about to turn away when one of the boys spoke again.

"Sure glad that stupid human kid helped us out," the teen laughed. Pierce pulled his hand back from the starter, deciding to wait and follow the two boys instead.

"Dang." Sali glanced at Ashe. Ashe was back to himself and Ren was shielded and standing beside him as they stared at the burned ruin of the Booth home. Mrs. Booth was leaning on her husband and wiping tears away. Mr. Booth seemed stunned as he held onto his wife.

Marco and Cori volunteered to go looking for the missing boys and had already driven away. Half the community had emptied for the same reason—adults had climbed into vehicles to search for Chad and Jeremy.

"Ashe, Sali can come with us," Adele walked up beside the boys. "Marcus and Denise are out searching with the others, and they said Sali can spend the night."

"Mom, do you think Chad and Jeremy did this?" Ashe swept a hand toward the smoldering remains of the Booth's home.

"I don't know, hon. Mr. Winkler says Director Jennings will send arson investigators tomorrow, to check things over. If we find those boys, Nathan will place compulsion. I think your father may be too angry to do it. This may have exposed all of us—two big fires so close together, not to mention the fireworks."

"Fireworks?" Sali turned to Ashe's mother.

"Somebody set some off in one of the O'Neill's pastures. We all ran in that direction to make sure the field didn't burn, and then the house blew up and burned to the ground. We got the pumper truck out but we weren't able to save much."

"Yeah." Ashe could see that for himself. "Where are Mr. and Mrs. Booth going to stay?"

"Marcie is moving in with Sali's parents, so the Booths can have Pat Roberts' old house," Adele patted Sali's shoulder. "I said Sali can stay with us as much as he likes. We have an extra bedroom that we don't use."

"Really? That's cool, Mrs. Evans," Sali was excited over the prospect of spending even more time with Ashe.

"Aedan, Nathan and some of the others will rebuild this house. They should have it finished in two or three weeks at most," Adele said.

"What will Marcus do, since Chad and Jeremy broke parole?" Ashe asked.

"Ashe, that's none of our concern. Come on, let's go home. It's way past your bedtime. But," Adele held up a hand at Ashe's protest, "You and Sali can stay up and watch movies and have popcorn if you want."

Ren, following along invisibly, climbed into the Evans' SUV right behind Ashe.

～

Pierce was tired of listening to both boys whine about being punished. He'd gathered early on that they'd sneaked away when they weren't supposed to, and were now drinking beer and throwing empty cans in a rural ditch outside Cordell.

Pierce didn't care that they'd broken the rules; he just wanted them to shut up and go home so he could follow them. They'd mentioned names of several children, calling them empties, and one of those names was the one Pierce most wanted to hear.

～

"That empty will pay sometime; just wait and see," Chad sneered, crumpling another empty can and tossing it into a weed-filled ditch.

"Yeah. It's always Ashe this and Ashe that. It'll be worse since he won that stupid contest and gave the money away." Jeremy threw his can farther than Chad, just to show he could.

"Come on, last two," Chad popped the tab on a beer and handed it to Jeremy before grabbing the last one for himself.

"Too bad; we shoulda asked for two cases," Jeremy hiccupped.

"Yeah. We'll know next time," Chad burped rudely.

～

"What's that—down that road?" Marcus pointed toward a car sitting in the middle of a narrow, dirt road between barbed wire fences. Winkler was driving a Winkler Security van with the lights turned off. The only things they'd seen on the road so far were a skunk and a raccoon.

"Let's look," Winkler shoved the van into reverse and backed up to turn down the road.

171

~

Pierce was hiding in brush behind a barbed wire fence. His motorcycle was parked and well hidden farther down. He heard the van before the two teens did; both were now quite drunk and laughing. Pierce ducked lower so he wouldn't be seen as the van slowly pulled near before turning its headlights on full, bathing both boys in a bright light.

~

"Both of them stinking drunk," Winkler muttered as Marcus hauled Chad from the back of the van, narrowly avoiding Chad's vomit as the boy threw up. Jeremy, still inside the van, began to vomit as well. Winkler cursed. He'd have to get the van cleaned before he could drive it again—a smell like that offended any werewolf's nose.

Aedan and Nathan watched as Chad and Jeremy were pulled from Winkler's van. They'd appeared after hearing the van pull through the gate into the community. Winkler had driven Diane Booth's car back, after helping Marcus shove both teens into the van.

The smell of beer had been everywhere when they'd picked the boys up—Chad and Jeremy weren't used to drinking and they hadn't been neat about it, either.

"Why are we here?" Chad had finished vomiting and only now noticed his surroundings. The van was parked outside Pat Roberts' old house, where Marcie Pruitt now lived.

"Your house burned to the ground while you were out drinking," Marcus growled. "Know anything about that, or the fireworks that were set off as a distraction?"

"Marcus, they're too drunk," Aedan muttered. "We'll have to question them tomorrow, after they sober up." Aedan turned and zipped away. Nathan shook his head over the entire state of affairs before following Aedan.

~

Pierce let his motorcycle idle as he sat outside a barbed wire fence, searching for the opening. He'd seen the van and car drive through, but the entrance had disappeared before he could reach it. He'd kept his headlight off and stayed far enough behind that his quarry hadn't seen him, and they'd managed to escape somehow. Now, he couldn't detect an opening anywhere.

While he was searching, his cell phone rang. That shouldn't be—it was a disposable phone and only one other person had the number. That one wasn't scheduled to call until the following day. Several seconds passed before Pierce decided to answer.

"Hello?" he said.

"I was hoping you'd answer, Pierce," Wildrif had a smile in his voice. "If you'll give me a week or two and agree to meet with my representative, I think we can arrange to get what you want."

"Who the hell are you?" Pierce growled into the phone.

"A friend," Wildrif replied. "And if you want to get your boy away from the ones that look human but aren't, then you'll do what I tell you."

"There's no cure for stupid," Sali muttered as he and Ashe sat down to breakfast. Sali and Ashe had checked their email earlier, learning from Cori that Chad and Jeremy had sneaked away the night before, convinced somebody to buy beer for them and then proceeded to get as drunk as possible before throwing up in Winkler's van.

Cori also informed Ashe through email that Chad and Jeremy had been too drunk to answer questions about the fire. Marcus was waiting until they slept it off before questioning them.

"Nathan and your father will be assisting Marcus tonight," Adele set a glass of milk down for Ashe. "That means Toby and Roger will be patrolling Cloud Chief until they're finished."

"Mom, I don't get that Chad and Jeremy," Ashe began (he'd almost said Chump and Wormy, but held back), "would set their house on fire. All their stuff was in there. Jeremy always talked about his video games, so I don't think they had anything to do with it."

"Are you defending them?" Sali stared at Ashe.

"I'm just saying that's not like them," Ashe spread blackberry jelly on his toast and crunched into it. "Jeremy liked his stuff too much. Chad, too. The fireworks, though, sound exactly like them."

"Your father says they found evidence that a mountain lion may be in the area," Adele interrupted. "Sali, if you find any evidence of a mountain lion, you need to tell your father. A real predator like that could kill lambs, calves or the Thompson's poultry. Marcus says he'll arrange a hunt if the mountain lion comes back."

"I won't get to go on a hunt for another year," Sali muttered glumly. Ashe judiciously remained silent and barely blinked when Elizabeth Frasier's ghost slipped through the kitchen window and stood near the sink, staring at him.

"Salidar, your time will come," Adele smiled at the young werewolf.

"Mom says the same thing," Sali grumped.

"A mountain lion could be dangerous, Sal," Ashe pointed out, and then lifted an eyebrow in surprise when Elizabeth's ghost nodded in agreement.

"But what will I get out of this?" Vince grumbled. He stood in line outside a deli in Silver Spring, Maryland, waiting to get inside and grab a sandwich for lunch. Wildrif had promised a lot of money after Director Jennings retired. After all, everyone was aware that a new Director meant a new staff, and Vince had worked for Director Jennings for nearly fifteen years. He was resentful that he might lose his job or receive a demotion when a new Director took over.

"I'll arrange payment. A half million if you keep funneling information in the same direction," Wildrif replied. "I told you there would be substantial money involved."

"A million would be better," Vince pointed out.

"You'll have to do more than you're doing for that kind of cash," Wildrif laughed and hung up.

~

Diamond was ready to strangle Hilbah. The seer was worthless and Diamond had no idea why Friesianna kept him at her side, dispensing information. Hilbah couldn't find his own shoes on a good day.

"You should be able to see the Destroyers, as close as they are," Diamond growled. "My medallion is groaning from being within a hundred clicks." Diamond grasped Hilbah's silk robe in his fist, bringing the seer's face on a level with his own.

"But something is interfering," Hilbah squeaked.

"Bah." Diamond shoved Hilbah away. They'd been forced to inhabit an abandoned cellar outside the small town of Cordell and the shelter was ancient, the walls cracked, steps broken, and with spiders and crickets inhabiting it before Diamond sent them scurrying with a blast of power. Ruby, Diamond's brother, stared distastefully at the brackish water standing in a corner of their claustrophobic, darkened refuge, expecting a snake to emerge at any moment.

"Brother, we both know the only talent Hilbah has is flattering the Queen," Ruby said, keeping his eyes on the small pool of water.

"I'll keep looking for them," Hilbah backed away from Diamond a second time. Both he and Diamond jumped as Ruby leveled a blast at the water moccasin snake that crawled from the standing water.

CHAPTER 16

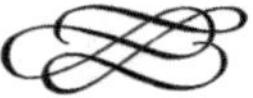

$\mathcal{A}$she and Sali watched from a distance as Director Jennings' arson investigators moved through the burned rubble of the Booth home. Cori and Marco walked up beside them and Cori offered a soda to each of the boys. Ashe gave Cori a grin before turning the cap on the orange soda she'd given him and drinking.

"Have they found anything yet?" Marco wore cargo shorts, sunglasses and no shirt. Winkler's Second, Trajan, was forcing Marco to work out and run every morning, so Marco was more muscular than he'd ever been.

"Nah. Not yet, anyway," Sali replied. Jonas O'Neill and Frank Dodd had come to help, but their assistance hadn't been needed. Now, both men stood beneath a shade tree nearby, watching the two investigators sift through burned remains of household items.

"Heard from Hayes that Chump and Wormy may be up and around," Marco grinned. Cori slipped an arm around Marco's waist and he bent his head to drop a kiss on her hair.

"Hey, no PDA," Sali grumped. "I'm blinded by syrupy affection, now."

"You wouldn't know syrupy affection if it jumped up and kissed your butt," Marco flipped Sali's ear.

"Marco, if you're going to wrestle your brother, I want to stand over here," Cori moved away to stand beside Ashe.

"We're not wrestling; the tapeworm would lose," Marco tried to flip Sali's ear a second time, but Sali jumped aside too quickly for Marco to land a second hit.

"I wish we could find out what's going on with Chad and Jeremy," Cori whispered beside Ashe. She knew that Ashe's exceptional hearing would pick up her words. Ashe stared at Cori for a moment.

"There might be," he mumbled, loud enough for Cori to hear.

"Marco, stop fooling around with Sali and let's take a walk," Cori moved to link an arm with Marco's. Ashe pulled Sali along, and soon all four were walking toward Cori's home, a quarter mile away.

"They're not looking," Marco turned to peer over his shoulder. Ashe took the opportunity to turn his three companions to mist before blazing toward Pat Roberts' old house.

"Mom, we only meant to go into Cordell. We didn't burn down the house," Jeremy growled over a large bowl of breakfast cereal. Chad, seated across the small kitchen table, was eating his own bowl of flakes and not talking. "It's that kid's fault—Philip or whatever. We just asked him to set off the fireworks. We had nothing to do with the fire. Why would we burn all our stuff?"

"Jeremy Alan Booth, you'd better be telling us the truth." Diane Booth was as angry as Ashe had ever seen her. He and his companions hovered in a nearby corner as mist, watching the exchange between Jeremy and his mother. Neil Booth sat at one end of the table, listening and watching both boys carefully.

"Do you think he was retaliating after that family's mobile home burned?" Neil finally spoke, his words thoughtful and deliberate. Ashe found himself wondering why Jeremy couldn't be more like his dad, even as he mentally nodded.

It made sense—all those kids liked Luanne. A lot. And Philip had asked to ride with her on the trip from Dallas. They all relaxed around

Luanne. She had something the others didn't. For Chad and Jeremy to be responsible for her house burning down, well, the others were likely still angry about that, only Philip's anger might be more volatile.

Arson, after all, was a serious crime in the human world and had Chad and Jeremy been judged by human authorities, likely jail time would have been handed out instead of house arrest.

We've heard enough, Ashe sent to his passengers and sped through the roof of Pat Roberts' old house. He didn't stop until they all stood on the back deck outside his home.

"You think this was retaliation?" Cori flopped into a lawn chair. Marco sat on the deck beside her chair to listen while Cori absently ran fingers through his dark hair. Ashe ignored the affection and hoped Sali would, too.

"It makes sense." Ashe flopped on the deck, too, allowing Sali to have the other lawn chair.

"I don't know how you turn everything to mist and still hold onto your soda," Cori toed Ashe's knee with a sandal.

"I'm talented," Ashe grinned. "But you can't tell Mom or Dad what we did. I'll get grounded again."

"My lips are sealed," Cori grinned back.

~

"How much?" The warlock schooled his face. He'd dabbled in the less than white arts, now and then. And for the right price, he'd go farther than that.

"Fifty thousand," Obediah Tanner said, pouring out a drink for his guest. "Seventy-five, if you bring your friends." Obediah trusted Wildrif's judgment in this, deciding that Wildrif would only contact the willing and talented enough, who would also settle for the money offered. "And no questions asked," Obediah added, handing the glass of whiskey over.

"And it's to take down a boundary and pick up a few kids?" the warlock asked his second question.

"Yep. Think you can do that?"

"Absolutely. Half up front," the warlock said, sipping his drink.

"A third up front and my guards stay at a designated location outside. Bring the kids to them and the rest of the money is yours. We have business to do with other clients after that," Obediah countered. "When you get the money, you vanish. Is that clear?"

"Completely," the warlock agreed dryly.

~

"You know what he looks like?" Wildrif spoke over the phone.

"Yeah. I know what he looks like. I've tailed him twice and he doesn't even realize he's being followed," Trina Lucas, a werewolf and a nurse for a clinic in the Washington, D.C. area, replied. She was a friend of Josiah's, and Josiah had given her name to Wildrif as someone who might be able to take Vince down as soon as all necessary information had been gleaned from Director Jennings' assistant.

"Make it look like an accident, or maybe mauled by an animal," Wildrif said. "Josiah will make it up to you."

"He'd better," Trina said and ended the call.

~

"So, you asked Philip Raymond to set off fireworks?" Nathan placed compulsion while Marcus, Winkler, Aedan and Director Jennings looked on. The arson investigators had pinpointed the cause of the fire earlier, and identified the accelerant. Neither Chad nor Jeremy knew anything about the house fire. Both agreed in their story regarding Philip Raymond and the box of fireworks, however.

"How did you get the fireworks to him?" Nathan asked. Marcus leaned against a kitchen wall in Pat Roberts' old house, growling softly as Chad explained that he and Jeremy had sneaked out when Diane Booth had left the house to run errands in Cordell. They'd left the box of fireworks in tall weeds behind the O'Neill's tool shed.

"The Raymond kid must have been keeping tabs on all the guards,"

Winkler whispered to Aedan as Nathan continued questioning Chad and Jeremy. Aedan nodded at Winkler's observation.

If the kid was smart enough, there were gaps in even the best of guarding jobs he, Nathan and the werewolves could do. After all, there were only two guards on duty most of the time. Aedan and Nathan had the entire community to guard at night. Granted they were fast and could run from one end of the community to the other in very little time, but they were at opposite ends at times, leaving a window of time for Philip to escape his home and sneak away if he were so minded.

"You don't think that kid can mist, like Ashe and Elizabeth, do you?" Winkler went on softly.

"No idea," Aedan returned. "But we'll find out later tonight."

"Yeah," Winkler agreed with a slight nod. Philip Raymond's house was now their next destination, after Marcus was satisfied with Nathan's questioning of Chad and Jeremy. Marcus would likely be in contact with the Grand Master quickly, to learn what additional punishment should be levied against both boys since they'd violated house arrest.

"Luanne, I think you need to be with Philip in the next few minutes," Ashe appeared in Luanne's bedroom, sounding out of breath. Ren, invisible to all except Ashe, appeared immediately after.

"Why? What happened?" Luanne dropped the book she'd been reading and stared at Ashe.

"Well, uh, I just came from Chad and Jeremy's questioning. Both say they asked Philip to set off fireworks. Now, everybody thinks Philip burned down the Booth's house and my dad and the others will be coming to question him in just a few minutes. I think you need to be there, Luanne."

"Yeah, I probably do," Luanne stared at the earnest expression on Ashe's face. "But how do we get past the werewolves that are guarding the community? And do we need to tell Mom and Dad?"

"Yeah, your mom and dad can come, too. I'll take all of you over and the werewolves won't know." Ashe almost jumped when Elizabeth Frasier's ghost walked through Luanne's bedroom wall and sat on the edge of Luanne's bed.

"I wish she wouldn't just show up like that," Luanne muttered to herself. Ashe, with his sharp hearing, heard Luanne perfectly.

"You can see her too?" Ashe stared at Luanne.

"She's been here for days," Luanne grumbled. "And she keeps doing this," Luanne held out her arms in a wide sweep, lifting them upward until they were straight over her head. "I don't know what that means, but she keeps doing it. None of the others see her," Luanne added, as she and Ashe both watched Elizabeth echo the motions Luanne had just made.

"Well, that's the first time I've seen her do it," Ashe chewed his lip in consternation. "But we need to get to Philip, I think. You might be able to calm things down a little when they come to question him."

"All right. Let's go tell Mom and Dad, and then we'll go."

As it turned out, Linda and Peter Jansen insisted on walking to the Raymond's house. Ashe, giving Luanne a nod, misted home after floating overhead until the Jansens arrived at Philip's house.

Roger and Toby, the werewolves, didn't like it when Peter Jansen explained that they wanted to visit with Jackie and Philip Raymond, but finally agreed, watching as the small family walked from one mobile home to the other. Jackie Raymond answered the door and allowed the Jansens inside.

"Dang. I wanted to be there when they did the questioning, but I took a chance, being with Chad and Jeremy," Ashe fumed as he paced inside his bedroom. His mother had already checked on him once, shortly after he'd gotten home. Ren, sitting on the bed, calmly watched as Ashe scuffled first one way and then another across his bedroom carpet.

"You're building up a generous amount of static electricity," Ren pointed out eventually, staring at Ashe's socks.

"Yeah?" Ashe reached over and touched Ren's shoulder, hearing a satisfying pop as the energy released.

"Thank you," Ren smiled widely. "Static is good for a quick snack."

"You're kidding? You ate that?" Ashe stopped worrying about Philip's questioning for a moment to gape at Ren.

"In a manner of speaking. Although such a weak charge will not sustain me for more than a few of your Earth seconds," Ren chuckled.

"Dude, that is seriously cool," Ashe breathed.

"I told you when we first met that I absorbed energy as a food source," Ren said.

"Yeah, but you said sunlight, with everything else being," Ashe didn't finish, Ren beat him to it.

"Broccoli," Ren smiled.

"Yeah. So, static is broccoli?"

"I enjoy static. It may be the equivalent of one of your fizzy drinks."

"Dude, that is messed up and cool at the same time."

"Marcus," Aedan held the Cloud Chief Packmaster back. Philip had just confessed under Nathan's compulsion, admitting that he'd deliberately burned down the Booth home in retribution for the Jansen's house fire. He, Marcus, Nathan, Winkler and Director Jennings had come to question Philip Raymond regarding the Booth's house fire.

They'd all been surprised that Luanne and her parents were there, and also surprised that Philip didn't even attempt to argue when Nathan placed compulsion. Philip hadn't complained or interfered when Nathan instructed Jackie Raymond to remain calm while they questioned her son, and then commanded Philip to answer all questions truthfully.

Marcus growled softly, but Aedan had a hand on the werewolf's shoulder as Philip expressed his dissatisfaction with the punishment given to Chad and Jeremy.

"Luanne could have died," Philip muttered. "And you just give those two a slap on the wrist. It isn't fair that we were dragged into this. It isn't fair that Lizzie died. It isn't fair. None of this is fair."

Philip's face was drawn in an angry frown and he tossed out a hand in a helpless gesture. "We don't belong here. Those two jerks made that clear enough. Lizzie told me they called us empty. They were out at the fence when they were supposed to be locked up inside their house. Lizzie said they were rude to her. I think they were rude to Eddy, too, but he won't talk about it."

Marcus cursed. Chad and Jeremy had gotten out multiple times, it seemed. He and Nathan hadn't thought to ask them about all the times they'd left the house. He was going to be more creative in his punishment after this.

Director Jennings rubbed his forehead as he listened to Philip. This experiment was obviously a failure, and people had died as a result. Not just Elizabeth Frasier, but three Cordell residents had died and one other was in critical condition in an Oklahoma City hospital.

That didn't include Agent Nick Lawford, who was still in a coma. "I've heard enough," Bill raised his hand, stopping Nathan in mid-question. "It's obvious this was a mistake. I'll make arrangements to have these families moved within two weeks. Winkler, if you'll come with me, I have to make calls to some of my associates. A safer place has to be found where we can move these people." Bill Jennings stalked toward the door of the Raymond home, Winkler following closely behind.

"We're moving again?" Jackie Raymond sounded close to tears.

Ashe, we're moving again. Director Jennings says it was a mistake to bring us

here. Luanne just sent mindspeech to me, Edward informed Ashe. *I don't want to leave. I like it here. It's quiet,* Edward added.

Yeah. I liked having you here, too, Edward, Ashe returned with a sigh. *Did he say when you'll move?*

Luanne says he has to find a safer place for us, but he wants to do it in the next two weeks, I think. This is awful. Edward was upset and it came through in his mental voice. *And I tried sending to Macy and Keith, but they don't seem to hear me.*

Dude, they'll know soon enough, Ashe kicked a toe against his desk chair. Ren still sat at the end of Ashe's bed, listening to Edward's mindspeech. He still was unable to hear Ashe unless Ashe directed it to the tall Larentii youth.

You're right. We'll all know soon enough. Ashe, we've moved eight times in the last six months. I want to go somewhere and stay, Edward said.

I understand, Ashe replied. Edward didn't send anything else.

"This is so messed up," Ashe pulled the covers back on his bed. "Dude, I have a sleeping bag if you want to spend the night," Ashe offered to Ren.

"No, I must go. I admit, this is far more perplexing than I thought it might be, and I find myself more involved in it than I should be," Ren confessed. "I will see you again soon, I promise." He disappeared and Ashe sighed again.

❧

"Those children are being moved again," Adele set a plate of ham and eggs in front of Ashe the following morning.

"Yeah. I got mindspeech from Edward," Ashe said, picking up his fork.

"Ashe, once they're gone, that killer may disappear, too, since they're the reason he came here to begin with," Adele pointed out. "And that means that we can go back to the store. Jason and Marcie are doing a good job, but I hate imposing on them like this."

Ashe knew his mother itched to get back to work—she'd already cleaned out closets that didn't really need cleaning and spent much of her day weeding and fertilizing the community vegetable garden.

"Mom, they still need to catch that guy. We can't just hope he leaves and follows those families. He'll kill again; I know it. I think Director Jennings and Mr. Winkler know it, too."

"You're right, honey. I wasn't thinking about that. I just," Adele's hand went to her throat. Ashe knew she was recalling the man's hands on her neck as he'd threatened her. He also remembered the other deaths; the body strangled with a chain—this killer liked to go for the throat.

"Can I go see Edward after breakfast? I'd like to spend as much time with him as I can before they leave."

"If you want to, hon."

Ashe kept eating, even as Elizabeth's ghost floated into the kitchen and settled against the sink to watch.

"Wynn and Dori came to see Luanne and Macy, and Macy hugged Wynn and cried," Edward swung his legs on the small porch of his mobile home. Keith and Bryce had joined Edward and Ashe, and all sat against the outside wall of the home, talking.

"Dori invited Lu and Macy to her house, so that's where they are right now," Edward added. "They told Philip he had to stay inside his house and not come out. I haven't heard what they're doing with those other two."

"Yeah. Nathan probably told Philip he couldn't go outside," Ashe nodded. He didn't bother to explain that compulsion had been employed. He knew that without having to ask.

Compulsion was likely employed to keep Chad and Jeremy from wandering off as well. Ashe hunched his shoulders angrily at the thought. If Chump and Wormy had just kept away, Edward and the others could have stayed all summer. Now they were being forced away from their homes again.

"It's just not fair," Keith muttered, surprising Ashe. "We were just getting used to this. It's nice to be able to go outside and throw a football around without worrying you'll hit a car. And you can actually see the stars at night. I never knew there were so many of them."

"Edward, there's something I've been meaning to tell you," Ashe said. "About your mom."

"What about her?" Edward was immediately interested. After all, he barely remembered her; he'd been so small when she died.

"My mom doesn't know it, but last year I found her unconscious on the passenger side of her old truck, weaving down a road outside Cordell. I had to mist in and drive her truck home. My parents still think Mom managed to drive herself back, even though she doesn't remember doing it. She didn't. Those Dark Elemaiya tried to kill her like that last year."

"So, that's what happened," Edward said softly. "Can I tell my dad?"

"When you're away from here," Ashe nodded. "I don't need to be grounded again if that information gets out."

"Understood," Edward said.

"They'd ground you for saving your mother?" Bryce stared at Ashe.

"For waiting this long to tell them," Ashe replied. He was grateful that Edward, Bryce and Keith hadn't been at the Awards Assembly to see how winning the essay contest had turned into such an embarrassing failure. All because he'd gotten upset over Elizabeth's death and misted home after saving someone else's life. "We're not destined to have normal lives," Ashe observed philosophically.

"Here comes Sali," Edward dropped off the porch as the young werewolf approached.

"The Queen would be better off without him," Ruby grumbled as they waited at a local diner for a waitress to bring their meals. Hilbah had been left behind in the cellar—most unwillingly. He was just as hungry as Diamond and Ruby, but Diamond was in charge and he'd left the whining Miriasu behind. Diamond ordered a third meal to go, and he didn't care that it might be cold when he brought it to Hilbah.

"Have any ideas how that might be accomplished?" Diamond studied his brother sitting across the small, Formica table in Betsy's Diner. "With Hilbah and his foolishness out of the way, she'd be forced to bring Rabis back. At least he knows what he's doing when he opens his mouth."

"Rabis won't come willingly," Ruby pointed out.

"But he is subject to the crown, just as the rest of us are. He'll be compelled to do as commanded."

"He'll resent it. After all, Gwynitha was his daughter," Ruby sipped the glass of iced tea he'd been served.

"Old news. Surely, he's over his daughter's death by now. And when she was Queen, she kept us in the regular guard, if you recall." Diamond halted his comments as the young waitress set a plate of food in front of him and asked if he and Ruby needed anything else. Diamond shook his head and waited for her footsteps to recede before continuing the conversation with his brother.

"We were always stronger than those fools Gwynitha kept around her. She never saw Friesianna coming. Too bad she never asked her father to look out for betrayal from within. She kept Rabis busy searching for King Baltis and his horde."

Ruby cut into his meatloaf. He'd been on worlds from one end of the universes to the other, and all of them had some variation of meatloaf available.

"She was always convinced that the Bright and Dark could never be on the same world together," Diamond agreed, dipping into a bowl of chicken and dumplings. "Yet, here we are. The only danger I see is that we kill some of them, they kill some of us."

"It is enjoyable at times to watch them die," Ruby observed with a smile.

~

Certain that he was being followed; Vince ducked inside the small bookshop and waited for his tail to catch up with him. Except it didn't —they'd stopped when he stopped.

Vince wanted to report this to Director Jennings, but that would require that he be honest with the Director. That would be a mistake —one that would lead to a prison cell. And there was always the possibility that the Director already suspected him of passing information to the other side; that meant the tail was sent by Director Jennings to begin with.

Vince didn't know which might be worse—having the ones to whom he'd sold information trailing after him, or the Director and his many operatives. Either way, it could turn out badly for Vince. Cursing softly under his breath, he barged through the bookshop door and onto a busy sidewalk to continue his journey.

CHAPTER 17

"Full moon is less than a week away," Adele Evans pointed out over dinner that evening. "Can you believe it? Honey, your birthday is less than a month away. Have you decided what you want?"

Ashe was picking at green beans while he listened to his mother make conversation. He and Sali spent the day with Edward, Bryce and Keith, while Macy and Luanne had gone to visit with Dori and Wynn. Cori and Marco had driven to Oklahoma City to shop for the day, but Ashe had heard Marco's car drive past moments earlier and knew they'd made it home safely.

"I don't know what I want," Ashe replied listlessly.

"Honey, things will work out."

"But what if they don't? Mom, those people are hunting Edward and the others. They already got Elizabeth. The minute those kids drive past our boundary, somebody could be waiting for them. Edward and the others could die, too. Stupid Chump and Wormy."

"Chump and Wormy will be locked up inside Old Harold's house. It has no windows and Marcus will hold the keys," Aedan walked through the middle door and sat down at the dinner table with a sigh. "Marcus phoned the Grand Master last night. From the conversation I overheard he was not happy, and it's likely the Head of the Vampire Council will not be pleased, either."

Ashe realized his father was more upset than his face or his words indicated. It had likely taken a great deal of money and work to get the housing trucked in and arrangements made through Director Jennings' department just to move the families to Cloud Chief. And now, thanks to Cloud Chief's two mischief-makers, they had to leave again, less than a month after they'd arrived.

"Aedan, surely they won't try to blame you and Nathan for this," Adele reached out a hand to touch her husband's sleeve.

"I hope this is not so," Aedan's Welsh lilt came out with his words. "We were promised another vampire to help us after Old Harold's death, but that help has not come. Nathan and I are stretched to the limit as it is, m'love."

Ashe stared at his plate, troubled over his father's statement. Aedan never complained about guarding the community. Never.

"You've called them already." Now it was Adele's turn to stare at her plate, half her food uneaten and growing cold.

"I left a message, Adele. I am obligated to report on the happenings here." Aedan rose from the table. "Finish your dinner, son," he said and walked through the kitchen door, closing it softly behind him.

"This could turn out so badly," Adele sighed.

Pierce used his small, handheld GPS to track the coordinates the new contact had given. Wildrif was an unusual name, but then Pierce had heard plenty of those over the years.

The location turned out to be an old, broken cellar in the middle of an Oklahoma field. A house had likely stood nearby long ago, but traces of it had disappeared beneath tall grass and weeds after many years.

Parking his motorcycle, Pierce cautiously approached the old cellar, worried that Wildrif might have misled him or sold him out. A raised, grass-covered mound with a cavernous opening on one side greeted him. A few brave wildflowers grew in the cracks of the broken concrete portal that once held a heavy door.

"Welcome," Ruby and Diamond appeared from nothing at Pierce's side. "Our accommodations aren't the best, but we won't be here long." Pierce was ushered toward the gaping hole in the ground.

~

"They plan to move the children in three days," Wildrif informed Obediah Tanner.

"So, we have to move in two nights," Obediah nodded. "I have Josiah nearby already, and I'll send out another six. That ought to be enough to deal with those kids. I don't care what happens to the parents. I'll let the warlock know." Obediah hauled a cell phone from his shirt pocket and tapped in a number.

~

"I've had word," Josiah informed Diamond. "You'll have to be there in two nights—the warlock and his associates will lower the shield, and I've told them to deliver the families to your coordinates."

"Nicely done," Diamond nodded at Josiah's words. Diamond was only now seeing Josiah in the flesh; they'd exchanged messages through the mundane method of cell-phone communications before. "I will bring a few others with me, and we will take the children and leave here. If a few Dark Ones die, so much the better."

"I and my associates want no loose ends," Josiah shrugged. "Do whatever you want with the parents."

"Dead," Diamond shrugged callously. "They're human. We have no need for humans. Those children will learn soon enough what it means to be warriors in the Bright Queen's army. She will search out their gifts and employ them accordingly."

"Is that how you learn what they can do? She tells them?" Josiah was very curious.

"This is information that we normally do not give, but the greater gifts must be sorted out by the Queen, who employs the power of her crown to search for them. I will not tell you what some of those gifts might be—a few have never been written down anywhere, they are so rare. Not that I expect any of those gifts to appear in these—they are only half-Elemaiyan, after all. Fodder for the war and little else," Diamond added.

"No matter to me," Josiah replied, uncaring that any or all of the children and their parents might die. He only desired the promised payoff at the end. Diamond had offered a great deal of money for live children; Obediah and the Dark Ones offered slightly less to have them killed. Perhaps all might be satisfied in the end.

Josiah intended to bring in the Dark Ones after turning the children over to Diamond, and the ensuing battle would likely destroy the children and their parents. Either way, he had already been given a down payment—by both sides.

"I'll have the gold ready when the children are handed over," Diamond promised. Josiah smiled.

Vince turned the key in the post office box he'd rented—the money he'd been promised should be waiting. He'd handed over one last piece of information to Wildrif, and Wildrif informed him when the money would arrive. With shaking fingers, Vince withdrew the envelope from the small box; it was the only item he'd received since renting it more than two months earlier.

Wildrif had been correct all the way through, Vince realized. Wildrif said that the opportunity would present itself so the six half-blood children might be moved in with the seventh one in Cloud Chief.

Wildrif knew that Pierce would contact Vince—Vince had known Pierce from years earlier, under another name, of course. *I want all the eggs in one basket*, Wildrif had joked with Vince.

Vince didn't get the joke until days later. Now, Vince would get the payoff and walk away from his job with no regrets. He didn't care who might come in as Director now. He could take his retirement and go where he pleased.

"Where's the check?" Vince pulled a slip of paper from the envelope, but there was no accompanying cashier's check. "What the?" Vince opened the note to read.

Surprise, the note said, even as he was hit from behind and taken down.

"Director Jennings told us to pack up." Edward shaded his eyes against bright Oklahoma sunlight. Ashe and Sali had gone to visit Edward, Ashe's old, lime-green Frisbee in hand. Keith and Bryce came along as soon as they saw Ashe, Sali and Edward in the field outside the mobile homes, tossing the Frisbee around. Sali had gone to wolf as usual, and Keith laughed every time Sali leapt in the air to catch the flying disk.

"So, how much more do you have to pack?" Ashe asked when Steven Pendley walked out with a small tub of sodas in ice for the boys.

"We're almost done," Steven replied. "Macy and Luanne are with Dori and Wynn today. I really hate to move away from here," he added.

"Dad and I don't want to go," Edward grumbled.

"We don't want you to leave, either," Ashe said. "All of you. Sali and I talked about that on the way over."

"Director Jennings hinted that we might be split up," Bryce sipped his cola. "I don't want that. Macy, Luanne and Edward feel like part of the family, now."

Ashe noticed that none of them had mentioned Philip. Ashe drew a heavy breath at the thought of Philip. Likely, he was feeling Luanne's absence greatly—after all, he was seeking revenge against Chump and Wormy's attack on her when he'd burned their house down.

Philip had chosen an ill-advised method of expressing his opinion about Chad and Jeremy's punishment. The Booth home was being rebuilt, too—many community residents had pitched in; building supplies and lumber had been purchased and the frame was already up.

Roger and Toby, the extra werewolves that Winkler had brought up, were providing guard duty at night so Aedan and Nathan could work on the Booth home while awake.

"You have no idea where you might go? There's no way to keep in touch?" Ashe toed the ground. Sali sat on the grass beside Ashe, his tongue lolling from his mouth as he followed the conversation, still in wolf form.

"Director Jennings won't allow it," Steven Pendley sighed.

You're a quarter child, aren't you? Ashe sent to Steven Pendley.

Yes. That was a very good guess, Ashe. And I have mindspeech. I only discovered that when we met you, Edward's father replied. *That makes Edward more than half Elemaiyan. I don't know what this will mean for him eventually. I have to worry about keeping him safe for now.*

I hope you can tell me about them, someday. The Elemaiya, I mean, Ashe said, sipping his soda.

I hope we live to tell you, Ashe, Steven Pendley replied.

"Director, I'm afraid I have bad news," the Captain of a local police precinct in Silver Spring, Maryland informed Bill Jennings over the phone. "We've located your assistant—his body was found in Chesapeake Bay, near Cape St. Claire. Looks pretty bad, sir. If I didn't know better, I'd say he'd been chewed on by animals."

Bill went cold at the news. "Send the body to the forensics specialists at the FBI, please," Bill said. "Did you find any personal effects?"

"His wallet, but the money is missing. Credit cards are still there with his identification. I don't think this was a robbery, sir. I get the idea that the killer knew who he was."

"And likely who he worked for," Bill muttered. "Get the body to the FBI as quickly as possible. I have some investigations to make. If Vince was killed for information, we may all be in danger."

"Understood," the Captain agreed. "I'll send word when the body is delivered."

"Thank you, Captain." Bill hung up. "Vince, what have you done?" Bill whispered, raking a hand through his hair.

~

"You'd better hope they don't tie the two incidents together," Josiah hissed at Trina over the phone. "I got a call from my contact, here, and he's ready to take everybody apart. The body was found, and found quick. What the hell were you thinking, letting somebody else do this?" Josiah raked fingers through his thick, brown hair.

"I had to work late," Trina snipped at Josiah. "And you said it had to be done in a certain place at a certain time. I trust the person who did this for me, so stop complaining. The human's dead. Wasn't that your goal?"

"You mucked this up. You owe me and I won't forget," Josiah snapped and ended the call.

~

"We have to move them a night early," Bill Jennings was on the phone with Winkler. He stood at the airport, ready to board a flight to Oklahoma City. He had assignments sorted out already—Vince never had that information, so it was still safe.

"I'll make sure Trace, Jason, Roger and Toby are ready," Winkler said. "I'll be there as well, and I'll inform Marcus and the vampires so we can prepare for the move."

"We'll move the families first—we can haul belongings later. Have them take one small bag each and we'll get them to the airport. I'll have private jets there to take them away. The trucks will come in at the time we originally arranged."

"I'll take care of things from this end, Director," Winkler promised.

"Thanks. At this point, I don't know whether to curse Vince or mourn his death."

"We'll investigate, Director. Let's just sort out the families first."

"Right."

~

"Are you capable of fireblasts?" Wildrif contacted the warlock by phone to ask the question.

"I and one other. Will we need them?" The warlock was puzzled over why they might be needed.

"Just in case," Wildrif shrugged. "Get those kids out at all costs, and meet at the designated location. Someone will take the kids off your hands and hand over the rest of the money."

"Good enough," the warlock agreed and ended the call.

~

"We have to leave tomorrow?" Edward looked up from the video game that he, Ashe and Sali were playing. Bryce and Keith sat behind them, waiting their turn.

"I'm afraid so," Winkler said. "Something happened and the Director thinks it's for the best. Pack one small bag to take with you; trucks will come later to gather your other things."

"So much for having a party before we go," Bryce grumbled.

"I'm sorry, son. The Director just wants all of you to be safe," Winkler apologized.

"Yeah. I get that," Bryce sighed.

"We can have popcorn, sodas and watch movies tonight," Steven Pendley suggested.

"Sounds good," Ashe said. "Can we help?"

~

Ashe was getting ready for bed later when Ren appeared inside his bedroom. "Ashe," Ren began uncomfortably, "I have to say good-bye, tonight. I can't come back."

"What?" Ashe was in the middle of reaching for pajamas when Ren made his admission. "But you can't just leave. You're my friend. I don't want to lose all my new friends at once."

"I do not wish to leave you behind, either, friend Ashe. But I must. The half-blood children are leaving, and they are the ones I am studying. My father and my uncle will not allow me to return."

"But," Ashe argued.

"I know. I feel the same," Ren studied his feet. Ashe looked at Ren's feet as well, noticing for perhaps the first time that the tall blue youth wore sandals made of woven fibers.

"Ren, we haven't had enough time together," Ashe mumbled. "I want to be your friend—always."

"Then we will remain friends always, Ashe. I will remember you as long as I live."

"Same here," Ashe said.

"I must go." Ren disappeared.

"Damn," Ashe muttered.

～

"We can't even give them snacks to take with them," Adele said as she, Ashe and Aedan walked through the field behind their home the following evening. Director Jennings had arranged to move the families as soon as the vampires were awake. Winkler, Trace, Jason and the other two wolves were already helping the families load into several black SUVs that the Director had sent to collect them.

"This is so messed up," Ashe said softly. His skin was itching, just as it had been when he'd known his mother was in trouble. "Dad, they shouldn't be going."

"Son, the Director is calling the shots. We cannot interfere."

"But Dad," Ashe breathed, scratching at his arms.

"They have as much protection as anyone can give them. Mr. Winkler and his wolves are going with them, just in case."

"Dude," Sali trotted up, leaving Marcus and Denise behind. "This is so messed up," Sali echoed Ashe's words as he stared at drivers and agents loading bags into cargo areas. Edward handed his backpack to an agent, who tossed it in with his father's bag.

"Come on, Sali. We have to say good-bye," Ashe trotted toward the SUV before Edward could climb inside.

"Ashe," Edward looked up as the two boys approached. "Sali."

"Edward, I, uh," Ashe didn't know what to say. He felt so uncomfortable; his skin continued to itch and he had no words to say, suddenly.

"Yeah," Edward nodded, staring at his feet. "I just, well, I never had such good friends before."

"We hate this," Sali said. "You should be able to stay."

Ashe blinked as he looked up at Edward—Elizabeth's ghost was standing at Edward's shoulder, making the same gesture she'd made inside Luanne's bedroom.

"She's here," Luanne came to stand beside Edward.

"Lizzie?" Edward whirled to stare at Luanne.

"Yeah. Right behind us," Luanne breathed. "She keeps doing that gesture thing. I have no idea what that means."

"It's kind of creepy," Edward shivered.

"What?" Sali didn't understand.

"Elizabeth's ghost," Ashe said. "She's been hanging around ever since, well, ever since." Ashe shoved his hands in his pockets and hunched his shoulders.

"You guys see a ghost?" Sali's eyes were wide and he took a step back.

"Sal, she hasn't done anything," Ashe said. "And only Luanne and I can see her, I think."

"She isn't dangerous," Luanne agreed. "She just keeps holding her arms out like this," Luanne copied the gesture, stretching her arms out and then pulling them upward until her hands were nearly touching, high over her head. "Nobody knows what that means," Luanne dropped her arms.

"Looks a little silly," Edward nodded.

"Everybody into the vehicles," Bill Jennings barked orders.

"Ashe, I wish we could stay," Luanne leaned forward and hugged Ashe tightly.

"Yeah," Ashe was stunned when Luanne let him go.

"Ashe," Edward stepped forward and awkwardly offered another hug. Ashe clapped Edward on the shoulder and stepped back.

"Take care, man," Sali held out a hand. Edward took it briefly and nodded once to the young werewolf.

"Ashe," Bryce and Keith had come to say good-bye. Ashe copied Sali, offering his hand. In minutes, all of them were loaded into waiting SUVs and doors were closed. Philip and his mother loaded in last of all; Ashe watched as Philip sullenly climbed into the back seat of the SUV and sat beside his mother.

Pierce and Hilbah waited for Diamond and Ruby to return with carryout from a local restaurant. The time had been set and they had more than an hour before the children were scheduled to arrive, but Pierce was hungry and if they didn't return soon, there might not be enough time to eat.

Pierce was angry and out of sorts while Hilbah sat huddled in a corner of the cellar, lit only by a camping lantern that Pierce had supplied. Hilbah stared intently at Pierce. It made Pierce uncomfortable. He was ready to snap at Hilbah when the strange, point-eared man spoke.

"Your death will come at the hands of one you know," Hilbah said softly, his eyes glowing strangely in the lantern light. The gun was in Pierce's hand and Hilbah was dead before Pierce even realized what he'd done.

"That saves us having to kill him; he was worthless anyway," Diamond handed over a bag from the restaurant. Pierce pocketed the gun he'd stolen from Nick Lawford and accepted the bag of take-out without a word.

"Is the ghost still here?" Sali asked as they watched five dark SUVs drive toward the entrance to Cloud Chief.

"It got in the car with Luanne," Ashe said, shaking his head over the oddity.

"Son," Aedan's hand dropped onto Ashe's shoulder, "Take Sali to the gate but not beyond, hear me? You can wave good-bye from there."

Ashe searched his father's eyes. "You mean I can mist us there?"

"I'm giving you permission," Aedan smiled.

"All right," Sali pumped his fist. In seconds, Ashe and Sali were mist and blazing toward Cloud Chief's hidden entrance.

"This is Sorrel's work. Strong, but it won't keep us out," the warlock muttered, pulling back the dark magic he'd employed to detect the barrier. "Ready?" he glanced at the line of six others, male and female, that stood beside him. "Then let's begin," the warlock said as each one nodded.

Ashe kept pace with the lead SUV, where Winkler and Director Jennings rode with Philip and Jackie Raymond, before ranging ahead to rematerialize beside the gate. The vehicles were nearly there and Ashe and Sali had hands raised to wave good-bye when the witch's shield fell and the first hurled firebomb upended Director Jennings' SUV.

CHAPTER 18

*A*edan barely had time to register Ashe's mindspeech as he and Nathan raced toward the blast. Marcus and many other werewolves were running as well, but they were far behind the two vampires.

"The shield is down!" Adele shouted to others who'd ran or driven up. "Marcie's on the phone; she and Jason heard the blast in Cordell and the Cordell Fire Department is on the way. This is awful," Adele waved her cell phone in the air.

"Come on, we may need to help," Denise DeLuca drove up and flung a car door open. Adele climbed inside Denise's small car and held on while Denise sped toward the gate.

Sali went to werewolf, Ashe turned to mist. Winkler was climbing out of the overturned SUV and Ashe registered that he was swiftly turning to wolf as well. Two warlocks hurled more fireblasts at the SUVs, but those vehicles were attempting to get around the one that carried the Raymonds and Director Jennings.

Winkler tore into one of the warlocks and Sali, seizing the

opportunity, leapt at the witch who was attempting to help the warlock against Winkler. Aedan and Nathan ran up at that moment, even as a hurled fireblast hit another SUV.

Think fast, Ashe, filtered into Ashe's misty brain—it was a voice he didn't recognize—it sounded adult, and Ashe only knew of one adult with mindspeech—Edward's father, Steven Pendley. This wasn't Steven Pendley. Making up his mind swiftly, Ashe flashed from one SUV to another, lifting all the teens and their parents inside his mist.

Jason, Trace and the other werewolves, along with Director Jennings' agent-drivers, pelted from SUVs, the werewolves turning to wolf, the agents with guns drawn. Director Jennings was the only one who didn't move; he was unconscious, his head cut and bloody. At the last moment, Ashe lifted the unconscious Director in his mist as well. Unsure where to take the children and adults he carried at first, Ashe turned in a complete circle while he desperately searched for a solution to the dilemma.

∼

"The plan's been compromised!" Wildrif's voice screeched into Diamond's cell. "The warlock and his people are fighting for their lives. You'll have to take the children away yourselves."

Diamond nodded to Ruby, and he and his brother each grasped one of Pierce's arms and disappeared before Pierce had an opportunity to shout at either of them.

∼

"We're on our way." Rend, the Dark King's Destroyer, ended the call he'd gotten from Wildrif—it was almost identical to the one Diamond had gotten from the wild-eyed clairvoyant. "Come on, those stupid spell-casters have managed to muck this up," Rend informed his three brothers. "Sorry, it will expend too much energy if we take you along," Rend informed Josiah and the six werewolves that stood before him. "Here's your money," Rend tossed a heavy bag to Josiah. "We'll be in touch." Rend, Slash, Grind and Crush all disappeared before Josiah could say a word.

~

"Quick, get in the storm shelter," Ashe had carried all his passengers to the shelter between mobile homes. They'd never used it until now, but it was built of strong material and buried in the ground, with a thick door that could be latched once they were inside.

Ashe could still hear the noise of fireblasts being hurled at the entrance to Cloud Chief, while werewolves, vampires and a few shapeshifters attempted to fight off rogue spell-casters. Steven Pendley and Rocky Hill carried Director Jennings between them; the Director still hadn't wakened.

"Hurry," Luanne and Edward were lifting the shelter's heavy door so the others could get inside. Bryce, Keith and Macy helped shaky mothers down steep steps after Director Jennings was taken in first.

"Son, shouldn't you come with us?" Michael Caldwell, Keith and Bryce's father placed a hand on Ashe's shoulder.

"I need to check on Sali," Ashe winced as another fireblast exploded at the gate.

"I'm not going in there," Philip Raymond announced as his mother attempted to pull him down the shelter's narrow steps.

Smoke from burning grass filtered past as Ashe stared at Philip Raymond. Philip backed away from the shelter entrance, refusing to go inside with his mother.

"Dang," Ashe breathed and prepared to mist Philip inside the storm shelter.

"You stupid," the sentence wasn't finished as a voice shouted directly behind Ashe. Jackie Raymond screamed as a bullet tore through her shoulder.

Ashe whirled to find the man who'd attacked him and his mother inside Cordell Feed and Seed. Behind that man stood two others Ashe didn't recognize, and both were just as shocked at what the man had done as Ashe was. None of them, however, were expecting what happened next.

Philip had been angry for a very long time, and his anger found an outlet that night. Turning to mountain lion, Philip hurled himself at the one who'd once called himself Philip's father. Philip Raymond Sr. had been a CIA spy for many years before going rogue and acting as a double agent.

Until he'd been discovered.

He'd disappeared after that, and Jackie Raymond had tearfully lied to her son, telling him that his father was dead.

Now, Philip slashed and clawed at Philip Raymond Sr.'s throat, even as the gun his father carried fired. Ashe and the others watched in horror as father and son fell to the ground, dead of their wounds. Jackie Raymond kept screaming as four more men appeared from nothing, immediately engaging the first two strangers in a firebombing battle. Only these blasts were fifty times more deadly than those hurled by the warlocks and witches at Cloud Chief's entrance.

A mobile home behind Ashe was hit and tossed high into the air, exploding with a resounding boom that flung Ashe to his knees and forced him to cover his ears. Michael Caldwell dragged a weeping, bleeding Jackie Raymond toward the shelter as the battle continued around them.

Another mobile home blew apart as Ashe struggled to stand. The remaining homes were hit and exploded while Ashe watched the battle between Dark Destroyers and Bright Jewels. He ducked flaming debris as it blasted outward and rained from a smoke-filled sky. A fireball was aimed directly at him and he was prepared to turn to mist when everything slowed and then stopped in midair.

"What the?" Ashe could move, but everything else had stopped where it was. Ducking away from the fireball that had almost reached him, Ashe studied it in terrified curiosity. He could have walked between other fireblasts if he'd chosen to do so; the fireballs hung in midair between combatants.

"We must hurry; there is little time. If I suspend everything for more than a few of your Earth minutes, others might suspect and attempt to undo what I have done."

Ashe nearly jumped at the eight-and-a-half-foot blue giant that appeared at his side. "Ren?" he whispered, stunned at the sight of his friend, who was now an adult.

"I have always been your friend, Ashe, and always will be," the adult Ren smiled, flashing brilliant white teeth at Ashe. "But we have little time. Bring your friends out. You are going to save them."

"But how?" Ashe stared at Ren. "How are you here and doing this? And how can I save everybody?"

"Adult Larentii are quite powerful, Ashe, but even they might not do this," Ren swept out a hand, indicating the suspended action surrounding them. "You might say I've grown past their expectations, although time holds no constraints for any of my race." He smiled again. "Come, you will do this. We must hurry."

"Do what?" Ashe still didn't understand.

"Open a gate, young Ashe. I believe you concentrate on making the gate, while sweeping your hands like this," Ashe watched in wonder as Ren imitated the very movements that Elizabeth's ghost had been making for days. "No other living Elemaiya is capable of making a gate anywhere they please; only you have that talent. The others must rely on fixed gates that exist upon certain worlds. There are two of those on Earth. Come now, time is ticking away. Make the gate Ashe, and call the others out of the shelter. We will send them away tonight."

"Send them where?" Ashe asked as he attempted to do as Ren instructed.

"Trust me, friend. All you have to do is open the gate. People will be waiting on the other side to take these to safety."

"All right," Ashe drew a shaky breath, concentrated as hard as he could, mouthed the words "*Open Sesame*," and pulled his arms up in an arc over his head. Shocked beyond comprehension, Ashe stared as a bit of light formed and then spread until a twelve-by-twelve portal opened before him. Even more shocking was what he saw beyond that portal—several people waited there expectantly, one of them a woman made almost entirely of light. She shone so brightly that Ashe couldn't make out any features; he could only see a female outline.

"Call them, Ashe. Command all inside the shelter to come out. Tell them it is safe," Ren instructed.

Come, Ashe sent mindspeech. *You will be safe. We will send you to a safe place*, he added.

In twos and threes, the families came forth, led by Edward. Stunned parents were helped along by determined half-Elemaiyan children, all of whom seemed to recognize the gate Ashe had created.

A beautiful woman; perhaps the most beautiful woman Ashe had ever seen, with black hair and piercing blue eyes stepped to the line where the gate stood, the edges of it glowing and crackling with energy.

"Hurry, come quickly," she said, her voice musical as she beckoned the children and their parents forward. Two more who stood behind the woman quickly took adults and children aside as they crossed over.

Ashe, watching his friends leave, noticed for the first time that behind the people on the other side stood trees, seemingly planted in neat rows. They reminded him of photographs he'd seen of lemon groves.

It didn't take long for the children and their parents to walk through the shining gate and stand among those trees. Luanne, Macy, Keith, Edward and Bryce turned to wave at Ashe. Ashe lifted his hand in farewell when Director Jennings' voice spoke behind him.

"Wait! Wait." Ashe turned to watch as the aging Director, with blood soaking his white hair and covering the side of his face, reached out a hand toward the gate. Ashe was worried at first that the Director wanted to stop the others from crossing to safety.

That wasn't the case. The shining woman stepped forward and held out her hand. Bill staggered the last few steps through the gate to take it, and the two embraced.

"They are old friends," Ren said softly. "She came for him. Close the gate, Ashe."

Ashe was about to close the gate, making the opposite gesture and reaching high over his head to create a sweeping arc downward, when two things happened. Elizabeth's ghost ran lightly through the portal, closely followed by the ghost of Philip's mountain lion.

The beautiful, dark-haired woman watched silently as the ghosts swept past, and then sent mindspeech as Ashe's gate closed between them.

I love you sounded softly in Ashe's mind as the portal disappeared. Ashe gaped, openmouthed, wishing for another glimpse of the woman, but only the Oklahoma prairie surrounded him, along with suspended figures frozen in mid-battle.

"There is one last thing you must accomplish, young Ashe," Ren said, making Ashe jump. For moments, he'd been lost in the music of the woman's voice and the burning desire to know who she was. Ren pulled him away from that brief and lovely reverie.

"What?" Ashe looked up at Ren.

"Turn these to mist and drop them several miles away," Ren indicated the four Dark Destroyers and the Bright Queen's Jewel Sentinels. "I have removed the memory of this place from their minds," Ren added. "They will not find it again."

"Want to come with me?" Ashe shook himself and grinned at his tall, blue friend.

"Of course," Ren chuckled.

"Dang," Ashe breathed as he stared at the suspended battle between warlocks, witches and the community. He and Ren had traveled to Cloud Chief's entrance after dumping their other cargo in a field on the far side of Cordell. "What am I gonna tell them—about Edward and the others?" Ashe turned to Ren.

"You won't have to tell them anything. Do you recall your game— the one in which automobiles exploded?" Ren asked, his bright blue eyes twinkling mischievously.

"Yeah," Ashe nodded.

"Watch this," Ren held out a hand and each empty SUV exploded in a fireball, making no sound at all. Debris rained down without touching any Cloud Chief resident. It even missed the witches and warlocks—those that still lived, anyway. Only two of those remained at the moment, although Winkler was about to take down the witch while Ashe's father held the warlock in a stranglehold.

"All will believe that the others perished in these blasts," Ren said. "Including the Director. You must keep this secret to yourself, young Ashe, or the children might still be in peril and our work to keep them safe count for nothing. There is one last thing," Ren went on. "The next gate you open upon this planet will be the last gate you open upon Earth. Make sure it counts. Good-bye, friend." Ren bent down and embraced Ashe tightly before disappearing. Ashe stared around him as the action resumed.

Ashe and Sali watched somberly as the funeral procession was displayed on television. A journalist spoke about the service that Director Bill Jennings had rendered to the country before giving his life in the line of duty.

Ashe's skin tingled slightly as the journalist mentioned Anthony Hancock, Director Jennings' predecessor, who had also died in the line of duty. Ashe pretended not to notice when Sali wiped his eyes.

Everyone in the community believed the children and their parents dead, and there were no announcements or news coverage of their demise. Even an altered account of Director Jennings' death was given—that he'd died in an explosion with his assistant, Vince Jordan. Ashe mourned with Dori, Wynn and the others, only for a different reason—he missed Edward and the others and had no idea where they'd been taken. He trusted Ren, though, and believed they were in a safe place for perhaps the first time in their lives.

At first, it was difficult keeping the secrets from Sali and the others, but he held them inside and it became easier over time. And he found himself hoping that somewhere, someday, he might see the half-Elemaiyan children again.

After the battle at Cloud Chief's gate, the Cordell Fire Department had somehow been misdirected to a field west of town, where evidence of a grass fire was found. Fortunately, the fire was already out when the firefighters arrived. Ashe figured it was the aftermath of the battle between the strange men he'd dumped there before all disappeared.

Somehow, too, the body of Philip's father had disappeared. Deciding that Ren had managed that in addition to many other things, Ashe thought he might be in the clear—at least for a little while.

As to the reason and purpose behind the shield being taken down, Aedan and Nathan had questioned the only living warlock after the battle, and he'd spouted off some wandering tale of revenge against Paul Harris, saying that Paul had offered him money for services in the past and then had never paid. The warlock seemed much surprised to learn that Mr. Harris had perished a year earlier.

The warlock was turned over to the Spell-Caster's Consortium for judgment and punishment afterward, for violating their laws. And somehow, the witch's barrier surrounding Cloud Chief had magically repaired itself. The last thing to come about was Jane Scott and Nick Lawford's waking in an Oklahoma City hospital, with no memory of what had transpired in and around Cloud Chief and Cordell.

Two days before Ashe's fourteenth birthday, Ashe walked along the path where the mobile homes had stood. None survived the battle between the Dark and Light Elemaiya and Nathan, Aedan, Trace and Jason had all pitched in to clean up the debris.

Ashe kicked at a few clumps of dirt and grass as he contemplated what had happened in such a short span of time.

Things were settling into a normal routine; he and his mother were back to work at Cordell Feed and Seed and Chump and Wormy were locked up in a windowless house for the rest of the summer.

Word had it that both boys snarled and spit at the ones assigned to take meals and clean clothing, including Diane and Neil Booth. Ashe shook his head over so much disrespect. Chad and Jeremy had nobody to blame except themselves.

The community breathed ragged, relieved sighs over the whole thing and Winkler, Trace, Roger and Toby had gone back to Dallas. Jason stayed behind and asked Sali's Aunt Marcie to marry him. She said yes. The wedding was scheduled in August and the community was already making preparations.

Ashe waded through knee-high grass where Edward's mobile home had stood. Now, only the outline of the foundation was evident, while new grass attempted to consume the imprints. "I wish I knew where you were, Edward," Ashe sighed. "I hope you're safe and happy."

Sali trotted up beside Ashe, panting a little since he'd run from his house as wolf. Ashe didn't speak to the young werewolf at first, pondering instead the beautiful woman he'd seen on the other side of his gate. Her image ran through his mind, as did her silent words for him. He also weighed Ren's final warnings. Had he ever thought of not befriending the tall, blue youth? *Thanks, Ren,* Ashe sent out in silent gratitude. There was no reply.

EPILOGUE

"So, young Renegar, have you learned something from your study of the Elemaiya?" Nefrigar smiled down at his brother's child. Nefrigar, Keeper of the Larentii Archives, was ancient, although his appearance belied that fact.

"Yes, Uncle," the nine-year-old Larentii child smiled back at his only uncle as he handed over a tiny crystal data chip. "You know the Legend of the Ir'Indicti?"

"Of course. We hold a copy of the H'Morr here in our Archives. Why do you ask such a question, child?"

"Because I found him. I saw the Ir'Indicti, Uncle." Nefrigar almost dropped the data chip, he was so stunned.

The End